THE MELODY OF THREE

Evercharm Trilogy : Book 1

S.D. Reeves

An Imprint of Sulis International Press
Los Angeles | London

Library of Congress Control Number: 2019912966
ISBN (print): 978-1-946849-62-5
ISBN (eBook): 978-1-946849-63-2

Published by Riversong Books
An Imprint of Sulis International
Los Angeles | London

www.sulisinternational.com

Contents

Well, here we are again. It's been two years, and I have been allowed to publish another book. Some of you can be forgiven, like editor C.B. Moore and my excellent cover artist Sean Counley. But my wonderful wife Alessandra? No, nearly a decade of encouragement has made her entirely culpable. Neither can I exonerate Sulis International Editor Mark McFaddyn, or really, any of you readers out there who bought my first book and supported me with your kind words. Thanks to your efforts people will read The Melody of Three and be entertained. Some may even daydream. I hope you are all able to sleep at night.

Prologue

Light from the flame spits and sputters, forcing Leon to move the candle away from his work. For the third time this night, the silence is broken by his furious editing.

Dandelions twirled around Calem like dancers…

The old man rubs his ink-smeared temple. Tomorrow he must present the translation of his client's will at Liverpool Crown Court, and here he is writing fiction. He picks at the feather of his quill. Dawn is a few hours away.

"'Dandelions and dancers,' this is what I've become now?"

The glow from the candle reaches toward the frosted window. His gaze drifts, seeing it illuminate a backdrop of snow and night.

"No. This time… this time it will be winter."

Snowflakes twirled around Calem, gracefully flirting with the ground as if to foreshadow the coming of a greater snowfall. Yet he knew it was merely a trick of nature; the white hag still slept. When the gray waters of the Dwem' aimá seethed, and a red sun breathed, her day would come.

"When the gray waters of the Dwem' aimá seethed, and a red sun breathed…" Leon's voice trails off. He stares into the flame, transfixed, as if he were channeling another person. "Dwem' aimá. Now, that is a ponderous word."

Snowflakes twirled around Calem…

His pen clacks hard against the floor, punctuating the silence as several sheets of paper scatter in a sudden draft. Leon sighs, shuffling court files away from his writing. His hand comes to rest on a loosely bound stack.

One.

He freezes as the old clock's chime ends. Slowly, his attention falls upon the paper. Leon blinks. "Am I losing my mind? I'm starting to hear voices now?"

Scribbled in his journal, is the word "one," but the style of the script is foreign as if written by another's hand.

"Ponderous."

A dark stain bleeds onto the margin of his newest work. His hands trace the scratches and marks on his desk. It has been a long day, and everything is making him jumpy. His client was especially demanding, checking on him almost every second hour. Leon rubs his shoulder and considers a knot in his armchair's hand rest.

Snowflakes? No. Chill winds from the hallway curl around his neck, and the journal flips to yesterday's entry. One page, written in a heavy hand, flutters. Outside, the weather is furiously trying to imitate his fiction.

An unseen shadow arose.

Leon fidgets. This wasn't his doing. This voice—clear and full of menace—, this intruder whispers inside his head with the slither of a serpent. "No more writing today."

It came from within.

"Maybe I should go for a walk." His eyes drift to the world beyond the frozen panes. Bad idea. Maybe he should stop for dinner? "What is it, seven? Dinner, yes."

But he can't seem to keep his eyes off the pen for long. Was it his inner muse speaking to him? Or the sandwich he had for lunch? A bit of bad turnip? Or a potato that had turned? As if summoned, five words, one at a time, bounce inside his skull: *and fell over the room.*

Separate. Alien. Not his own. Leon hovers over his paper. His concern, buried by curiosity, falsely believing the voice benign. The rattle of the window is louder than the sound of crumpling paper and the return to determined writing.

Long fingers ink around dusty corners.

Leon leans closer to the candle after transcribing word for word what the voice is telling him. The smell of tallow turns his nose away, and the thick smoke blurs the lines. Dark shapes whip around him in the haze of the little room. The old man shivers. "Long fingers."

There is something here, cold and hard. This is hate; smoke risen from the dying embers of unloved dreams.

Leon slumps onto the desk. The voice is making a play at his own prose. The light from the candle flickers and shakes, casting obscene shadows against the paneling of the window. Tree branches, abused in the winter storm, mock him as he continues copying the strange, disembodied timbre.

Tendrils crept over the tomes, curling around the old man's feet.

It was chilly this night. Freezing, perhaps. And even through his woolies he could… *feel the bitterness.*

"There's a blanket here, yes, I left on the drawer. Just… just over there." But he does not turn around—while behind, the chime of the clock is overstepped by feet making no attempt at silence. Leon's hand twitches on the desk. He is no longer alone in this room.

"Who are you? Why are you here?"

A pair of intruders pace beyond his reach. His clock chimes in the background, like a mechanical herald announcing their presence. One. Two. At the stroke of three, Leon musters the courage to speak again.

"If you want money, I have none," he insists.

One approaches. The soft mesh of his foot on the hardwood floors would otherwise go unnoticed, yet Leon's ears are keen on it. The old man finds the strength to lift his right hand, but quickly falters and returns pen to paper.

Until the intruder whispers, "…and at last, cold hate touched warm flesh," into his ear.

The pen rolls away. There is a thud, and a wet slap from Leon's head hitting the desk. But no scream.

•••

Culsan looks down at his handiwork and watches the man's lifeblood swirl together with the black ink on the unfinished manuscript. He takes the blade in his right hand and wipes it against Leon's back, while the left tugs at the corpse's shoulder, letting the weight carry the body to the floor. The elf's fingers fly over to the desk to glance the leather spine of a book.

A metallic note rings the count of the hour: eleven. A growl from his companion reaches over his shoulder. "We don't have time to browse."

Culsan stiffens and casually regards his tall, clean-shaven fellow elf. Sethlan has been his constant companion and *irritant* this whole turn, thrust upon him by their Matriarch. Or, more rightly, the other way around; he is Sethlan's jailer and brother. Culsan's gaze follows the parade of buttons on his partner's vest to finally stare him in the eyes.

"There might be something we need—a clue, perhaps, in this fairyblood writing," Culsan says. "It would be a waste to leave it.".

"You talk of waste when you spent all that time toying with your prey, and—" Sethlan halts his pacing to look down at Culsan. "I could have flushed more answers from him alive."

Culsan sniffs. "The portal will hold."

"Look up," his brother says, and Culsan follows the suggestion.

Stars wink at them from a faux-night sky, and the marble-sized dot of planet Verdu blushes red. The true night sky of their homeland, the Elfsea, shows clearly. Their portal is unstable.

"The Matriarch is not yet strong enough for this," Sethlan continues. "Our time here winds down like the man's device. The only thing that matters is the Evercharm." that cursed Lyre of old."

"The old man doesn't have the cursed lyre," Culsan's voice says in a snarl, motioning towards the corpse. "This pile of blubber may be fairyblood, but he could never play such an instrument." The Travelers' Stars appear over the crown of a bookcase, and an intense pulse beats upon Culsan's temple. "Fairy kind are all tied to one another, and these stories—"

"I do not care about your hobbies," Sethlan growls again. "I should be doing this alone."

"Stories." Culsan's eyes rise to meet Sethlan's. "Are magic. They are life, and here they may give us insight. Or a trail. Is that fair to you, Hunter?"

For one moment, his companion appears to be ready to protest. Then, he relents in a sigh.

"That is fair," Sethlan says. "But be quick. This keepers of this world will not tolerate us much longer. Sooner or later, the Curatorium will find us."

Culsan stands and slides over to the bookcase, now half engulfed by the portal they used to arrive here. The veil had weakened, allowing them to bend the rules of the old pacts and the will of the Artisans. Culsan's fingers slide past thin leaflets, around tomes and journals, until they rest upon a copy of *The*

Seventy Nights' Campaign, by Grey Um Kimbesh. His lip trembles as he tips the spine forward.

"This one." He turns back and smiles. "And all the others on the table too."

A brass strike ends the sentence. Sethlan freezes, and Culsan tries to speak when another tone from the clock forces him into a stutter.

"Ti… Time is distorting. The way-passage is turning against us. It's going to send us back soon." The air trembles again with his voice—but something else steals the following moment: silence, succeeded by a sharp chill. It crawls over Culsan's toes. It slides up his legs and digs deep into the calves. The feeling creeps to the small of his back. "The others, now!"

Sethlan sighs and collects the stacks of ink-soaked and now blood-stained papers. "One day we will be able to return, and the Queen shall use the Lyre to seal these E'tah in a prison of *our* making."

The portal collapses with the utterance of "making." Bookcases break silently on the right and heave with the floor. Culsan slides when he pivots, nearly crashing into the other shelves on his left. He reaches out, bracing himself against a wall that vanishes a second after. Travelers' Stars and distant planets, painted on a wall of darkness, engulf both elves, then withdraw with them inside.

Culsan clasps his hands together to stave off the bite of a sudden chill and stares through the edge. The world of men retreats like a wandering firefly. Buzzing, buzzing away, until he can no longer see anything of the room.

Sound reemerges with a thump that makes his head throb, and finally, warmth returns, along with the feeling of wet grass beneath him. Somewhere close by, Sethlan groans.

Chapter 1

"Hold fast."

The shout crashes against the deck with another wave, sending men scurrying up the ratlines. Further cries from the captain of the maintop join with the bosun's, and in between flashes of lightning, the silhouettes of the crew dance upon the sails.

Inspector Rein holds fast, yes, to his spellbook. "How bothersome. Can't this ship wait to sink until after dinner?"

"I don't think your appetite enters into it much, sir," says Higgins, whose soggy mustache droops into two points, making him seem like the caricature of a young walrus. Ruddy cheeks and square jaw set the rest of the picture nicely. "But you may like to know that I don't think the ship will, in fact, sink."

"Well, la-de-bleeding dah."

Three weeks spent on the East Indiaman, *Worley*, have soured Rein's disposition. Time spent to buy secrecy. He told everyone with clearance—which largely was only Higgins, his apprentice—that his qualms about the voyage had nothing to do with the cramped quarters or the length of time rolling around the decks. No, it was this rationing of magic by his bosses in the Curatorium that irked him. As a result, Rein complained loudly of anything and everything. No one paid much attention. Not the captain, his steward, or even Higgins. And now the Inspector is using British curses.

The steward's vague shape appears at the entrance to the lower desk. "Come off that, you daft ninnies," he yells.

The Inspector cringes as the steward's yells are drowned out by the roll of thunder and the more harrowing cries of the men around. He could have helped them ten years ago. *Hell, even last winter, maybe.* A strain. A bother. A downright sodden year, full of inconveniences like that. But the worst of it was when he couldn't find his slippers a fortnight ago.

Sheets of rain wrap themselves around the man's side, and Rein just stares through. At his side, his assistant's focus alternates between the deck of the rolling ship and the men's struggle to furl the sales. In the midst of a coughing fit spurred on by the damp, the Inspector catches Higgin's eye.

Higgins shrugs, hovering just below Rein's shoulder. "I think our friend still wants your attention."

"Let him have his tantrum," Rein says, now observing the steward. "What a strange little Irishman. Say, with all that jumping and hooting, I wonder, might he have once been an owl?"

"Don't make the rare common and the common rare."

Such magic was a deeply personal subject to Higgins. Why, his own wife had been a fox. Not the adjective to an attractive lady, although she certainly is that now, but a foxy fox. He had met her one day on a hunt.

Outside, the steward hasn't given up. "Will you get back into the bloody cabin? Fools."

And nearby, the creak and groans of timber answer. The helm is fighting the storm with some success, but the two men are hesitant to leave. Rein acknowledges the steward again with a flitter of his fingers.

"Connor is just a man," Higgins says. "And an angry steward, trying to get two of his deranged passengers out of the weather."

"And he is a good man, I agree. Not like his captain."

"Who was a fine man himself," Higgins snorts, "before you made him into a foul monkey."

"Orangutan."

A shift at the helm forces the apprentice to throw out his hand so as not to stumble into his friend. "Orange, what?"

"Orangutans are not monkeys, my friend. And they would be entirely appalled that you might call them such."

"Forget I asked," Higgins says. "But what will the Curatorium say when they find out you were the cause of his transformation? And using unsanctioned archaic magic?"

"Oh, come off it. I'm going mad with all this as it is, can't I have a little leeway? Besides, the potion isn't permanent. Why, he will be back to his feces-flinging self in a month, at worst."

"At which time he will already be sold to some heiress as a pet."

"She'll hardly know the difference."

The apprentice's eyes roll in response, but a strike of lightning splits both the conversation and the foretopmast. Rein and Higgins share one knowing look. "Right," the former says. And then, amidst falling timber, the Inspector nods and steps away from the bell post.

"It's time to go. And Higgins, do remember to hold on. I don't want a repeat of the Seulawah-Volcano affair. Re-growing you is getting damn expensive on many accounts."

"As you say," Higgins agrees, almost under his breath.

A handful of the crew watches them step up to the starboard gunwales. One or two are even able to get confused over the Inspector's procurement of a bucket. All for naught An errant wave turns their attention back to a listing ship, and Rein secures the pail to the deck with his foot. He taps the lid with the ferrule of his cane and steps in, unmindful. The bucket rattles with magic, ready to take flight.

"What a time for a flight through the heavens." The Inspector picks at a lock of gray hair that has fallen across his nose. "Do you think they will manage without my guidance?"

"Better than average chance."

Nearby, the previously ignored chaos erupts into furious harmony when the ship lists. Present danger helps bring Higgins back to the real world, and he throws his arms around Rein's skinny midriff.

"Higgins?" The apprentice stares up at his friend's furrowed and unfairly dry brow. "You're pinching."

That is enough. A stream of profanities from Higgins flows, just as the bucket—with his assistant fighting for purchase on its lid—lifts off into the stormy night. Cloud speaks to cloud above. Man to stoic man below. And the sea rolls on. And the storm beats on. Slowly, and surely, they pass beyond the topmost mast. Rein here, in a rare moment of wistfulness, takes a chance to reach out his arm. The white ensign of Her Majesty's Royal Navy flutters only inches away from his fingers. Then that, too, does fall away.

"God save me and my itinerary. Ships are much faster and more comfortable than this mess, what with those vicelike, meaty claws you call hands."

The apprentice sighs, squirming on the edge of the bucket. "Does this help a little?"

"A little," Rein allows with a wince. "You know, Higgins—to be honest, I did not have much of an opportunity to fully read my agent's report."

"Did you not?"

"I'm afraid I might have only nibbled at the edges, so to say. I had been bothered by a bit of indigestion from the other night and could not sit through it. Damn it, Higgins, stop that infernal wiggling! Wiggle, wiggle, wiggle. Are you trying to catch a fish?"

"If so, why the trip to—" Higgins' scream as he plunges off the bucket is broadsided by a double shot of thunder.

And Rein just ignores the broken howl, mistaking it for his friend's usual disapproval of small talk. If he had only looked to his left, he would have caught the man plummeting towards the ocean and certain doom.

"Because of the musician. Or should I say, *The Musician*. When she sends me a letter, to pox with the details, I need to be at the scene. Certainly, before the Curatorium's dogs get a whiff and tie it all up in regulation."

A trio of clouds like celestial pompoms coaxes him to stretch. It is a wonderful night for flying. Folds of dark clouds ripple ahead in the dullness, and he is at once reminded of the ball at Kneuterdijk palace. And a woman: Mrs. Sofie Van Co-everden. Her dress writhed like midnight on a heavenly stage. Dark. Flighty. Dangerous. It was the second time Rein ever felt small, as if his own magic was merely a dalliance. "This," *This was real.* "She was so similar to—"

Changing the subject, he continued despite the silence from his long-departed friend, "He felt the Chords, you see. That was in the second letter. The plucking of the Chords, can you imagine it? In Liverpool? An absolute thrill, don't you say?"

The last hints of the ship disappear beneath a veil of clouds. There remained only a quiet friend, his thoughts, and the task ahead. Feeling lighter, either from the quick jaunt down memory lane or from a break in the storm's relentless attempt to dampen his spirits, Rein taps twice upon the bucket. *I think we can risk a little more oomph.*

The sky tears in long lines with his ascent. Clouds billow. Flow. Then, with no ceremony, the stars orchestrate a display. *It is truly a good night*, he thinks. One for romantic thoughts. *Dreams.* He allows a gasp to escape his lips as the storm disappears below, and he is struck by the cold, strong currents above. Spread out over the horizon, the top of the stratus ripples.

"Astounding," he says. Rein purses his lips, while nimbi continue to stream behind like vaporous extensions of his cloak. "So nice to be able to actually breathe."

The Inspector pulls his cloak tight against his chest. "This case will be a dastardly one. The chords! Chords." Then, quietly, "No one has whiffed at this sort of thing since the capture of Brielle by the Watergeuzenevolt . Yet here I am, and here this is. Dangerous times are afoot, Higgins."

Dangerous times. For every Artisan worth his or her salt knew that any plucking of the Chords, must by some fashion, involve a true musician. And those were often fairykind, or worse, elves. "Our reality, the Curatorium's reality, could be threatened. Wouldn't that be a bad bit of beef?"

A chance opening gives him a glimpse of the real waves far below. *I wonder, how they are going to cover up my disappearance from the ship?* Then at once it hits him: the ceasing of that awful pinching, the lack of poorly disguised cynicism.

"What in the—?" Rein spins around on his bucket and lifts both shoes. "He cleared off!"

Chapter 2

The bucket lands with a solid clop, which rolls to a clatter as Rein steps onto the docks. Fog is everywhere "…bloody everywhere, and cold," but still warmer than last night. Besides, he'll take the Mersey's mercy this morning and report to the Curatorium later. *Much later.* And with some luck he can cut his time dealing with bureaucracy short. The Inspector raises his arms above his head, squeezes out a yawn and takes a deep breath.

"Good God." Rein's fingers move past the fake pocket on his coat and into the inside lining to pull out a handkerchief. "I think I can taste the bloody city."

The short pauses between coughs provide time to gather his thoughts and steal a look around. It is early morning, and the city—while never fully asleep—prefers this moment to stir, roll over, and vomit out the usual sort of obscenities. *Vagabonds, and ink blotters.* In less than a half-hour, the warehouses and offices will be open for business.

Unremarkable buildings stretch on past the horizon set by his gesture. Tidy streets appear here, alleys teeter there. And untidy sailors muster every which way. There are ships behind, refuse everywhere, and many, many barrels of fish.

Choices stall Rein, and he turns his head towards the seabirds hovering above. *Finding my way to the pub on Hacken's Hey might put me in touch with the Musician. The bitter ale there is also palatable.*

The line of nerves along his back triggers, causing him to shiver. The Inspector rubs his neck, looking left just in time to see a light flicker in a bed of mist. "Higgins…"

Wisps of light and fog coalesce into a round form and then erupt, leaving behind a high-pitched growl. This noise drops in tone, before collecting itself into the voice of his dead friend. "You stupid sot," it says. "Bloody ill-conceived, spotted boil on a peddler's dog."

Rein rolls his eyes, about-faces from the ghost, and steps towards the middle of the street. "Still using the same bit," he says over his shoulder. "Voltaire. Diogenes. Byron. Do you not mingle at all?"

"Byron isn't dead."

"Shame." The Inspector halts, letting a cart and its oblivious occupants pass. "I was expecting you an hour ago."

The voice follows him past a group of men offloading from a jetty, none of which notice Rein, his assistant, or their conversation. And neither he nor his Higgins act as if they expect anything else.

"I had difficulty," his assistant explains. "My connection to the Construct is weak."

"Damn Curators," Rein says. "Rationing even for the dead? What's next, taxes?"

A thought occurs to the Inspector then: *maybe the Curatorium really is stressed? Could the Construct, the instrument binding reality to the Curator's will, be weakening?*

"Preposterous," he squawks to himself, then lowers his voice to address Higgins. "So, what should it be, Apprentice? Should I seek out the Musician, or head straight to the crime scene?"

A dockhand notices him, waves hello, and the intrusion of social interaction flusters Rein. He tip-toes past the man, mumbling his own short "Good morning," then busily returns to his conversation with the sky and his assistant. Around, the mist is slowing, blown by a riverside wind. He could not have arrived at a more fortunate time. *A better time would have been never.*

"I'd personally find your contact first," Higgins says.

The Inspector sighs. "All that walking, though."

If it weren't for the emergence of this primal magic, the Chords, Rein wouldn't be here. Much like those English beefeaters who yearn for a good beer, Rein has always found more disappointment than anything else in the search for truth.

"I will also have to get a room at the coach inn." The word "coach" puckers his lips as he steps past a vagrant. Then an able seaman. Then a gaggle of them. By the time he rounds a corner, running smack dab into the sign for Fenwick Street, he's just about assembled an entire ships' allotment of sailors, with a splash of marines thrown in for the coloring.

Higgins' voice hovers just above his left ear now. "Could they be from Perch Rock?"

His friend sounds distant compared to a moment earlier, and Rein almost doesn't hear the comment. He answers first with a scowl, his eyes sailing past the dockworkers and out onto the Mersey.

"No..."

A ship's bow thrusts out, emerging like the tip of a hero's spear from a dragon's lair. The second follows, then the third. Fourth. Rein pauses, letting the handkerchief slip. Even at this distance, he can see the boats ferrying men ashore, and a tide of Redcoats spills from their bellies as blood from a gaping wound. Their boats wash up upon the shore with waves, and in waves.

A grainy, Dublin accent smacks Rein from the left, making him jerk his head as if it were on a ship's wheel. *"Old Boney's gone and done it this time."*

"I beg your pardon?" Rein says.

An aged man, half stooped, pulls a cart overflowing with breeches, shirts, doublets. "You were gawping like a seagull, so I thought I'd throw you a fish."

Just a slop merchant. But for Rein, he is also the second person to have noticed him. *Or is there more than meets the eye?*

Middle-aged men normally go unnoticed, and he should have blended right in with the crowd. Especially since the Inspector *does not want to be found.*

"Gone and escaped Elba, the Frog has," the old man says. He fusses with his hat. "They say he has got the whole place a-buzzin'."

"Has he," Reins says, closing his mouth with a clop. "That means press gangs."

And the trader raises his hand as if to slap the ships on the river with the back. "Means more shore leave, means more business."

"I suppose it does," the Inspector says. He stares hard at the man's face, almost rudely so. *Yes, just a slop merchant, peculiar.*

The image of a leathery, sun-worn thing with rivers meandering out of every port unfurls in his mind, aided by the merchant's face. *A map.* Directions. *There's a fellow in Fenwick's Street that—*

"Jane Ellison owns a fine drinking establishment there," Rein barks, more for Higgins. "And the Curatorium's customs is nearby, too."

The Inspector grunts as diplomats sent from the far corners of his body meet. Somewhere in that instant, the representatives from the stomach, liver, brain, and tongue all come to a quick decision. He raises his finger as if to make another point, then spins on his heels.

Behind him, the merchant mumbles about strange folk as Rein propels onwards to libation. More men fill the streets, heading towards the docks. The Inspector, forced from the middle of the road, pivots once, twice as he tries to keep sight of Higgins. Nearby, the ghost struggles with remaining in contact. His light pulses, winking in and out of existence as a thick line of soldiers jostles the Inspector.

"Wait for me near the crime scene," Rein yells, fighting with the crowd. "Yet not too near. Remain at the Athenaeum, and when I am close to you, join me."

His friend's curses drown in the growing chatter, as soldiers, workers, and others chat about their various catches, from women to fish. Almost carried by the course of the throng, Rein slips into a side street, then joins another major road at a cross between alleys.

Cirrus clouds flatten on the horizon, their bottoms touched with a red rim, as if some ancient Titan had spilled his rum and let it settle. Rows of men march around the dock, loitering near closed doors, waiting for their superiors to let them in as one might a cat. Rein, preferring the Romantic, keeps his head in the clouds. But this is short-lived, and he is almost immediately dragged back to this world's stage. Barrels of salted pork obstruct his first foray into this street. Rein dances past these, a pile of horse droppings, and a quadroon of children. He steals a breath. A lady with too much rouge waves to him from a balcony, and a courier nearly steps on his shoes. Both he ignores, moving from the middle of the street to the left as if tracing a jigsaw puzzle. Somewhere in the distance, church bells strike eight o'clock and an exciting murmur, almost a chirp, answers from loft windows on either side.

Dodgy men with batons, which are more like poles, stare his way. Rein shrinks from sight, using the back of a cart to hide his progress. Soon, they pass. As do a string of men being paraded by some ragged-looking gentleman. *Yes, I called it:* a press-gang. Hereafter the flow of the street thickens, and the grind of the throng bothers. An incline, thanks to the layout of the old town post, provides a moment's refuge, allowing Rein to step onto the raised edge of the pillar and use it as a sailor might a mast. From that vantage, he finds his way too—

"Ah, the pub," eyes sweeping from the tops of heads to the establishment's sign. The contact lives nearby too, but it isn't the thought of maps or idle chat that brings a smile to Rein's lips. He can hear the tavern's call.

Or the drunken louts singing outside: *"Some say women are like the seas..."*

Some the waves, and some the rocks. Rein presses his cane to this bottom lip. The tune steals out of windows, swaggers from the open door. It parts the masses for the Inspector and lends him a hand.

"Some the rose that soon decays..." they continue.

Sailors, roused early, wander past Rein, leaving steins in windowsills. Fat whores prowl the streets, and fatter bums waiting for them. But at each group that washes out, the tide inevitably brings more. The Inspector comes in with chaser of blue petticoats and is immediately splashed by another round of the song.

"Women are witches, when they will. So is wine, so is wine..."

Above his head and the entrance door is a sign that reads: The Fly and the Weevil.

The sailor's chorus follows the Inspector to an empty table. A few plain-clothed gentlemen nod, and a serving waif notices him. She sets down a dirty rag. A hand, Rein's, reaches into his coat pocket. He knows just the sort of spell for quiet, and the details of it are available at a flip of the page.

Two marines, Redcoats now beer-stained, stumble past, slurring the next line of *"They make the statesman lose his skill. The soldier, lawyer, and divine..."* And upon the departure of their trailing coats, the serving maid appears as if by magic.

"How's your stout?' Rein asks her.

The Inspector coughs, nervously, as the woman smiles at him and leans forward. Red lips. Fine, but plain clothes. His hand withdraws from his pocket.

"Do you have anything you can recommend?" he asks into her ear.

That smile. Those lips. She's a different sort than Sofie. But Rein's heart still skips when she smiles—and time and all manners are forgotten and lost in the sway of hips. Around, the song has begun to die down. Only one lone, gap-toothed salt in the corner continues it. His voice croaks: *"What is it that makes your visage pale..."* and dies off into a drunken slur just as a new tune is taken up.

Rein's drink arrives in between another chorus. A man mixing liquor calls out the serving girl's name, and Rein smiles.

"Merci, Abigail," he says, only to watch her expression sink, and eyes dismiss him. The Inspector quietly curses and fiddles with a pocket. The scratch of his coin on the table is loud against the backdrop of cheer. Loose in the lining are the remains of his assistant, preserved in glass, for the eventualities of the position.

"Higgins," to her back. A vial, filthy and old manages to take some of the light from the fireplace as it is spun between his fingers. Toenails, hair clippings, and piece of something indescribable drift, suspended in an amber liquid. Rein raises his arm as if he is about to smash the fragile glass, then gently sets it down next to the mug.

"You're never here to have a drink with me.," to the vial. The mug is cool. A sip tells him he was brought a lager and not a stout. "No matter," he adds sadly.

Abigail spins by to serve another customer, and he can't help but stare casually, hopeful for something. Her passing without so much as a hello makes Rein return to contemplating the chill of the porcelain.

Ale is soon replaced with liquor, liquor that flows thick and black as the storm clouds creeping over Liverpool. By midafternoon the clouds have arrived, along with a slurring of his own speech. Rein chuckles, his head hanging low. The crowd of sailors has thinned. Regular townsfolks, clerks, traders, sneak in. Some stay longer. Too long. He runs his fingers languidly over the rim of a cup. Fine wine this, uncorked only after the larger portion of the scoundrels had left. Quietly, ponders the lingerers till his glass is too heavy. *That man, in the corner—I say a week till he's a beggar.* Somewhere a chair moves too quickly, and a heavy thud shakes his own.

The Inspector shifts uncomfortably in his seat, then taps the top of the vial containing Higgins. "You will be a better Artisan than me, my friend," he says.

A man in a checkered attire helps the fallen up. There is thunder in the distance, but no rain yet. Rein sniffs the air and leans back, deep into the chair. Abigail buzzes again around the emptying tables. The bartender is with her, busy righting stools and tables. She's cleaning the mess left by a patron who was unable to make a pot.

"Though you are going to have to stop this expensive habit of dying…"

Chapter 3

From the perspective of one's purse, walking to customs gives the same sort of empty foreboding as walking to the market, gambling den or whorehouse. To a human being there are of course levels of enthusiasm to be deployed at each. Rein's trudge to the Curatorium's checkpoint is laborious and uneasy. This is only partially influenced by alcohol.

The road goes one way but the Inspector's feet another, tripping over themselves to deposit him against a wall. There his stomach negotiates a settlement with the pavement, leaving behind last night's meal. Opposite the façade of the building he just graced is a door. There are no signs above saying, "Behind here is an inn," you just must know. In Rein's drunken state, he knows quite a few things.

The first droplet of rain splatters at his feet, teasing his eye upwards just as his fingers wrap around a knob. The creak of the door is answered by thunder, much closer and threatening. Rein removes his hat and pushes inside. A man moves from an alcove to him. The Inspector raises his arms, the doorman removes from his pocket a measuring tape bound neatly to an acorn-shaped spindle, and like a tailor, sets about measuring this and that.

"I've not adjusted my height with a potion, nor made any use of any fat-slimming confection," Rein says. "Could you tell the clerk that Inspector Christaan Dei Rein is here to declare?"

The doorman's lips flatten over non-existent teeth as the corner of his mouth pulls back in a smile. "Tell him yourself," he says, nodding towards the counter.

Barliman. Rein's own smile is much more practiced. *I'm about to be lectured about quotas by a man who takes shifts in every custom house in Europe.* "Barliman, my old friend. How's the wi—*dead?* How is work?"

"Slow," the clerk says, without looking up from a stack of papers. "You'll need to declare all your normal magical expenditures in triplicate this morning."

"Triplicate? You mean, paper?" The fake smile is gone, replaced instead by the same expression Rein had earlier upon catching a whiff of Liverpool. "You can't tell me they've even stopped the weighing service?"

The clerk finally looks up from his paperwork and his eyeglasses slide down. Rein braces for the incoming speech on magical taxes and luxuries, but it never comes. Before Barliman can open his ample mouth, someone behind them answers, "He can't. They've lost contact with the Forum Magicae earlier this afternoon."

"Lost contact? Will this week of inconveniences ever end?" Rein pivots towards the voice. "Inspector Paxton, I should have recognized you." A jar of ink clatters, toppled by Rein's sudden outstretching of arms. "In from the Americas?"

"Inspector Rein." Paxton grabs his hand with vigor instead and shakes a crumpled roll of parchment at the counter. "All the regulars left this place a little past noon."

"I'm woefully uninformed. And bored. I had no knowledge of any meeting," Rein says. "I just came in from the East myself, though."

"We wouldn't be invited anyhow."

The other inspector walks past Rein to slam his stack upon the counter. It is only now that Rein notices exactly how empty the place is. The customs building is the de facto point for all members of his guild, as well as for other outcasts. For him, it is as close to the office of the Curatorium as he is allowed.

"Those misers have been making it a real pain to do my job," Rein says. "I was obliged to take that dreadful old ship, *Worley*. Liked to have sunk—"

Barliman perks up behind them. "That was a wasteful use of resources." His needle-thin voice stitched its way into the conversation. "Oh yes, don't look surprised. We are aware of your liberal transgressions, Mister Rein."

"Transgressions?"

But Paxton's hand keeps Rein from continuing. "It's only going to get worse," he says.

"Indulgent, greedy old pox stains. They just to make our jobs too expensive, then they retire us."

"More to it, I think, Rein," Paxton says. "There's something very real taxing them, so they're taxing us."

A quick seriousness and change in the other inspector's demeanor takes Rein by surprise. He leans forward, then backwards. Then, as if the clerk were about to pull a weapon on both, he withdraws a crumpled letter from his coat.

"I received a dispatch," Rein whispers. "Can I trust you with my sources?"

"I've no love for bureaucrats," Paxton remarks.

"It's from the Musician." At once the other Inspector's mouth tightens. Rein pulls in closer, pressing his cane against Paxton's chest. "I know what you are thinking, but this is important."

Paxton tilts his head towards Rein's ear. "She's fairy folk. You know how that looks?"

"I'm aware." Stepping back, Rein again catches Barliman trying to lean in casually. "Would you like to get a drink—"

"Later," Paxton interrupts. "Maybe tomorrow? Inspector Smith is waiting in the drawing room, and both of us soon to be heading over too. 'sides"—he nods towards the clerk—"I'm afraid you'll be tied up for a bit."

He looks to Paxton and to the clerk. From some hidden shelf below, Barliman produces a binder of paper that makes the other stack appear as the foothills to a mountain.

"Bloody hell," Reins says.

"That's the spirit," Paxton says, slapping him on the shoulder. "Cursing like one of old George's. Before long you'll be a proper tea tipper."

"And here I thought you were my friend," Rein says. Then quietly once more: "Tomorrow, same place, noon? I found a lovely and quiet spot down the way."

"Rather thinking you found a lovely woman there," Paxton says. "But it's done."

Rein turns back to Barliman and adjusts his collar.

Chapter 4

Culsan releases the woman's head, letting it fall to the ground with a wet thump. Another night, another fairyblood, another body. This one was a performer, *a singer,* he notes. His fingers slide over a playbill of her last performance in the human city of: "Liverpool."

"I grow sick of this," Sethlan says, towering over the smaller Elf. "Was she really the last?"

For a moment Culsan considers. He lets his fingers slide over an inlaid desk, eyes poking every hole of the antechamber. It is a light place, airy. Paintings of dead women hang on paneled walls, and a large, keyed instrument dominates the center of the space. He walks towards a chair with swan motifs engraved on the rests and wipes the dust from the wood.

"This was the last on Earth."

"Yet we are no closer to finding the Evercharm." Sethlan stalks past both elf and corpse. "At least our trial and execution will be interesting."

Culsan snaps towards the taller elf, teeth barred in a quiet snarl. "Your trial, my execution. We are close," he hisses. "I just need more time to riddle this out."

"Riddle? Is this a game to you?"

The air between them feels thin to Culsan—suddenly thin and hot. Sethlan regards the widening portal that threatens to send them back to the Elfsea. His tone thickens to match the heat as the words slide from his lips. "There is a tale here, one that I think stretches across worlds."

But how to explain this to Sethlan? The song this one sung, the statues from the sculptor, and the writings in the fat man's chambers. They twine together, as if—

"When you hunt your prey brother, is it always easy?" Culsan continues. "Is the flight from your arrow the only thing you chase?"

Sethlan stops on the quarter turn of a third step. "Rarely." He squints, as if trying to crush the image behind his eyelids. "First there are the traces; the droppings, the tracks. Rumors and hints of a passing. Mists in the wind."

"I believe I have the scent of our prey." Culsan smiles. "Her name is Niena, but we are in the wrong forest."

"Speak plain."

His brother leans closer. Dark features recall their mother. Tall, thin lips. *Sethlan the fair. Sethlan the strong*, with his high cheekbones, and steely gaze—as compared to himself, whose perpetual frown and dwarf-like eyes help sink a face already dominated by a nasal mountain.

"Each of the Fairy-bloods we killed were working on part of a tale. The writer with his novel, the sculptor, and now this singer. They all speak of a Fairy lord and a girl named Niena. To be able to touch this many Fairy-bloods requires power. The girl is the one who played the Evercharm. But I do not believe this Niena is in this world. She can only be in Hearth."

Above, the portal widens with hunger. "You own a lot of beliefs," Sethlan remarks. "Thankfully we do not have to rely upon them."

"What do you mean?"

"Words can fly where we must walk," he says. "You see? I can speak in riddles too."

Culsan's answering gasp dies, as if lost on some trail, then erupts: "Cultists? You reached out to them?"

"The Evercharm is a tool of the Gods, and our enemies are numerous. We are two. I worry about the Artisans. They should be harried. By hounds, if I must." And then, more quietly, "By worse, If I dare."

The portal throbs and draws Culsan into a brooding silence. He paces between his brother and a stack of clothes hanging from a divider. Blood tracks wherever he walks. Sethlan's face is stoic, calm, reserved. The exact opposite of how Culsan must appear.

"Hounds," Culsan says, facing the hunter. "Hounds, unattended, will wreck everything and shit in the yard."

Sethlan's chuckle is worse than his growl, while Culsan's hands clench the edge of the chair. The whirl of the magical storm snatches bits of paper, dust. And the command in his words, as he speaks, "In the meantime, we must hunt down all possible leads."

"You still wish to travel to Hearth?" The force of Sethlan's comment mirrors the violence of the portal as it takes the last chain of a candelabra. "You see this, because you desire to. The simplest answer is like the best loosed arrow: straight and easy to track. These are all just stories, shared dreams or other nonsense. You have not lost the trail, you never had it!"

"Are you afraid?" *Wrong question.* Culsan's next words are louder, and fast. "Would you go home now? The great Sethlan, refusing to hunt?"

His brother scratches his nose. "You are as brash as an E'tah. Let's say I agree to this foolishness. How do you propose we do this?"

"Through the Fairhome."

The Fairhome. Culsan can see the wonder spread across his brother's features. The Fairhome is closest to the origin—before the pact that lead to the construction of the two worlds. This reserve, this leftover from ancient times, belongs to the Fairy-kind, who are nearly no more. It is a place of power. Yet is a dangerous gambit; the humans' Curators will know the instant the elves puncture this veil.

They move in unison. Hand painted wallpaper rips and flutters gold and yellow in the magical breeze. Sethlan nods slightly. "We may have time, but not much. Few Elves endure the corruption of Hearth long."

"Once we have the Evercharm, it won't matter. We can remake reality as we see fit."

"The Matriarch shall—" The portal ripples, revealing the Travelers' Stars. "We must begin at once."

They shut their eyes and reach out. A shared dream arrives on a warm wind, and beyond the portal an imaginary thicket takes shape. Trees thin out while the forest spreads. Leaves fall, and branches stretch to the changing reality. But darkness reigns here, and between this and the portal, patches of light burst and die like boils on a pale face. In these moments the scape looks alive, chaotic and dancing to some alien will.

Sethlan starts the spell. "And the skies flow gray…"

"As the sea, and the night till morn," Culsan says, joining.

A soft rain falls on the dreamscape, drizzles. The Elves, united in thought and song, take a step towards it. Thunder rolls in the distance, behind unseen mountains of the Fairhome. They take another. The smell of blood dies to a gust, and the fresh scent of leaves newly wetted overpowers them.

"Light carries the days—like leaves lost in the wind," they sing.

With a third stride they open their eyes. Ahead the stars rest in a flowing night. Neither looks behind, to see the portal fall— but they can instead feel the collapse. Like a hole being pulled close with a plug.

"And the waves crash—against shores, heavenbred."

Culsan scowls at the Fairhome, and it, too, adjusts to the mood. Once open and inviting, the trees begin to twist and turn. Already, thin saplings become wraithlike, whipping to a bitter wind. Oaks leer every way he turns. Even behind, now, where the portal and world of man used to be.

"Fairway, come again," he says with a sneer.

Chapter 5

Clouds hide the retreat of the sun and disguise the march of evening in bands of rain that rattle the glass. Rein's plans for the day are behind by at least a tumbler of scotch and a sip of wine; a two-drink minimum. The local cartographer has likely gone to bed, and his fingers are numb from filling out forms.

I'll go to the inn, find a room for the night. It may be too late. *I'll walk until I find the crime scene.* In this mess? Muddy puddles lurk beyond the reach of the pub's lantern. Rein leans lazily underneath a balcony overhang, confused, and fearing what the water might do to his French leather boots.

"Pluer op." He's soaking wet. "Kak!" First it was the common folk noticing him, and now nature defies him. The inspector loses a sock from wrinkled feet and slaps it hard against the wall behind.

Thunder interrupts him as he pulls it back over his sore foot. "Fine night for this klere, Curators." The wind, quiet until now, builds into gusts. One such breeze catches the splatter of rain on tile, cobble, and else, and whips it into every corner of the alley as a fine mist. The musky smell of the street mixes with the taste of warm, briny droplets.

They did this. A ban on magic. It's happened before, but not in many years. He can't remember the last time such an edict was used to pacify an area, but these are queer times. *I can't feel the Construct, I've been cut off.*

Other random thoughts permeate his mind too. He could take off his shoes. *Maybe.* Lose the trousers. *Well.* Throw off the damn heavy, soaked-through jacket. *Yes!* Run naked, screaming through the streets. *No, no.* Rein chuckles at himself, picturing a younger self in Harlem. His mother was not as amused as he.

But that was before his father's debts forced them to leave, and he to take up residence with a family business contact in Venice. Then Milan. And finally, when the Borromeo family had grown tired of the odd things that happened around a young Mr. Christaan Dei Rein, he ended up in a small manor on the equally tiny Isola Dei Pescatori. Until his master came. Rein would never forget the smell of fish, or the little daily challenges, like fighting the swallows for his morning bread.

He grimaces, pushing off the brick wall and into another made of rain. The swing of a lantern from a shopkeeper's hand shows a glimpse of his expression, smile wavy as the old glass. It takes a bit of further force to get Rein's foot back into the leather. Near, and far, the patter of the rain stops. The Inspector taps his foot into the last boot, then he, too, halts. The fast change in weather is more than out of the ordinary.

Everything is still. Not just quiet or calm, but physically *still;* lumps of water hang as if stuck in a spider's web. And the sounds, the baying of the storm, once muted through the veil of drink and the stuffed ears caused by a change in pressure from his earlier descent, are gone. He tilts his head left and presses his palm against his ear.

"Oh!" Thankful that the feeling of being underwater popped away, yet here he is, wading through the air as if he were a fish in an aquarium. Slowly one thought crawls its way up: "This must be magic."

"Took you long enough."

Curtains of water part, as if lifted by a string. And from be-hind, a tall, vaguely lamp-pole-shaped figure, steps forward. "I was beginning to wonder if you'd ever riddle it out. What was your first clue, Inspector?"

"Chancy," Rein says. "I should have known. Is this your doing, sir? A little brazen—"

"Right on the Curatorium's doorstep, I am aware," Chancy says, punctuating his sentence with a jab of his umbrella. "Funny how all our meetings fall the same way. You may not have your kinsman Vermeer's observational abilities, but I have no doubt you will leave your family the same legacy."

"That's rather kind of you to say, I—"

The edges of Chancy's smile drop. "I was sent by Lord Pembly. There is a coach waiting for you."

"Pembly?" *A Custodian, one step below a Curator.* "What would the Custodian need from me?" It was a fair question, in Rein's eyes. "You are aware I am not allowed upon the grounds?"

Chancy adjusts his umbrella. "I am aware. You will come with me."

Curators to Keepers. Keepers to Custodians. Those fools all had the same opinions of the Princeps Inspectorum, the age-old guild to which Rein belongs. He and other members were on a short leash. Rein's had nearly run out of lead. *Best to not pull too hard.*

"After you, then."

He is led down another side street, around a corner occupied by two cats stuck in mid-fight, and then back to dockside. There a plain black coach waits, surrounded by a menagerie of frozen Liverpool citizens. Through this trail, Rein's eyes scarcely leave the back of the Attendant's head.

There was a time he and Chancy were closer; not friends—hardly—but on good speaking terms. However, these feelings died long ago, killed by the delicate hands of a woman. What remains lies somewhere between indifference and the Attendant's dagger-like stare. Rein in his turn averts his eyes first to the driver, whose toothy smile contrasts with the blackness of the wagon, then to the musty compartment as he enters. A creak to his left announces Chancy is stepping in, and Rein turns at once to the window.

Beyond the glass were the better representatives of world culture, from Nova Scotia to the West Indies, from Guinea, to the Baltic. There were the silks, the spices and the exotic fruits. Beyond was also independence, free from the meddling of the Curatorium. Rein quarters himself hard against the other side, and hums three bars of Hadyn's Creation. A single door, held by the gangly coachman, finally closes behind him at the last note, and he, accompanied by Chancy, is left in a world of red velvet. Frozen people appear, left, right, as their coach lurches along.

"Ann Radcliffe could have written this," Rein says over the clip-clap of the hooves and the grinding of wheels.

A jolt from the coach forces both men to grip their accessories, and Chancy's strange English accent overwhelms Rein's muttered complaining. "How many times have you brought that apprentice of yours back. Six, seven?"

"It will be seven soon."

"Six," Chancy says, the 's' dragging. "I don't believe you will get any more chances, thank God."

Rein turns his attention back to the window with a snort. *We'll see.* Though it would be a terrible thing to have to break the news to Higgins. And as the wheels crunch through the debris-strewn road of one of Liverpool's choice neighborhoods, he idly counts the necessary merits an exorcism will require. *I'll have to pay twice to rid myself of his portly ghost.*

The carriage turns once more, and here the horses pick up pace, trotting down a long stretch of road. Last night's rain seems to have washed away most of the dirty snow haunting

Liverpool for the last couple of weeks. Tonight's may finish it. The drab can then sink deeper into the bricks and cobble of the city, with a chilly morning to preserve it.

"By God," Rein complains. "Couldn't you have frozen the smell too?"

In the New Quay slush has mixed with the scourings of a fire that swept through the district only two months prior. From the height of a roof, the corner of Lancelot-Hey and Chapel looks more like a bowl of porridge than a proper neighborhood. Chancy's spell also seems to stop at the line here, or else it is coming undone; Rein can hear voices. He cranes his neck and pushes closer to the glass, before the appearance of two old ladies and the sudden jump of thunder startle him back into his seat.

"Mourning bread, I said he got. Nothin' to do with the time o'day," he hears from one of the ancient creatures as the carriage comes to a stop. The coach sways back and forth until it settles.

"Course it's prime, straight from the whore—horse's mouth," the other woman says. "He got done in."

The clack of the door opening is barely acknowledged by the Inspector. He waits, staring at the two women until Chancy's hand finds and pulls him, thought and all, away. He slides to the Attendant's door, while his own latch groans with protest from the driver's efforts. Outside, the flip of Chancy's umbrella announces the return of the rain.

"I don't think I'll ever grow nostalgic for English weather," Rein remarks, but the Attendant doesn't answer.

The men share one look to the sky, but afterwards the Inspector's eyes lazily follow the back of his escort. Only the driver's gesture snaps him out of his lethargy. Afat droplet splatters on his hat.

Odors from the nearby dock flow back into the quay, straddling the little line of houses and drowning then in a tide of fish, spice, and other smells that can be only labeled as "peculiar." Reality further seeps in with the chill air. Towering warehouses—not old trees as he remembered—wall out the view of the Mersey. The Inspector paces.

"Every time I come here, I think the same thing; how could the representatives of a power that quite literally puts order to the world justify such a dismal location?"

Rein's fingers close around the pommel of the cane, and his attention wanders. The rain comes, harder. It patters against the refuse and fallen tiles. He closes his eyes. Carriage, man, horse, and building drown in the moment. One cannot tell between them. There is just the rain. Always the rain.

Nine years since my banishment. The last word ends his count where it began; his thumb. *This lord, he may hear me out. If I am careful and convincing enough, I might have a chance to see the library again.*

Visions of a great dome supported by two immense trees, one silver, one gold, sprout. Where their foliage should be, there are instead books upon branches laid out as shelves. And as many of those as there might be knots in the wood, or dreams of children. Fixed starlight casts shadows on the ground, where the grass is sweet, smelling like spring, lazy in the early morning. He rolls his thumb over the palm of his hand, then opens his eyes.

When he does, the images are gone, but so are the horse, carriage, and Chancy. The hoary buildings are the sole hosts left to greet him. Puddles gather ahead, surrounding the structures like shallow moats.

"I'll show myself in, I guess," Rein says.

Chancy's disappearance doesn't go unnoted; the lack of an escort, and the Inspector's inability to perform even the simplest magic weigh heavily, along with a damp cloak. Rein secures his hat against the downpour and rounds the small porch of a tenant house, where the two women from before huddle, keeping themselves warm with gossip.

Passing these with a tip of his hat gains him only hungry glares. A gentleman has money. And this one is alone. The exposure sends a warm flush into his cheeks and Rein suddenly feels overdressed, sloshing in the wet garments. He tucks his cane under and doubles the speed of his steps until the ladies are lost in the periphery, and he has squeezed through a small passage between buildings.

Long time since I have been here. What passes for a garden fills a gap laid bare by hands greedy for materials. Potatoes and onions occupy nearly every measure of tillable ground—along the few standing back walls, and even within the ruins open to the sky. A shed, cobbled together from the remains of an outhouse, provides a momentary relief from the storm.

"Not as overgrown there," he says, searching for a path through. "Could lead to the street behind."

Approaching Bryth Hall isn't a matter of finding the right lane or taking the left street. It is an adventure of perspective. For the homeless there is no such accommodation. The streets are the whores of the spread of industry, and the few businesses their last customers. There is no grand hall. No gathering of sorcerers.

Only with the right perspective is Rein able to look around the bedraggled people, to see the empty guard tower—what for anyone else would be another boarded-up hovel. The Forum Magicae exists by the will of the Curators, mostly separate from the world. Just as the prison of the elves does for them.

"At least I can still find it," he says. His eyes pick at the brickwork of a storefront's entrance. Red. Dirty. Broken—like an opium addict's mouth. But inside, the Artisans are the keepers of another sort of addiction, and Rein, with effort, looks past the shamble to see the truth.

Memories unwrap with the same care as his footsteps into this other place. Layers of bad masonry peel in the small first corridor. Brittle clay firms seamlessly in the strongest granite, and the skilled etching on the main chamber's door is a fitting frame for the architecture inside. Rein lets his toes brush the threshold frame. From within a burst of voices sparks and then spasms into acrid murmurs, like a tallow candle. When the door stops creaking, the room shows itself to be empty, and the Inspector is left to chew on this new worry.

Chapter 6

A creak of a door. A flash of light and sound. And then?

Rein steps into the fortress, treading illusion like water. "Hello? Anyone care to take my luggage?"

The echoes in the hall are real enough, as is the draft. Braziers hang lifeless from the ceiling, offering nothing, while the help from the windows stops at the corners of the great room. A few moments pass before his eyes adjust. The Forum Magicae is empty of people.

Rein scratches his lower lip. *This isn't*—a breath catches from an expected trick; the click of a lock, metallic and ringing. Teeth unclench, fingers loosen upon the pommel of his cane. *Right.*

"Right," he repeats. "But the rest of it? No, can't say it is right. The way should be illumed, now, in a sudden Ovid-style flash. Where are the guards? Where are the greeters?" Then, darkly: "Who set the automaton door?" It is not a thing that happens by itself.

There is no sign of the storm beyond the windows' opaque pane, or of Chancy in the hall. There are, however, pillars. Rein stops between two, one representing the Papal States and the other a hodgepodge of the Ottoman Empire.

No dust, so it has not been lonely long. Gold leafed and towering, this forest of marble inhabits a hall filled with mosaics. Each pillar is gilded in fine detail, festooned with a local myth.

Rein's fingers follow rivers of lapis, mountains of jade and opal in raised engravings as he passes. Double-wide stairs sweep up, and sweep him up from the tiled jungle through doors looming large that lead into the courtyard Their brass handles—shaped in the form of bent gnomes—are cold to the touch. He pushes in.

Stillness. Quiet. Calm. *Ruhiger.* But that is German. On each side of the corridor there is a procession of arches like at an abbey. Yet the craft of the Artisans is at work here too; beyond their dark recesses other lands await. The Curatorium has halls in many countries, and rumor has it, other worlds. Rein shudders, remembering the last time he walked past.

"I should have dried my clothes," he thinks, shivering near the first arches on his left and right. Rein looks to his feet. A yard of snow lays upon the marble, touching both the entrances to the Russian Lodge and the Arctic Circle Outpost. His own tracks through the slush retreat almost to the great double doors.

Black.

Ahead, only a few lit braziers remain, dangling from the ceiling center. Blackness rules to the right. A forest reigns in the expanse to the left, and gray snow with leaves packs the ground tightly. The Inspector can feel the dulling of his magic in his bones, and nothing stirs but sound, and the limits of dying embers try to fill the gap. So the Inspector turns at the snapping of twigs, or the flirting of a shadow, when he leaves these two portals behind.

With good reason. No one is watching the doors as he traces along the edge of worked stone. *No one human, that is.* The history of these "ways" supposedly stretch to the formation of the two worlds by the Artisans. *How long have they been left unattended?*

Winter grips his hands and walks with him past the duo of arches. Rein rubs his knuckles rhythmically. Myths and legends weigh and tease his senses, as does the snow. These extremes of temperature seem to dominate the corridor.

"There had better be tea at the end of this." His voice is quiet. "Lots of alcohol"—almost a whisper—"and Shepherd's pie." His voice dry and cracked like ancient wood.

Forlorn are the entrances beyond. Gaping, gap toothed and open *as the mouths of the dead.* Each seems worse than the last. From the cold of the north to the bite of sandstorms. And the gloom steals the last mirth from Rein. When a lonely nightingale sings to him from a nest of thorns, he stops and listens, entranced. *Must be somewhere in Africa,* he guesses. *Wintering still.*

Rozwi Imperium, says a milky, glowing description above the portal. The letters sink when he finishes, as if the stone behind them were quicksand, then re-emerge in another language. "Rozwi Empire."

A creature's shrill cry rips him away from the plaque, and he shrinks to the middle of the corridor. At his back he can feel the mist from another arch. And the many eyes upon him. Unsteady feet sweep him forward, forward. Faster, and faster. Until a raised tile sends him to one knee.

The floor of the corridor is smooth, cold. *This will not do.* The Inspector's right hand feels down past his mock pocket, and into the lining. Fingers tweak the edge of a spine, flip over the pages of his grimoire. He faces the pillar between two arches on his right, and of the rightmost choice there is little to see: wide expanses of sand lit by starlight and wind. The breeze from this one is hot and dry, rushing into the corridor. The other is different, and though the wind from there too is hot, it is also wet and heavy. Stale. The mix of the air oppresses.

But what if this is a test? The Construct, a power all Artisans tap from, was built from the older divine magic of words, stories, but blessed and empowered to work for lowly man. The same as those found in his book—a book that is highly illegal. It would be a spectacular failure to be both excommunicated forever from the Construct and from the world itself in one day.

One breath.

Two portals vie for his attention. Desert, bathed in starlight, and the other a jungle steeped in leaves thick as shadows. Rein's head flits between one and the second. Searching, probing. Finding. Black shapes roll past great patches of briar. The grimoire calls to him.

"No," he says, or thinks—unsure which. His cane trembles violently, reunited with the hand what had been inching towards the book. *Only in dire need.*

Two.

Slender figures, willowy, appear twixt the space of interloping branches. *Just trees, trees in the wind,* but the sound of him shrinking back and up onto his feet betrays terror.

Three.

Nightingales, other quiet fowl and clouds steal the starlight. The moon, though, is too much for the nimbi to secret away. Pale light picks at the canopy and blurs the line between the sky and the ground.

"Are those creatures leaving?"

Rein can't hear them now, as their shapes seem to slide between the trees. He stares long and hard at their lengthening strides, mesmerized—and then startles himself. *They're coming closer!*

Four.

The Inspector scrambles, his boots slapping stone as his pace picks up and flight quickens.

Five.

Other arches fall away, and their sounds and sighs are overshadowed by a shrieking in the wind behind him. The hallway dwindles, and the sight of a set of doors dominates, but he does not slow quickly enough to keep from landing hard against it. Iron handles jingle with his effort to grasp them.

Six.

Rein manages to open a crack big enough to shimmy inside. He enters in alone, surrounded by blackness worse than before. A moment's worth of heavy breathing is spent back against the iron, braced. His hand fumbles with a dry pocket and withdraws from it a match safe, then returns for a vial. Liquid sloshes as he uncorks the tube and dunks a thin timber in, and quickly out. With a spark of hiss and flame, a small portion of the way is illumed.

This hall, memory tells Rein, is more practical. Several passages freckle the sides, leading off into offices, dungeons, and even the great library. But one, unseen here, looms in his mind. Should he continue walking straight, he will come into the presence of a marble door. It is a large yet unadorned feature what occupies this precise location in every building of the Curatorium. And always leads to the same place. Beyond that door, the Curators convene.

"Devil—" The bite of the fire dies with its light, like a bee without a stinger. And the Inspector spoke loudly. Too loudly. He sucks in his gut, as if by holding his breath he can subtract from the noise already made.

A second flame, the second of a dwindling supply of matches. He raises the spark, extends it as far as he can. The hall remains in silence, broken only every other step by the clop of Rein's heel. Each second of light threatens his fingers, but the Inspector's interest lies in the stonework; the corners and hidden crevices where imagination is fed.

Something happened here. Fear of confrontation turns into something else, and cobwebs obstruct closer examination. Rein, retreats, stumbling away from a wall. A quick turn wicks the edge of scripture above a Sheela-na-gig: a vulgar depiction of a woman, commonly found in Ireland. The reveal of the spread legs ends with the extinguishing of the match, and the jerking of his feet. A plate of uneaten food clatters away from the errant move, and the smell of wine and spoiled egg follows him further. He pauses, then lets out a breath when nothing answers.

He won't be facing the council. That's what his gut tells him. It isn't a self-important Artisan or panel staring down at him from a round chamber he must fear, but the unknown. Light returns with his sigh. More abandoned meals around the base of the rescued stone, used as a support pillar, litter the area. Broken porcelain, scattered bones, and shattered goblets sparkle near.

This is a court of ghosts.
The silence deepens. It walks with him. To the end of the hall and near that fabled door. Empty. To the tapestries, hanging at the sides of a passage leading to the library. Also, empty. To the worn carvings above a Gothic door, marking the entrance to the old laboratories and some of the earliest construction. Through that forgotten door, and half-way into another match.

He snags his left foot while turning a corner. The match flies from his hand and splits the dark until it lands lifeless upon the stone floor. Yet, before the flame extinguishes, the culprit that tripped him is revealed.

It's an Artisan. Rein reflexively moves to the body, then stops just above the prone figure's torso. *It was an Inspector.* He dips the last stick into igniting fluid. Matchlight glints off silver bullion thread in the robe's embroidery. And sinks into a ruined face. *Paxton.*

A scream from behind. An unwholesome, shrill cry between that of a great cat and a hunting bird causes the abandonment of the body and the vial in one move. His footsteps drum after, faster and faster. The hall is narrow, and yet he ricochets off the walls as if he were a bullet fired wildly. Sweat stains his sleeves.

A door leading into a small chamber provides the first barrier. Soon it is joined by a table, chairs. Books, and random assortments with effort. A former monk's dorm, or so it appears, but he takes little time to study the architecture. The barrier becomes a barricade, though Rein is not calm. He watches another exit on the opposite side, unsure if he should continue, or guard it as well.

Where the klere *did that come from?* The arch-lined walkway? *Maybe.* The main hall. *Different screams, I think.* Somewhere deeper? The door opposite his barricade seems to hang, slightly ajar. Rein swallows, and his last match burns out in his hand, forcing him to muffle a cry. The room is plunged into darkness once more, and his mood is hardly lighter.

The narrow ways of the chambers hold the creature's renewed haunting call. Efforts to strengthen the makeshift fortifications are abandoned. Soon after, so is the room itself. Rein's panic leads him through the remaining exit—and into a chair, a bookcase, and another chair. At the end of a long list of furniture, he is tabled.

Glass vials flow like parted water, then shatter. Rein's arms slap the wood tabletop. More vials threaten to spill, but these he catches, sucking air in long gasps. It is at this moment that his hand finds its way to his spell book. And after, his mind to a decision.

Rein mutters, "I hope this won't be the last test I fail" as he grips the leather binding. The words on the paper flittering between his fingers are impossible to see in the pitch dark. But the book in hand is more for comfort; the weight of the power contained in it burdens his mind, not his arm. He closes his eyes and wraps his thoughts around the spell for "light."

"Sol Lochrein."

All corners of the room are immediately dipped in a strange luminescence. Vases, vials, the hardwood table appear in bursts. A lonely door, presumably leading deeper into the dorms and laboratories. Flasks, tubes, scroll cases—and other as sundries lining the walls—unblur more slowly. The implements of an Alchemist's table spread out before him. "Down here? Wait—" a peculiar name for an ingredient makes Rein blink. "Henry Woolworth?"

It's not an Alchemist's table. The vials, the samples—these are people waiting resurrection. "Necromancy." One of the few ancient practices allowed, satiating the Curatorium's need for foot soldiers.

Heavy thuds echo behind—someone, or something, is throwing their weight against the barricade. The Inspector's short-lived calm breaks. Papers litter the floor from his earlier stumble, and these get bunched, and shoved under arm. The remainder of the match-fluid, and the paper provides a needed material for his next—

"Sol an lochhrein aleanta," Rein recites. A hand's length from his head a luminescent ball erupts in a growl of magic. Hidden reagents suddenly shine on tables, books appear on dusty shelves, and long-forgotten devices wax into view in every corner, often stacked upon one another. The Inspector rushes towards the sole remaining, and unexplored door. Sweat prevents him from turning a knob with one hand, so it is an awkward juggle that finally reveals the passages beyond.

From the laboratories to the dorms he leads, and the light follows. Seconds pass in silence as he navigates the tight passages. The hall turns sharp right. Then levels. The signs of whatever pursued him disappear, but his knowledge of the layout is scant; he never came by the lower levels this way before. He stops momentarily at a barred window, arching deep into the floor itself.

"That must have been on ground level of an outbuilding once."

The window leads deeper, into the catacombs and cellars below the dorms. The Inspector touches the rusting iron. Through the cellars is a way out, but he cannot get past the iron bars, rusty or not. Rein leaves the window behind regretfully.

Eventually, another doorway crosses him. But it is the hint of light creeping underneath that sends him into a panic to end his spell.

"Fa'an—"

Shadows seem to move behind the door. Twitching, dancing. Rein swallows

"Fa'an dorchad."

His boots are loud on the rough stone floor. His breathing louder. The air in the tunnel is acrid; he smells smoke. And the crackle of a fire almost masks his approach as he rests his palm on the door's latch.

The handle rattles. Rein sucks in the bitter air and shakes off thoughts of preparing a spell of warding. Instead, he opens the door, cringing at the squeal. Immediately, he regrets his choice to enter.

"Good lord," he whispers. In the right corner is a well-stocked and busy fireplace. It would be cozy, inviting, if not for the corpses. The room is large, circular and thirty feet in diameter. Almost a hall. At the opposite end, another door lies splintered upon its hinges. With the placement of the bodies behind upturned tables, chairs and the sort, Rein is quickly able to deduce what happened.

His cane now serves as a different crutch—poking, prodding amongst the dead. The Inspector sifts through the gnawed remains of his colleagues. Shadows contort at the edges of the room, and every pale face, every mouth is open as if to say: *Leave.*

"Certainly, there will be a second link to the Forum Magicae proper from here," he whispers, concentrating on a darker shade of gray on the wall. Rein jerks his head left, up, then slowly back to the ground. Dead eyes stare back.

There are books here too, mingling with dirt, grime and more on the floor. Upturned from tables, possibly during the fight. *Or just carelessly tossed aside.* Rein spurts to action, and quickly rifles through the discards. "Students, maybe."

A distant crash hurries him. *But this isn't a school.* On the walls of the dank room, a silhouette lengthens from the shadow of a table leg. The Inspector holds his breath and squares his shoulders. One hand clutches his grimoire protectively, while the other withdraws a vial. The silhouette stretches around a corner. More join it, wrenching themselves in jerky motions from walls, shelves or such. And a low growl, like stones being dragged over cobble, accompanies their movements.

Rein slings the contents inside an arc. Words follow right after, seasoning the ash in the air with energy. The room appears to tremble. *"A tiginbo selladh neochionta."*

Shaky hands weave voice, dust and the firelight into magic. The Inspector eyes slink from corner to corner, stealing glances expectantly. He sees nothing, but hears more than he cares for. Low sobbing replaces the crackle of logs, and Rein steadies himself against the fireplace's mantle.

"A tiginbo selladh neochionta."

The sadness in the voices fall away in response, and then, as the sobs turn to angry wails, the room shrinks—the walls, never fully lit but now drenched in darkness, retreat and close in with the loss of light. Rein's hands dance upon lingering clouds of glowing dust. And it is as if the very blackness is screaming at him. From walls, from the floor. And from where the bodies lay.

"*A tig—*" the spell slips off quivering lips. Misshapen forms appear out of the dark. Hands, arms, and fingers crawl from cold mouths. *Demons, monsters. Same as those in the hall.*

"*A tiginbo selladh neochionta.*"

To the shelves. The Inspector strains, trying to turn the stream of magic to ward his escape. Tables and upturned chairs harbor the horrors too. He never sees them in full to this point; no more than a twitch at the edge of sight is granted. Instead, Rein senses their presence as you might a finger along your temple. They are everywhere, pressing nearer as his spell retreats, weakens. *The door!* They, close in. His eyes skip from corner to creeping shadow as he works furiously to anchor the stream to the walls. But changing the *Étincelle, Forme,* and *Mort* of a pre-Artisan spell is not this magic's strength, and the best he can do is loosely tie the ends to the door.

Their screams, growls—and the faces of the dead—are shut behind the door as he backtracks. Diminishing around the first corner. Diminishing, then rising as he slams another door behind him. Rein wheezes and fiddles with his pockets. The room he is in descends into a deeper gloom with every breath.

Kak. His light spell from earlier is fading fast. *Kak!* He is almost out of ash. Rein scans the tables, looking for anything he might use. "Dead rats in cages, a mounted cat a…mounted *cat.* Deftly, the Inspector works to set another ward on the door, hoping that these monsters might at least be polite enough to use it. On his way through to the other side, he snatches a handful of the stuffed cat's fur.

"There's no quantifying how corporeal they are," he says. The wailing and screaming stops at the room behind. But somewhere else, something far more physical ploughs through the passages, filling the narrow halls with the sound of shattering wood.

By now his gentlemanly pride has been abandoned. He runs, feels, and as the last light from his spell departs, crawls his way back to the laboratories and to the window half buried in the floor. Surrounded by darkness, Rein discards the rest of his trappings.

The wailing, screeching mass turns a corner. Off come his hat, boots. Thirty meters separate him from the end of that hall. Near, there are heavy footsteps. The breeches are next, the jacket and shirt.

"This isn't the weirdest place I've been found naked in," he muses as he lays his cane gently aside. His grimoire he shoves through the bars, to hear it thump on the floor below. If he were to return, best not to leave that in a hallway. The vial containing Higgins' remains is fast wrapped into a cradle made from his cravat, with the pages of his grimoire as stuffing.

Rein kneels, flitting the cat's hairs between his thumb and index finger as it will, combined with his concentration, serve as the reagent and *Forme* of his spell. *"Agusan,"* he mutters, and he tries to mouth the rhythm, hoping that his lips might remember the proper start. "That's the Étincelle. And here I become, which translates to—"

Crockery shatters somewhere. *There were vases, urns, in the alcove ahead.* The wailing comes closer, opposite. "Become, is *fas,* what is also the *Mort.* Here in the old tongue it's *Setha.* Yes, *Setha* in the old tongue." He closes his eyes and inhales slowly. *"Agusan setha mia fas."*

Rein, naked in the corridor, lays the wrapped bundle of his friend's remains on the ground. The air is stale, but cold. The hour, late. He swallows as the magic raises goosebumps all over his skin. The noise that approaches first is the one from the laboratories. Scratching, growling, and huffing—*It's a ghoul.* Though it isn't fear that brings the inspector to all fours.

Each stone under his paw feels like lightning, and the smell and sounds that flow over him, as he reaches the ground, are nearly overwhelming. A second step. His ears twitch, and his long tail frizzes in mid transformation. Walls seesaw in a strange display of color and perspective as his body makes the final shift. The next move brings him face to face with the bundle.

While footsteps approach from behind, he bites down on the cloth, slips through the bars and lands in the water below with a splash.

Chapter 7

Many adjectives that can be used to describe an alley are equally representative of a tunnel or catacomb. Damp, perhaps. Cold, certainly. Maybe even dreary and lonely. But Rein is focused on the first two, and having been forced to leave the lion's share of the grimoire behind, he is also feeling decidedly at a loss.

Murky water laps at his chest. Now his face. Rein drags himself out of the filthy water, losing fur and more on a sharp paving stone. The spell that maintains this form requires only concentration after a successful cast, though this is difficult while half drowned in freezing water. He shakes his coat, taking account of the run-down alley and its distinct trade, tanneries, which inform both scent and scene.

Dusk. A dirty moon greets him, choked by the belch of a hundred chimneys. The light only seems to reach the top of a facing wall, as if scared to wander further. *This place isn't safe.* He scans the alley for purchase up, finding it in the form of a broken pipe.

Debris, sagging floor tiles, and decay leer everywhere—there is seemingly nowhere up for him until he remembers: *I am a cat.* The dirt and stonework become perches, the drain a ladder. With the vial of Higgins jingling off rock and more, he mounts the wall.

And towards a retaining wall he goes. And up into the black he ascends. When Rein finally crests into the moonlight, he looks down. From here, the alley appears more like a red-bricked canyon, leading into the nearby waters. In that direction, the masts of several ships rise above the low dock buildings like rows of pines on blasted, bare hills. Sails and flags replace leaves. The foliage on the shore is positively exotic as several nations' flags ripple.

The moment of peace gives clarity. With the damper on Artisanal magic, the infiltration of the Forum Magicae, and God knows what else, he is left with few options and many uncertainties. But there is one fact he can count on: Chancy certainly led him into that trap. *Why?* Summoning ghouls and other archaic beings lies in the realm of the older powers. Which means *Cultists.*

Wind, fouled by rotten fish, briny water, and possibly fowl shifts his direction, and Rein skitters up a patch of tiles to get onto another roof. There are many such groups who would love to take control of the Construct. Yet, he's never heard of any Cultists that could succeed or even have the bravado to attempt such a siege. There is still the why.

His ears twitch. Footsteps in the direction of the quay could be anyone, or anything. Chances are that soon they will know he escaped. Rein hunkers behind a chimney, using it to block the breeze. He must leave Liverpool, and quickly—but to depart without investigating the incident that brought him here… *they are connected.* Old magics. The fall of the Forum Magicae. *The Chords. I must risk a visit to the crime scene.* It would be folly otherwise.

But how shall I find it? Bloody bastard brothers, if they had at least waited to be gutted, I'd have an easier time. He had never been to this part of Liverpool and only knew to find the crime scene by a few landmarks and the vague directions between.

Two orbs flash across the way and Rein backtracks up the slanted tiles behind him. In the space between the chimney and roof-wall to its opposite, something moved. He hesitates, and for a few moments there is nothing in his world but those lights, and him. Shadows around the chimney lengthen. Those are not orbs.

A ghoul.

Luminous eyes follow him as he retreats. Rein turns left, then right. The pale form of the creature stretches into moonlight, and its clawed hands wrap around a gutter. Back, now, focused on the monster, the Inspector's fur stands on end. He dithers.

The ghoul leans fully into the light, unafraid, letting strings of black hair dangle over a withered jaw. The second it waits there, watching, is over in an instant—as hands, shoulders, and arms lurch into action. And in that second Rein's indecision is also done. Cat, vial, and parts of the roof tile flee as the ghoul lands almost soundlessly on their side of the divide. Dashing left. Dashing right. The creature easily overtakes him at every change. From rooftop to gutter. From gutter to street and back again. Missing only thanks to the reflexes of instinct. Backdrops of the city disappear in blurs of gray, taken with the wind and rooftops under paw.

At the back of a corner building, Rein halts, recognizing the façade of the Lyceum behind the shades of trees in the distance. The ghoul does not, spinning out around the chimney and sending a barrage of broken shingles, nails, and more from the digging of its claws. The growl in the Inspector's throat comes naturally as the monster stands between him and easy escape.

Step after step, the ghoul creeps forward. Rein backpedals while peeking left and right. But he is on a flat roof now, with uncertain drops on all sides. The only chance is the chimney pipe the creature has against its back. *Which may be big enough for us both.* If not, he will have to leave Higgins behind.

He has nothing else to regrow him. The ghoul shifts its weight from left to right, watching Rein with hungry eyes. The Inspector crouches and pins his ears back by reflex. He will only have one shot at this. *On the count of three.*

One. The corpse-like skin of the ghoul glows in the moonlight.

Two. The inspector's claws dig into shingle, and he shifts the weight of Higgins to his left ever so slightly.

Three Rein takes a half leap to the right. The ghoul strikes from the left, and he flattens just enough for the attack to fly high. Off-balance, the creature lurches stiffly with the right. Rein dashes up the extended arm like a ramp, launching off and onto the chimney. The sound of the creature's claws striking metal and a long, sick hiss are what follow the Inspector down into the pipe.

A moment squeezing through the dirty ironwork spills into another, falling and sliding along the chute. The adventure ends in a soft thump as he tumbles into an abandoned fireplace and room. Neither he nor his cargo is injured, but Rein, once white, is now a dirty sort of black. He shakes his body, licks his paw —then coughs. *Bloody cats.*

Not much remains of the furniture, made in a style fashionable before King George's time. A chair sits against the wall on his left, a desk on the right. Mold is everywhere, for though it is rather dark in the interior, Rein can smell rot. There are no open windows.

Glass breaks somewhere nearby. His eyes dart immediately in that direction, but there is a door in the way, decayed and broken. *This is not over* —another crash and annoyed screech follow—*I am going to need to fight.*

But not as a cat. He releases the image of the stuffed feline he had been holding all this time. Paws grow into hands. Fur gives way, and the familiar form of the Inspector fills the small room.

"Kak—" A shrill howl makes the man cower against a rotten desk.

"Listen very closely," Rein says to himself. "There is a ghoul in the other room. Do not panic. You are naked, without any weapon and woefully unprepared magically. Good news, though, you won't have to worry about soiling your pants." Bare feet on wood patter just outside the door, and the Inspector's voice drops to a whisper, "Ghouls are made by a circle of twelve Necromancers. In short, I am doomed."

The Inspector overturns a wicker chair nearby and breaks off a long reed. He winces. The noise stirs the beast, and his efforts are mirrored in the crash of rotten timbers at the door. Rein, trembling, stumbles to the chimney.

The door shudders. Wooden shrapnel flies, and the gnarly face of the ghoul appears through a break in the wood. All teeth and madness, shining glibly in the night. But the Inspector only stirs the soot with the tip of his stick.

I must find the needle; I must find the creation thread. The ferrule of Rein's stick glows like embers as he removes it from the flames and swings it towards the beast's face. A withering hiss reaches through the hole, followed by the sound of claws rending wood. The Inspector's mouth moves as if working a spell, but the ghoul bursts through just then.

The creature slashes at Rein, yellow claws biting into the floor. Fast the ghoul recovers, driving forward again and again and forcing him to circle the room. His makeshift wand threatens the monster's flailing limbs with fire, here, and again, but to little real effect. Two milky-white eyes stare into him, unblinkingly.

Rein trips, and the ghoul rewards him with a deep gash in his left side. *"Insdo draheach."* He utters a basic spell, requiring no materials. Lines, traces of stitches, and deep crevices glow on the monster, giving it a strange, unreal bearing to go with its undead horridness.

A surprise lunge sends him to the floor where a struggle immediately ensues. The wand saves the Inspector from the beast's ferocious attempt to bear upon him, meeting it with flames. Yet every attempt to escape is unsuccessful. Driving, pushing, gnashing—the ghoul swabs the floor with him like an irate sailor.

Everything that is animated unnaturally has a thread. The last lesson of his mentor, Gabriel, who showed him the magic of the cultists, flashes between the pain and blackness.

Dizzy and bloodied, he peers upon into the yellow-toothed maw, losing focus. Losing strength. "Sofie." Delirious. "Anna—" He squints and strains more, nearly pulling a muscle in the fight to keep those fangs from him. It is here that Rein sees something. A single, lone strand dangles from a mane of grizzled black hair.

The hallmark of its creation.

This time it is Rein who lashes out, pawing at the mangled mass while the ghoul's claws find his flesh. Pain makes him focus. The inspector wraps his hand, mind, and will around the creation thread and pulls it out, needle and all. Screams fill the room. The monster's. His.

And then it is over. He pushes the once-more lifeless corpse off his body. Exhausted, Rein's head thumps against the wood floor. "I think I am done for tonight."

In this case, the flesh is already provided. Gabriel's voice fades, fades, then quietens to a sound below that of the wind whistling through porous walls. *For the animus, Necromancers prefer using a needle and thread.* Rein sits up. He regards the corpse through tucked knees, then closes his eyes. The gash on his left side is found quickly, but he doesn't have the strength to mend it. Rags, fashioned from the remains of drapes, serve instead. Until infection sets.

I'm too busy to die. His gaze drifts over to the boarded-up windows on the east side. Soon, the rest of him follows. "But of what—?" Lanterns out on the street wink in strange regularity and there is a hue to their light which he finds unsettling. "What worse fate I must face, I cannot be certain."

Chapter 8

Faster. Branches strike Sethlan' face, and their leaves, thin and needlelike, grip at his clothing. Faster. Over a rotten log, through a narrow pass of boulders. Faster. As if he could outrun the dusk. But that is impossible; it is always night in the Fairhome.

His mad pace halts at the edge of a ravine, where fresh air catches up with him. Starlight touches the top of trees, left, right, filling the horizon. There is no visible way down. Sethlan breathes deeply, and his lungs burn from the effort.

"Almost there," he whispers, risking a glance over his shoulder. What he sees is an encroaching darkness. Creeping, creeping—and close now. *Are these the same men I knew, so long ago?* Sethlan closes his eyes, takes two steps forward, and jumps.

Air whistles in his ears, and the sound and feeling of branches snapping, leaves shredding, complete the world around him as he plunges through the canopy. Sethlan lifts his arms, letting the rush of wind fill his otherwise tightly wound tunic. "Halfway."

The ground is approaching rapidly, but the elf is unconcerned.

"Here."

In the Fairhome, reality is always what you make of it. The very world is shapeable to a strong will. The elf smiles and imagines himself landing safely in a clearing near his brother, Culsan.

There is a soft thud. The cease of the whistle, and the loss of the chill flow of air. What replaces it is the smell of grass, untouched by the morning's mist. Sethlan opens his eyes.

"Where have you been?"

Culsan. "Have you done as I asked?"

"I have," his brother says slowly. "I never thought I would need to remind you that the longer we tarry, the colder the trail will become."

A butterfly flits around a tree, landing and launching in turns from wood that squirms, while vine-wrapped branches move jerkily. They are too slow to catch anything. In the background a little bird cries out for a mate, not realizing his loneliness. It is the canopy that rustles an answer. And sitting on a log is the elf scholar, Culsan. His face is framed in the light of the Travelers' Stars. His black hair is changed, now tied neatly behind, and as he looks up at Sethlan, it is impossible for him to hide his concern. In his hands is the writer Graham's book.

"This is important," Sethlan says. "You wished to know my allies? You will, now."

Dust gets lost in the light as pages flap with a one-handed slap. Culsan stands. "What do you mean by that?"

"They are here."

"Here? Who is here?"

Strong gusts carry the bird call away and tilt Sethlan's head in the direction of the wind. Beyond the second line of trees he can see little; for there, somewhere in that line, those he summoned approach. And these guests bring a different stain. He rolls his right shoulder and glances at the outer line of the circle he asked Culsan to prepare. Toadstools surround the two elves.

The bird call stops. The wind stills. Sethlan, sensing a change in the air, clears his mind. He is not entirely successful, as the forest breathes oppression back at him through the filter of shade and gloom. This is natural here; it is born of the thinning of the fairy race who are tied to it. A second, other intruding presence is alien, unnatural, and evil.

"What have you done Sethlan?"

Culsan's demeanor betrays a lack of trust. *Wise,* Sethlan thinks. Also, fear. Even so, a strange sensation makes his stomach roll too. His long fingers pick at the linen strings in the tunic, as a shock of leaves rolls ahead. He is thankful for the extra caution with the ring of toadstools.

"Have courage, they are only men." *Powerful Sorcerers,* Sethlan thinks. He inhales slowly. The ground around them darkens, as starlight is stained by something earthbound and dreadful. He strides along the edge of the wards, the toadstools protecting them. *They've become devils.*

"We meet on neutral ground," he says. "In the land where three thrones once stood."

A breeze. A sudden chill. A prolonged silence

—and then, an answer from the forest: "We shall sit upon the throne of dreams."

The voice rushes from the undergrowth, on a gust of air that is hot and thick. Culsan, whose curiosity had lifted him to almost the equal of Sethlan near the edge of the circle, falls back at the pressure his brother's hand, and whispers past his ear, "Anyone who can enter this world is a rival in power. And we should not deal with rivals."

But he ignores Culsan, The question "Who are they?" and later, when several blurry figures approach the line of darkness, "What are they?" make Sethlan push his brother further behind him and step forward. He clears his throat.

"The Artisans—"

"Dead."

Nearby trees twist away, one by one, from the queer nobility dreamed by Sethlan to something more sinister. But the hunter has no time to check Culsan, and though he is sure his brother is causing the change, his eyes still find their way to the end of the circle. "And what of their masters, what of the Curators?"

"They remain." Each syllable the figures utter is labored, heavy. It is an old accent. "And in time shall be handled, as we agreed."

Sethlan clicks his tongue, considering. "Keep them occupied, keep their eye upon you. Do so, and you will sit upon that throne once more. This I promise."

You idiot. Culsan's eyes say as he pulls his brother face to face with a yank of his collar. *You can't*—But the hunter turns away, not interested in reading his expressions.

"We must keep in contact," Sethlan says to the Others. "I can —"

From the edge of the woods there is a flash, a rare light. It wobbles in the middle of the void and drops, rolling along the ground to Sethlan's feet. He looks at an orb, then at the darkness—and without turning from the latter, reaches between his legs and recovers the ball of light.

"I am to use this?" Silence. "How?"

A long moment threatens to leave them in more of the same: silence. Yet this time, an answer comes. Branches wilt on the edge. Darker strains of blackness peel back, and in these Sethlan can see shapes. People. One emerges from the forest. He is not at all what the elf would expect. *His attire is similar to those Manneligs', those E'tahs' back in their city.* The figure bows low and removes his strange hat.

"I apologize for the conduct of my colleagues," he says. "They haven't been socialized in at least an eon. Forgive them."

The elf takes a tentative step forward. "Give me your name."

"Oh, I never give," he says. "Especially not to elves or fairies. All that contract business can get tedious. Lending, though? I might lend. You can call me Chancy."

"Lending then," Sethlan says. His right foot brushes against the orb and reflexively withdraws. "You represent whom, precisely? "

"The Teamor."

Sethlan grits his teeth. "The Teamor, interesting name. Yet when I made my call, I did not know it. Where is Erasthmus?"

"Old and weary," Chancy says. "Rest assured your message reached the right address. Oh, it may have taken a little longer. The post always drags its feet. "

"This is not what I asked," Sethlan says, then gestures at the wood. "I do not know you."

"Names," says Chancy, laughing. "What is more important than that nothing has changed? You could get to know your new friends. Do you gamble?"

"It is important that I know the nature of those I have bargained with."

"The deal is already done," Chancy says. From the night surrounding him, an umbrella appears, and is taken by this representative of the Teamor. "You called, we answered. You agreed to the terms; it is late."

Chancy had been flexing the umbrella shaft up, sometimes opening the device or casually regarding the elf. His polite smile is the only thing remaining. He steps to the edge of their wards and pierces them with unblinking eyes. "The Forum Magicae is undone, the Curators sieged. All who have the power to oppose you are gone. Your Matriarch must only break their stronghold, and together we can both reclaim what is rightfully ours. Is this enough?"

Culsan tries again to gain Sethlan's attention, but those long arms throw him back easily.

"I suppose it does not matter who sits on that throne," Sethlan says, finally. "So long as they do not again try to take ours."

"That is another deal, for another day," Chancy says, flipping his hand up together with a shrug. "As for the orb, when you need us, when you are ready to strike, peer into it and think of your new friends. We will answer. We always do."

As quickly as he appeared, Chancy melts back into the forest gloom. At the line, the figures follow. There is no longer a breeze, but the hot, fetid air remains. Sticks. Sethlan tilts his head, trying to peer into the line of trees, the tunnel beyond, and into the meaning of this moment.

"It is a Seeing Stone," Culsan says. "Wrap it in cloth—do not hold it with your hand, fool."

"Be quiet." Sethlan snaps. And then much lower: "They are still here." Both look beyond the circle, eyes feeling through the black, touching leaves, branches. As they watch, the oppressive turn of the forest lingers for a few moments, and then in a quick breath falls back through the tunnel like water down a drain.

"The art of the Stones' making"—Culsan pauses, and rolls his eyes, as if trying to pull the words from the air—"is guarded jealously by the E'tah Curators. They are made without song, without story or phrase. That is the work of an Artisan. But what Artisans are these?"

"The worst kind," Sethlan says. *I am a fool.* "The best. An old enemy."

Culsan's head tilts again and at almost the same time his eyes light up, and his manner is caught between confusion and understanding. "We must hurry to Hearth."

"Yes, we must."

Chapter 9

Where is she? The Musician always kept strange hours, but Rein was sure she'd be here tonight. He stares up towards a dark balcony, shivering in his nakedness. *Might be hiding. Lord knows I should be, too.*

His wounds need better treatment. His stomach as well. And cold nights are hardly a remedy for either. Rein hobbles into the alley between her building and another, contemplating burglary then deciding he has neither means nor strength to attempt it. All the time, he can't shake the feeling that he isn't alone.

"At least it isn't pouring down any longer, but what am I supposed to do now?"

Chancy. Rein's thoughts turn dark, and he again finds himself looking towards her windows. "I bet he had something to do with this. With all of this." *I should find him, I should*—"No, I shouldn't. That's in league with my other bad ideas."

A gap between the old building and a newer construction provides concealment and access to a private garden. Water drips from drains above, pattering alike on refuse, Inspector, and dirt. The passage is damp, narrow. Each inch threatens to open his wound, undo his weak spell of healing.

Rein stops just before a tumble of brick and roof tile. "There have to be others still alive." The body of Paxton comes to mind unbidden, the face a bleeding mess but recognizable. "Barliman? *Kak*, no. I'd rather kiss a Cultist."

He inches ahead, forced to progress nearly spread eagled. *I could find some clothes and go to the smaller post in London. Organize a resistance.* That idea makes him bite his lips, which evokes a growl from his stomach. "They'll make me fill out forms for that. I wonder which one it is to report the eradication of the Forum? Green or blue?"

Lord God, I will have to, though. The garden opens ahead, and he crashes into it face first thanks to a raised bed. The sweet odor of fresh dirt is the first thing to hit him, then the pungent bite of rue, and some winter herbs. Rein lies there in the dark, wrapping himself in the smells. Forgetting the carnage.

"Maybe she will find me here in the morning," he says. "Among the leeks, the wintercrest salad, and—"His stomach growls again, and the next moment he is scouring the garden, ripping out ripe and unripe vegetables. The onions never tasted as sharp. The wintercrest so bitter. Rein spends equal time gorging and apologizing for the ravages he inflicts. But the food is fresh, if dirty, and he can feel strength returning to his limbs.

He lies on his back, exhausted. There are no lights here, not even the stars above, as they are still cloaked by a drizzling rain. Slowly, Rein feels the need to be taken into sleep. He counts the droplets. Feels their tickle on his skin. Shivers.

"Which opera did I see her at?" She wasn't performing. They met at first in the hallway, before the opening. They met after in a corridor. On the stairs. Later, in her apartment. He never learned her name. They spoke through their love of music, and magic. A chance friendship, he thought, until learning she possessed gifts like his. Gifts which they both used for the Curatorium.

Thunder sounds far off, and a slight breeze visits him on the ground, rustling the many herbs, filling his nose with the remains of lavender. *One, two.* Again, another grumble from either his stomach or the sky. *The sky.*

"She was a cultist." His whisper is taken by the same breeze. *They weren't all executed by the Inspectorum.* In some way that made their connection far more intimate, so he didn't need to know her name, only that she was a musician. Thus later, in small circles, he gave her a name: the Musician. It stuck, and her influence grew. He no longer had to protect her.

Except from himself. *Turning her in would have been wasteful then. Staying here, and having her killed, wasteful now.* The rain picks up as if in agreement. Droplets patter, touching leaves, earth, him. Then just as quickly, die back to a drizzle. It is too cold to sleep, and he is still on edge.

"Just another in a long line of strange partnerships, that is the life of Christaan Dei Rein," he mumbles. Fleeting, random chance, and often unfulfilling. *Save one.* Rein sits up. Throughout his musings the peace of the garden never cleared the feeling from before. If anything, the sensation intensified.

An iron gate bars the exit, but neither it nor the longing to remain provide much of an antidote to fear—fear which encroaches, fear that swallows the leaves and beautiful smells, as surely as he did the vegetables. He reaches over, undoes the lock, and then steps into another alley between buildings.

Thunder returns. "How many seconds was that?" Cats yowl everywhere, and if he listens long enough, he can hear drunks answering. *Four, or fourteen? No matter, it is retreating.*

Through uneven lanes he limps further; their paths are worn down by years of storm washing without any proper drainage. Here, too, the buildings are older, and uneven—*limping,* he thinks, noting again he is anthropomorphizing.

With the food came strength, vigor, but also a willpower. *To London?* No. *Round up any survivors in Hackney?* "It won't hurt looking." Even though, deep down, he's made the decision to go the rest of the way alone.

The friendly breeze from before changes, howling its way down the straight path he just turned. He doubles his pace, mentally. His feet nearly triple it.

Chapter 10

Down forgotten lanes, and behind decrepit buildings. Deeper. Beyond the touch of stars, the reach of wind. Onward. Away from the smell of the Mersey, but closer to the dank underbelly. This portion of the city is small, yet unknowable. The Inspector has never been here before.

Rein jerks around, trying to follow what he thought was the sound of feet. *Nothing there.* Or nothing there now. *Paranoid. It's just,* "No, I'm not crazy. I've seen things, heard them in the dark. Whispering."

Sobbing.

"They are never there when I look."

The unusual appearance of a lantern casts shadows on an opposite wall. He approaches, cautiously, his nerves landing somewhere between flighty and panicked. Long limbs project onto the plaster wall from a gap, and wild thoughts churn in his head. *A back end of a tavern.*

"Or a portal to hell." He's unaware he is talking out loud. The shuffling of feet though, is real, and there is the splatter of water, possibly from a drain.

The creak of metal stops him, and he watches the lantern sway on its own post. There isn't any wind here, or even a slight breeze. He saw no hand, but really, there's little chance he could if it came from the gap. Rein's fingers dig into the mortar of a bricked-over doorway, inching his way finger by finger to get a closer look. The shuffling gets louder with each foot of progress.

A piece of wood stubs his toe and clatters into the quiet alley. He yelps, dumbly, then tries to melt into the wall. Poorly. Out of the gap, an old man stumbles left, right. The two share a quiet moment as the drunkard buttons up the rest of his pants. He then tells Rein to "piss off."

The Inspector wipes his eyes but decides to "bugger off" instead. Here, smaller streets abut into larger, so he must be careful how quickly he moves. By now he is closing in on Hackney street. The air is unusually acrid.

Rein stretches around a corner as the first gray flake settles on him. The way is clear; only broken pots and a march of boarded-up doors wait for him along this passage—*but that sky.* A second flake falls. Then a third. The Inspector stares at a red crest of light poking over a roof. He turns another corner and stops.

It in is the air. Ash and flame; fire and death. A torrent of gray falls here, even deep into a narrow alley. Rein's legs buckle, yet he manages to make the other side. A wider street opens onto his, and he can make out the charred remains of a block of houses. This part of the Mersey is well lit still as Liverpool's volunteers battle the raging fire.

"I don't know why I thought it would be different," he whispers.

The bucket brigade works tirelessly, their shapes moving between the flick and fan of flame, reaching even Rein's little slit of an alley with obscene shadows.

"There will be no help tonight," he says, too loudly. Somewhere in that menagerie a head turns, forcing Rein to retreat further. Voices come to him then, over the roar of fire, while he can feel his heart pound against the wall.

"I'm afraid I am of little help, Officer," comes a familiar voice.

Rein leans forward to risk a glance, but a flash of flame and light makes him retreat even further, for fear of discovery. He holds his breath, trying to calm the beating of his own heart, which surely must sound like drums. *Chancy, the devil take him.*

"I was on my way to another establishment, when I noticed—well, I mean, how could I not? It reminds me of London 1666."

He will be ripping us out, root and stem. Why? The bugger's motto had always been "Quid quo pro."

"Well, no, of course not firsthand. What type of thing is that to ask? I read about it, naturally."

Ash continues to fall on him like a dread mockery of snow. *Can't go to the customs house either, not that old Barliman would cause any trouble. Unless he touches the ledgers.*

"And there I did see the houses at that end of the bridge all on fire, and an infinite great fire on this and the other side of the bridge," Chancy's tone dramatic and sweeping.

I must do this on my own. But how can I make it there before him?

"Samuel Pepys, or would you prefer something biblical?"

The bastard likes to talk. It strikes Rein now, this: that maybe he isn't speaking to the officer. He's not heard a single reply. The Inspector angles his right foot. Never has he feared that man, but right now every inch of his body is screaming to run. A gulp of air is half filled with ash. With the talking he had ignored his instincts, which were telling him that, far from being watched, he was hunted.

Chancy coughs. "And throw them into the blazing furnace, where there will be weeping and gnashing of teeth."

The Inspector coughs and seethes. *I am not dead yet.* The ash sticks to the mud at his feet, already clumping. Rein is fast taken back to their time in Amsterdam, where both studied their primaries. It was there that a trick he played on a then teenage Chancy set him on his current path.

Rein bends over and gathers a gob of the ashy mud. Along the wall he, too, finds the remnants of a pallet and quietly sets to break off a timber.

"But the beast was captured, and with it the false prophet who had performed the signs on its behalf."

Lord preserve us, why won't he just shut up already? From the mud, Rein forms a little round ball. This he mashes onto a piece of timber. More timber, more ashy mud gets pressed together. Until he holds in his hands a very crude and nasty doll.

"Of course, it has nothing to do with fire, I just like how it sounds right about now."

The ash comes thick, and heavy. And there is a constant breeze his way, bringing with it both the smell and taste of charred flesh. Rein wipes his hand over his face, then over his wound. He mashes the traces of fresh blood on his fingers into two eye pits for the doll.

"Thord homsagus a fureac," he says to the puppet. He closes his eyes, connecting with his double, even as the doll wiggles and struggles in his fingers.

Gently, he sets it down, and faces it back the way he came. The Inspector opens his eyes, observes his creation's first movements, and smiles. It won't move fast; there's no guarantee that it will be able to navigate the streets. "With a little luck…" he hopes, looking past the opening in the alley, towards the fire to see if Chancy is coming. The former Attendant has stopped talking, which is never a good sign.

"It will have to do." Rein turns back to the puppet, watches it stumble off in the direction he came. Then, quietly and carefully to mimic the same path, he follows. When they come to their first intersection, he takes the opposite path to the doll.

"Hope is not a plan," he says, as his decoy disappears into the black. "But it is something. Right now, I will take it."

Chapter 11

Seven streetlamps guard the manor where the murder happened. Their acorn bulbs don't produce much, only enough to form a small barrier against the night, but Rein can't risk being seen. He takes a glance over his shoulder, then pivots back towards the street. Dirt rubbed on the end of a makeshift wand is half the *Forme* this time. With a few words and a tap of the stick upon the cobbled ground, one light fades.

Pain from the wound is stoked by sudden movement. Rein pulls the bandages tighter. His vision blurs but he continues snuffing out the lights.

Four remaining. Wind rattles the lanterns on their hooks. Three. Damp air finds them, sticking to Rein's exposed arm and raising goosebumps wherever it travels. He presses his face against the cornerstone of a building. The last sign of the weather turning arrives with the pungent odor from the whale-oil lamps.

He lays his hand against the stone and picks at the mortar. The setting evokes an inner-city decay with an amount of antiquity that easily summons a touch of nostalgia for him. The manor sits at a corner lot, protected on one side by a small garden with trees. Between its first and second floor there is a slight bulge, owing to the aging wattle-and-daub construction.

"No sign of Higgins. Of course, he wouldn't be here."

With a sigh, Rein approaches the manor purposefully. The last three lights snuff with a drum tattoo on the cobble so that street, alley, and house plunge into darkness.

"Be on your guard," he reminds himself. "If there are more ghouls, do your best to bleed on them properly."

Movement at the gates turns out to be only leaves, and shadow, and he coughs the main entrance's red door upon approach. The inspector avoids the lion knocker, circles his finger around peeling paint and finally lands upon the handle. He closes his eyes as his hands wrap around the brass knob, muttering, "God preserve me."

A whisper fills his mind. Short and sweet, it simply says "Amen." Thereafter put aside by the click and groan of the door, which opens into a wide hall. *Without the Construct...*His thoughts fall away with a shake of his head. Rein, hoping against reason that Higgins is somehow with him, walks in, closing the way behind him with a gentle push.

Open doors sag on hinges. *Could use renovation.* A parlor stands open on the left, but Rein slides past this, making for the stairs immediately before him. His eyes, still closed, remain so as he places his right foot near the worn landing. There are no more sounds, however, and he instead feels with senses other than sight, sound, or touch.

The ghost of Higgins though, against all odds, finds him. "Are you going to sleepwalk through this whole investigation?"

Shock. Relief, and wonder. But not *ruhiger*, or any other German word for calm. "Firstly, keep quiet," he says, blinking his eyes open. "Secondly—" He loses track of where he is, after viewing his face in a mirror. "I can feel the Chords. I can feel them!"

Higgins' ghost snorts. *Snorts?* The Inspector ponders: *How does a ghost snort?*

"You can feel them," the phantom says. "Yet your connection to the Construct is cold."

"Time makes all things cold—first your coffee, then your corpse." Rein places his hand on the baluster. "Difference sources of magic. Mankind does not reign over nature. Speaking of which," he continues, "how did you find me?"

"Death is an older magic than the Construct," Higgins answers. "That's a story for another day, though. What should I do if you come into trouble?"

The Inspector's attention returns to the stairwell. "Pray I survive."

Only one flight separates him from the second floor. One flight, and Rein can already feel the power of the spell that was woven here. His hand quivers, his feet move in a hesitant stomp.

Now, the Chords. The last word fills him with marvel and wonder. Even with the present danger. After so many years of false leads, dead trails, and hints, he was here. His talent, finally being used to its utmost. The Inspector's chest swells with more than air as he plants both feet onto the landing of the second floor. He takes a steady, long breath.

"How peculiar."

Beyond the tick of an eight-day clock, and beyond the sound of wind throwing itself on the walls just outside, a strong pulse of music plays for his ears alone. Rein steps out, following the lead past a doorway whose open maw he teases with his fingers. Through another threshold, where the magic weaves into a distinct melody, and he gasps because of it.

"The Musician was right." The rhythm of the old ways hushes him. *I can feel the Chords here.*

Higgins though, interjects with: "And you still can't dance."

The pulse grows stronger as Rein enters the room. His feet feel instinctively around the fallen books and toppled furniture while the melody rushes past. Unable to sustain himself, Rein nearly collapses on the ruin of a desk and rubs his eyes in wonder.

The emotion of whoever was responsible strikes him. "Whoever?" *Yes.* It is rapidly clear to him this was caused by a "who," as opposed to a "what." The knowledge makes him shiver, and he reaches with his own emotions to gently sort the strings of the memory like a weaver pulling threads.

Cold tears of rain stick to the window as the memory of the events that transpired here play out without further urging. The milky droplets harden, throwing the view of the garden into meshes of green and brown. But Rein waits, and the rest of the song overtakes him. Blinking away his own waterworks, he lets the raindrops fall away, replaced by snow as this man must have seen. There is a raging storm just outside the window.

Footsteps at his rear make him spin around. But there are no ghouls.

"You must be Leon Broadhurst," says Rein.

A vision of a what was once a man, enters the room. He is tall, but slightly crooked. Neither portly nor thin, and his translucent banyan with floral motifs draws attention to a small pouch of a belly. For the face, there is little to tell. This Leon could have been a banker, a lawyer. A judge, or a priest. He has that everyman chin, and the only thing hinting at his profession would be the stack of papers scattered around a resurrected desk.

As the memory settles back into this reality, so too, does the past recolor the scene. Ghostly luminescence disappears. The green and gold of fine silk seep past the gray. And finally, life returns to the cheeks of Mr. Broadhurst. Rein looks on, curious. The man, the vision, walks past him to the desk, carrying a candle whose light manages to fill the small room. The only hints that this is still a dream over reality is the lack of smell from the tallow candle, or the warmth from a passing brush of the hand.

Rein watches Leon. Observes the man scribble. Hem and haw at whatever he is writing. After several moments, a disturbance disrupts the man from his wistful gaze through the window. The Inspector turns to see this new devil, while the ghost continues with his writing, muttering to himself. The door hang opens, as does his mouth.

Sliding into competing versions of reality, there is another man. Rein squints. Two men. They stand in the hallway before the room, and between the present, which the Inspector occupies, and the memory. These men bring chaos. Lines of furniture, debris, bend. Colors splatter his sight as if tossed from an artist's pallet. Pulsing music, warping scenes are followed thereafter by a sensitivity to touch that turns the weight of his clothes into a trial of sensations.

Rein digs his fingers into broken wood. His hands sweat, and every inch of his body itches, but the colors slowly stabilize. He grits his teeth. His pulse races. The stress builds and builds like the draw of a recurve bow. Chance takes his gaze to the ceiling.

"A portal."

As the men in the hall join the room, they become more and more a part of the memory. Their approach is different from Leon's. Menacing, predatory, and—*aware?* For an instant Rein was certain they saw him, recognized him. He steps to the side as one stalks to the chair where Leon sits.

When the first, a sly, lithe creature passes, the reason for the feeling becomes clear. *Elves.* A flash of a smile, a short glance his direction are enough. Rein cowers to the window and pushes against the scene with all his emotion, like a man trying to hold back a dam's flood with his bare hands. Bottles roll out from underneath him. Wood splinters, and the Inspector falls back against the windowpane, knocking it open.

The stumble throws his head half out the window, enough for him to recover and see shadows and shapes melt from the surrounding streets. *That's now, that's now.* Terror takes him away from the edge, and he spits out a garbled cry at the approaching elves. Rein shifts his weight upon his left leg and flails through both memory and debris.

At first there is only a little change in the predicament of the room. The elves advance, Leon stiffens—then relents. The portal widens. But the moment he is free of entanglement, Rein rushes past vision and ghost. Away from the room. To the next door.

Wailing, like before in the Forum Magicae, closes in from outside as he leaves a bedroom. Rein rushes to a third room, then a fourth, and finally casts open the door to a small, rectangular antechamber. Just underneath a paltry window sits a bathtub. Higgins is nowhere to be seen.

The Inspector bites his thumb. "It's not a bucket—"

Raging sounds of inhuman misery from the garden interrupt him, but it's the wind coming downstairs that gets Rein chanting: "it will do, it will have to do." Immediately he sets wards on every wall, corner, ceiling and floor. But these are weak, without true *Forme.*

From the cravat where Higgins' remains are held, Rein withdraws a litter of papers. Furiously the Inspector paws through them, before finding the one that will serve. It's a modern variant, written in pidgin French, a poor, and unstable choice for a work of scholarly creation. Rein's laughter blends into the shrieking at his door to terrible effect.

With his hand against the wall, Rein can feel the trembling and bulging of the wards. *"Animer, ruminer et laisser voler à Navan,"* his timbre rising. *"Animer, ruminer et laisser voler à*

Navan." Blood from his own wound supplies a part of the *Forme.*

The hand movements, the repeated intervals of foot positioning. The strange, markings on the tub required. They all come together to make Rein look as if he is practicing some new sort of interpretative dance instead of a spell. When the last syllable flees his tongue, the bathtub rocks. Then creaks. Howls of rage, and whispers of promised torment flood the room as the wards falter.

The Inspector hops over the brim and slides to the middle. And in answer to his cold rear on colder metal, the bathtub lurches forward and up, crashing into the wall below the window. Wood puckers. Rein pushes himself up to lie properly. The tub flies into the wood again, and again the Inspector slides back to the middle. But this time wall, window, and everything else gives way to open air in a thunderous shattering.

Over the edge of the rolled brim, a naked sorcerer looks upon the streets of Liverpool. The former manor retreats, streets sweep by as the tub lumbers through the air like a bumblebee. Rein, happy to be away, is nonetheless somehow unsatisfied.

"Ireland," he says. The night air is invigorating. Using the moonlight, Rein rifles through his papers for resolution. "Don't have the *Forme* for that one or, this, or—A cloud, or something else, rolls between him and the moon. Rein stares ahead, immediately sees the "something else" and the unfortunate rigidness of his spell.

"Oh—" The looming steeple of a church comes closer, closer still. Rein sinks back into the middle of the tub and utters a prayer, in different veins, for the sturdiness of tub and church.

Chapter 12

A candle tries its best to light a windowless room. It fails. Maybe it should stop. Or maybe just set its sights lower—like illuminating the pages of Chancy's journal. Lower still is the desk itself. Perhaps the aged oak would even benefit from the ambience.

His pen dips into the fountain, only stained black before, dripping after. Over the plain desk. Onto the yellowing paper. The flame reveals more of the former Artisan. Up a line of steel buttons cut in star shapes. Up, and onto hunched shoulders and tightly pinched arms.

The first letters written are fat; drunk with ink. Almost illegible. The rest complete the pattern, forming sloppy, squashed words, phrases. The man rubs his temple. Creases created by years of fake smiles are smeared black. And at the man's brow —the ink makes them look like muddy ruts.

"You think you will always escape," Chancy says. "You think I've forgotten, forgiven. You would be wrong on all accounts, Mister Rein."

Anyone else looking upon the page would never be able to decipher this scribble. But for Chancy, it reads: "There is neither sanctuary for justice nor safety from the truth."

Memories of the explosion in Birgu, Malta, of the destruction left behind at Porta Marina, play. Luring Christaan Dei Rein into that trap was easy. Sabotaging the investigation, difficult.

Yet it is Chancy's masterful work, placing the sole responsibility for the catastrophe upon the Inspector's recklessness and negligence, that stirs a nostalgic chuckle. The pen taps again as he daydreams about what the court hearing must have been like. *If only I could have been on the council, if only I could have seen.*

Rein will still die. "I am a patient man, my old friend," Chancy mutters over the creak and pop of the chair's joints. *Necessity has required me to be pragmatic so many times, I...*

The pen strikes the edge of the desk, adding another stain. Chancy shakes his head and brushes flakes off his velvet collar. "May the devil take you," he mumbles.

Again, it's happening again. Instead of standing, he hovers over the journal to bear down on the last line written with his thumb, smearing away the word "justice." *I know where he's headed. And because I know*—"I can use him; I must use him. My Masters would expect it."

Somewhere in the dingy cell a clock sounds the hour. The pen is put away. The journal, closed. Chancy stands and straightens his suit, but a small cachet near the candle glints invitingly, and he hovers there, considering. His fingers trail along the desktop, follow gaps where the different boards have separated. Manicured nails tap lightly on the lid before flipping it up.

A woman's image stares back. Long hair pinned up and dusted, and a dress that indulges far too much in light pastels for modern tastes but draws attention to an elegant neck and innocent smile. Chancy cups the tarnished silver brooch in his hand, then lifts it gently. Without further ceremony, he fixes it to his breast and departs.

The walk from here is short, but unlit. The path though is familiar; he's trodden these halls since he was a little boy. Warehouses are hardly palaces, but when the fickle nature of business abandons them, they have a way of coming together. *Just like orphans.* Somewhere above this cellar there is a toppled roof and lower floors that are open to the sky. The buildings separate themselves there at street level, but here—here the rot has combined them into modern catacombs.

The former Attendant turns another corner and steps through a hole expanded with the use of strong hands and hard iron. Neither is his. Beyond, a faint glow beckons him. Chancy climbs into a low tunnel. Water lives in the walls, and trickles in rivets to the plain flooring. This place isn't rare in Belgium. Though the open space that teases him at the end of the tunnel is surely prime property. If anyone else knew of it.

The ferrule of his umbrella reflects the bioluminescence in a chamber. There is one path breaking a ring of paved stone, marble *purchased in Spain.* Chancy takes in the room's ambience—the dim light cast from strange mushrooms upon the rotting walls, the old stonework, but most importantly the sea of smoke that lingers beyond the broken circle.

These would be his associates, patiently waiting for the meeting he called, obscured by hoods and veils. As the face of the Teamor, he has no anonymity. It is a dangerous boon in any secret organization, but he wears his recognition with pride.

"Brothers, sisters," he beams, soaking up the muttering as if it were cheering. "I am absolutely tickled that you all answered my request so quickly. I'm afraid I did not provide any confections, so you have my sincere thanks for your commitment to our cause."

Our cause—the figures fast go silent at this, but he is used to it. His acceptance into the Teamor was less an induction than a pact. *They'll warm to me.* "I also want to express my gratitude for leaving your thralls—"

"Get to the point."

The command could have come from anywhere or anyone; follower or rival, left or right. Chancy does not react. His features are still as bright, his smile seemingly inviting, and his voice cheery when he says: "—and other pets behind."

Servants. The majority of those here would never have been allowed the magic to even glimpse the Fairhome, let alone been trusted to deal with elves. *These do not even know whom they serve.* Their place in that meeting, was instead supplanted by his own will, and enhanced by the power of his Masters.

He takes a step forward and one over a bag laying in the middle of the circle. *No better than thralls.* "So, orders. On the task that was given, what have we learned so far?" The assembly stirs once more, the muttering threatening to grow. Chancy fiddles with the handle of his umbrella, then jabs it towards a figure at the far left. "You there, what have you found?"

The room goes quiet again. At length, the man answers. "The elves' prison is weak, failing—"

"Old news," Chancy says, turning away.

"You did not let me finish." Chancy stops. "Their prison falters, because the Curators are dying and cannot control the Construct."

"A theory. A poor theory. Our masters are just as old…" With the implied threat of *I dare you to call them weak* hanging.

"They could be drained by their usage of the Construct."

"It's as easy to say that they might have eaten too much cake and have indigestion. If it were as you suggest, we would have been up to our ears in elves in 1666, the last time they had a little spat amongst themselves. Let us consider another angle," he continues, pausing only for effect. "Why haven't we been summoned? The elves could assault the Curators now. Instead, they spend time passing through the Fairhome and killing fairybloods in Liverpool. What do they gain by doing this? *Cui Bono?*

"Eliminating threats." This time, the answer comes from someone on his right. The voice is lighter, more feminine. He turns around on his heels gently and regards the small hooded form with a smile.

"Awful poets shouldn't be any concern, I think," he says. His finger replaces the jab of the umbrella, and he arcs around the room, pointing them down.

"They are looking for something," His arm continues the turn while the rest of him stands up straight.   "And I propose that something is the Evercharm."

Murmurs threaten to take over the discussion, but a series of strikes on the ground with his umbrella breaks the momentum. "What could disrupt the Construct?"

Tap.

"What could weaken the prison of the elves enough that the Matriarch would send her fools on missions?"

Tap.

"Only the Evercharm."

"It's a legend," someone says.

"There's no proof," yet another.

"Legends, myths," Chancy snaps. "If you haven't the stomach to chase after the unknown, then you are no better than the Curators' lackies."

The former Attendant wedges the ferrule into a crack in the stonework and leans heavily on the handle. "Follow the elves. Report what you find to me."

Several different spells of obscuring overlap amongst the listeners. Chancy's mustache twitches, and his hands fidget on his brolly's handle.

"Another opportunity has presented itself which I must attend to," says Chancy. "I am the voice of the Masters, and the Masters require this of you."

One by one they disappear, leaving him alone the middle of his circle. The lights of the fungi dim, falling between a dull glow and faint glimmer. He sniffs and checks the room for any lingerers. Once satisfied, he bends down and shoves his hand deep into a burlap sack.

Chancy's body spasms when he first wraps his hand around the orb hidden within. He breathes in, and out slowly, pulling his fingers back from the sphere. *Again.* And again, his arm plunges into the sack to once more touch the device he uses to speak with the Teamor—the true Teamor, not these pretenders that serve them.

The cold glass warms almost instantly. He closes his eyes, struggling against the contact, as waves of heat flow into his arm. The umbrella dislodges from the crack with a pop and clatters on the stone.

"One of the Inspectors has escaped judgement: he had arrived late to the scene," he announces, sensing the question from those creatures, those former men that still linger in the breathless void. "I feel there is an opportunity here."

He opens his eyes. Fire-rimmed smoke swirls in the center of the sphere. For a second only Chancy, thinks he sees them; a flash of silver, the edges of a crown. Impossibly wrinkled faces and black, soulless eyes.

"This Inspector has a rare gift; he can sense the Chords. Or so I have been told by my late, former Master." The pain of several questions draws Chancy's lips back as if to scream. He, instead, gulps air, then continues in one long breath, "The elves, this Inspector. If led right, they can be our hounds. If it is the Evercharm they seek, it can be ours."

Chancy reaches into a hidden pocket and wipes his nose with the handkerchief found there. "Yours," he corrects himself, staring at the crimson smear ruining the cloth. "It has already begun; he's fleeing to the only person left that can help him. Yes, I will see personally to the operation…"

And be responsible for its success, or failure.

The Speaker of the Teamor thrusts the orb back into the bag then remains, letting the quiet of the room seep in. Finally, when several minutes have passed, he leans down and retrieves his umbrella.

Chapter 13

"You know our Hearth isn't the only world, right?"

The old man's attempts at conversation are ignored, as the barmaid continues to clean the worn table. She must have seen a lot of men like him pass through this tavern. The joke is on her, however, as Oberon is a fairy.

"Earth is a real place," he says. "More than just a myth you've read—Oh, well, actually you probably can't read."

The rag manages to soak up some of the ale he's spilt, but most is swept into a crack. And his shoes. The codger's hands are also still wet from the last time he tried to take a sip. Bony fingers pin the mug like a spider might prey.

"It's a strange place," he says, following the movement of the towel as if charmed. "Full of weirdos. Most of them live in city called London."

Long ago he would be doing something else than bothering some young barmaid, but youth, with the greater part of his magic, is gone. These days his remaining power is spent guiding his granddaughter, Niena,—a girl who has more in common with a cat than a fairy. He hates cats.

"What the bloody…"

An outburst staggers through the closed doors of the tavern's kitchen, spilling over the chatter. The ancient fairy tilts his head to listen, picking up the same thing as everyone else, a male voice. None too happy: "What are you doing in my larder?"

Oberon coughs. Most of the patrons' attention remain around the circle of their own mugs. "But Earth. I'm sure you have heard the fables. Told to you by your mother, perhaps? A father? No?"

The woman squeezes a dirty rag over a bucket, ignoring his insistent, high-pitched voice. Mumbles from the other tables hint at growing tension. Near the fireplace a man complains loudly at the lack of service.

"Would you believe me if I told you there were adventures happening right now?" Oberon asks "There, in that other world?" Over the sound of crashing plates, Oberon continues, "Though saying 'right now' is a bit simple minded. Time between the world of Earth and of Hearth is a fluid concept."

The ruckus piques the bar maid's interest, and she leans back to take a sideways gander at the door. Oberon can guess what is happening: the tavern owner, or the cook, is struggling to hold on to a teenage girl he caught stealing. He pulls at the wench's sleeve just as another crash shakes the floor.

"It's not exactly relative, you see."

"Yeah," she mutters and lifts her arm. But the fairy latches on.

"Though still related."

"Are you crazy? Let go now, or I'll—"

The door to the kitchen slams open, and there is a terrible roar beyond. A figure bursts from the opening, leaps over the table and tumbles in a calamitous string of curses to land at the fairy's feet. Close behind her is another.

"Think of it like a third cousin once removed," Oberon says, his eyes narrowing while all others are on the teenager—a thin creature, with long black hair. His granddaughter, Niena. "Sometimes they are part of the family."

Her chaser climbs over the bar after, toppling steins and mugs as his rotund self flops over the counter. He struggles to his feet, but no sooner than he is able to stand, the man storms towards the girl on the floor.

"Tam?" The barmaid cries, accidently stepping between the girl and the bartender.

"And sometimes not." Oberon slides towards Niena, who smiles up at him sheepishly. By human standards she's a pretty child, with curious eyes and high cheekbones. Tapping twice on his nose gives her the code for "It is time to go."

"You idiots, why don't just stand there and drool?" Tam bellows.

That's Oberon's cue. He releases himself from the wench and steps over Niena. His arms stretch wide, and his chest puffs out. The edges of his sleeves billow.

"I think you should leave my granddaughter alone." Torches around the room sputter in rapid fire with a wave of the fairy's hand, and in the sudden darkness the fairy looms large.

"Bless us," the bartender says. But this wish is drowned by the panicked shriek of a patron. The ground trembles. The wine bottles clatter. Before, Oberon had been little more than the picture of a dotard. People would look at him, see the shriveled features, the spectacles. They would mock the long gray beard that clings to his chin like a weed. Maybe even laugh at the pipe hat, and the one bit of fancy wear he possessed: the bright-red vest. Not now. When the old fairy lifts his staff, it is to gasps of "wizard" and "sorcerer."

Those nearest to his table stumble over each other to get away from the wisp of light, emanating and spreading from the top of his staff, and the sound of the great oaken entrance door rattles with the fevered attempt of a few to escape. Faces light up under Oberon's scrutiny, and the air seems to fill with the expectation of terrible things. Magic. Strange, weird, and curious—but certainly terrible; after all, who ever heard of an angry sorcerer summoning sticky pastries?

Instead, he sings: *"A shepherd's pie with butter again, bet the toilets roar back. A shepherd's pie with butter again, bet the toilets roar back."*

And it is a terrible thing.

"Ripped your trousers down the main, now you're exposed to the crack. Don't forget yer sewing mate, rabble rabble rabble rabble here she blows!"

By this time, the entire common room is staring at the fairy. Niena, under the cover of darkness, crawls to the exit. The torches towards the front burst back to life and cheerily burn away the gloom. The fairy, once imposing and ominous, shrinks.

His song continues. *"Greasy sausage barely browned, two years old or more, that. 'Twas ere a more raucous time, stuck with the privy chore, black. Ripped your trousers down the main. "*

A bread roll bounces off the fairy's head. Then another.

"Now you're exposed to the crack. Don't forget yer sewing, mate, rabble rabble rabble rabble here she blows! Jelly strained with—"

"That's enough," an old woman yells. "Blessed Chords."

Quick glances around the room reveal it is about time to leave, but this doesn't stop Oberon. *"With vinegar rum, Ole navy provisions. "*

The first non-edible thing tossed is a mug. The shatter of the ceramic at his feet and the spray of ale fast get his attention.

"You can call them sticky buns. "

The next is a full bottle, and it crashes into the side of the table, breaking the rhythm. Oberon gathers himself.

"Back," he yells, waiving his hands at two men ambling too close, making as if to toss him out. "Back, I'm contagious."

Someone yells, "With what?" And the fairy responds with a gesture that implies, "All you see here."

A chair overturns nearby. He stumbles right, and the move elicits a healthy crack from his hip. On his way to the door, a soggy vegetable skips across his shoulder. Thankfully, the aim of the assailers is of the same sort as their walking: curved. Bottles miss their targets. Insults however, hit their mark, and these follow the old fairy outside.

Yet, forgotten in all of this is Niena. When Oberon has finally escaped the last of the throng's ire, he drops the doddering act and slinks into refuge. Around the corner, and into an alley flanked by dilapidated rows of tenant houses, he slumps against a pile of timber. Age has not been kind, especially since mortality leaped rather than crept upon him. Since Shenan some strength returned, but not enough. He is an ancient fairy in the body of a dying old man.

Breathing comes heavily in short, fast gulps. His arm trembles. At the corner, just beyond a cart, a crop of raven hair emerges. The fairy immediately straightens. The raspy breath quiets down.

"That was a fine mess you made there," he says,

The girl appears more interested in playing with the hooks on her blue overcoat, which is too warm for early summer, than being lectured. She shrugs.

Oberon signs. "I can't keep this up."

"Would you rather have paid for the cheese?" Niena asks. From the folds of the coat she presents a chunk of Wendel's finest, an expensive import.

Oberon snatches the morsel from her. "You're forgiven," he says through a mouthful of cheese. "But let's go home."

Home. He knew the word had a different meaning for her. For him? Home had always been wherever his children were. When they died, it was with his granddaughter, Niena. Oberon leans on the crumbling debris and stares at the back of her head as he turns to leave. *Soon.* He must warn her, soon. The passing of a fairyblood touched him in the only place where his magic still reigns: in dreams, alerting him. *Worrisome things creep ever closer. Set in motion by this child's innocent actions.* The playing of the Lyre. Yet the fault lies with him. To save her then, he might have doomed Niena now.

The Lyre, he thinks, nodding, but his lips form other words. "Yes, yes, let's go. We have much to do."

Chapter 14

A piece of parchment in Niena's hand fights back against her attempts to unravel it in an alley where clay-brick buildings lean. She responds with curses, as her fingers press down against a wall, dragging a brittle, black substance over the hide.

She sneezes, having accidently rubbed her nose. Charcoal. The workings of the spell stain everything now, but if she has done this right... *"Gadwich Imi basi."*

Nothing happens. Above, clouds roll past the midday sun, and fairy and granddaughter are treated to a succession of shadow and sun. Light. Dark. Light. Dark. Repeating for the span of twenty breaths, until Oberon decides to walk over to the wall, and shade Niena with his hat. The gesture doesn't make reading the scribble any easier for her.

"I know I'm doing this right," she says. Her good humor from earlier is going, going—seeing Oberon's wry smile brings on a glare that is sharper than anything she can stab him with. Gone. "This isn't your idea of entertainment, is it?"

Oberon props up his elbow with his other hand. "Absolutely. Watching you spout gibberish at a wall is high theater."

"This was your idea," she says. "So, if I look silly—"

"It might be important for you to learn human magic," he says. "It is either that, or dance lessons. And you always look silly."

Niena straightens her dress and the parchment again, mouthing the words silently before finally repeating: *"Gadwich Imi basi."*

That should have worked. But a strange feeling is the only result. Corkscrews? She can't name the sensation, and analogies and metaphors jockey for position in her head. *Like someone's walking around the outside of my bedroom.* Oberon leans further in, and whispers.

"Only one way to be certain," he says. "You'll need to back up to the end of the alley, get a real head of steam going, and charge the wall full on."

Her eyes climb down from his hooked nose to the march of buttons on his red vest and back again. The fairy's smile slides away with the tilt of his head. Niena, without blinking, taps the quite solid wall.

"Eh, as I feared." He shrugs. "Fairyblood is apparently too potent. Or we need a human sorcerer to teach you, because honestly I don't know what I am doing."

"I'd rather have used that parchment for something else."

Charcoal flakes off her fingers as she rubs them together. It is a dangerous job stealing from a temple. Also, something about stealing from the gods—with everything she has since seen—made Niena uneasy. She crosses her arms.

"Maybe we should stick to what we need first," she continues as she rolls back against the wall behind. "Like food. And blankets, and heating for winter."

"What is cold to the sorcerer who holds the fire of creation?" Oberon says. "What is food, water, to the magic that feeds this world?"

"What is a frozen corpse of a starved old fairy, to the girl who has to bury him? I think—"

A sunbeam lazily wanders over her grandfather, and a brief image of him as he was back in the castle of Shenan's jail imposes itself. She softens her tone and runs her fingers along the brick at her back. Paper crinkles on the rough wall. "I think our magic is enough for what I want to do."

"Words of power are quicker," he says. "While we must tell a tale, or sing, humans can just rattle off a few lines. You never know when something like that might come handy."

The edge in his voice, the concern—both are the bait for memories living in the deeper pools of her mind. Remembrances of loss.

"I might not be around to protect you," he adds.

"Let's not talk about that today." She rubs her temple. Distant sounds of cheering and music disturb the peace while Oberon settles against the brick wall. Niena, instead, lifts her head to listen. *The Eventide Parade.*

Next week it will be a time of fasting as the bay waters turn purple with algae, and the fish die off ere mating. Little will be harvested from the sea for the next two months. And then, it will be some real rough footing. For the Eventide marks the beginning of time before the start of a new year. Oberon and Niena will need to move inland until autumn if they want to eat well. And that is not an easy prospect.

As if sensing her distress, her grandfather moves to comfort her, but the sounds of the parade come closer. Music mingles with the voices, growing vibrantly in pitch and volume as the procession marches through the nearby streets. The event is early, and a twinge of regret is bitten back by pursed lips as the music and shouting drop.

Oberon steps back. "If you leave now, you might still make the opening ceremonies."

Niena grunts. This last year she was early and got there before all the good spots were taken. Last year things were different. They had food, water to spare. She had taken a job in a weaver's cottage during the day, as no one would hire a woman for scribing, and worked nights at a tavern. But the scandal of the latter had gotten her removed from the former. Word moves fast. It scurries along the streets with the beggars into every home. Soon, Niena's reputation preceded her at every interview. Now, thievery was the only way forward.

Amidst her self-loathing, the pomp returns with the *thomb, thomb, thomb* of heavy drums, enticing Niena to bob her head unconsciously. "Wrestling contests and jugglers. Once was fine, more than fine."

"Well, we need to get inside, and as usual I must do it myself."

Fallen leaves and other trash shift in a gust. Niena moves away, slowly. The fairy rarely works his magic anymore. Her own craft, though similar, feels different, looks different. She steps further back into the alley and watches her grandfather approach the wall. And then Oberon sings.

"Meet with me, my loyal friend."

She blinks. He buzzes along, rising in a timbre and tone similar to drunk bees. As she watches, he works his fingers into the grooves of the mortar.

"Show me the home, where we shall spend. An hour? Or a day?

A memory nibbles at the bait like a fish. Before she can react, the line jerks up, bringing it violently to the surface: her own first song. She had not been able to perform anything with such power since.

"Open to me, my loyal friend."

A twist of the fairy's wrist. A tug on his sleeves to pull them back. Then, with the sun threatening to sleep, he thrusts his hand out and through what once was solid brick. Mortar falls away under his fingertips and leaves no dust or debris.

"Remember, Granddaughter, feel the magic. Tell the story."

"Yes, Grandpa."

Gray bricks sink away. The reek of the inner building hits. She stumbles in, and the entrance closes behind. The fairy pushes ahead, leaving Niena's fingers to explore and fumble around a small crevice in the dark. Then a hole, searching for something she left there earlier. After a few breaths, she withdraws from it a worn, roughly oblong piece of clay. Unlike what she's seen Oberon do before, waving hands over the tapered end does nothing. Her raspy breaths break into coughs—the odor of mold seeps in.

"Rubbish."

A moment of searching through a bag finally brings a sigh of relief. With a strike and a sizzle, the oil lamp awakes. Dull light steps out and swirls its fingers in the inky black. Walls are revealed. Real rubbish. Niena lifts the lamp high over a piece of roof lying in the center of the room.

"I'm really looking forward to some sleep," the fairy says. But his granddaughter has already caught up and passed him. Her eyes move reflexively to an arch set in a far wall, then beyond stairs previously hidden. It takes a moment for the feet to follow, and it is instinct more than sight that guides her down into a tunnel connecting to the ruin. Oberon, this time, trails behind.

I'll never get used to this place. Sunford, a city alone; never a part of the fallen Empire of Naroth, which was shattered by the same dragon she helped slay.

"The Empire of the Nine Spoked..." her whisper echoes as water from ruined brickwork drips on her head. She glares at the interruption of her translating and moves on, seeking the roots that will lead her home.

Sunford at least was mostly safe, or safer than traveling south where former principalities and kingdoms fight for supremacy of the scraps. *Or north, but for other reasons.* But the main reason they stayed, since coming here two years ago, were the roots. They restored vitality to Oberon whenever near, so she didn't begrudge staying.

Brick eventually gives way to earthwork, stone stairs, and a dirt corridor. The tapered end of a tree's root introduces itself in the middle of the path. The wood is first gray against the light of the candle. Flecked with silver later. Thereafter, it breaks from the floor and climbs to the left wall. Thickening. Flashes return the light of the candle at every curve, and the wood is even seen to give off its own shine here and there, without the aid of the lamp. Unlike normal roots, these do not appear to be going up. They stop at the split of a false intersection, before the leftmost passage. Niena lays her hand upon a spot of twisted wood.

"Not so—" Her whisper quickly dies, almost joined by the weak flame. *Bad, ugh.* The wall is wet, and the air chill. But the latter rushes through the passage, winding down to this point from a distant exit or shaft. The draft touches every inch of exposed skin. She shivers. Then, a different sort of feeling caresses her leg.

Niena lifts the light as a familiar orange blob slinks past her legs. "You almost made me drop the lamp."

The skinny little cat sneezes on her.

"I'm sorry," she adds. "I haven't made your dinner yet. Can you wait?"

But cats are not known to be happy about waiting. After yowls of protest, the tabby launches itself onto a protrusion of roots near her. The sound of claws rapping along a crack in the wood sends shivers up Niena's arm. Veins of silver glow retreat and return as she jerks back. She passes the lamp back to her right hand. "Shi—"

Both her own hand and the flame are nearly jabbed into her face from fright. Faces emerge from the knotted root, as they often do in dark places. But the wood in forests is steeped in shadow, and brown kissed. Dark, dreary, but not quite as alive as here. The twinkle of silver gives these knots character. And menace.

A woman's eyes appear in a bend. Ferocious shapes follow the glint. The longer she waits, the more they seem to shift under scrutiny. Niena isn't certain it is just a trick of the light.

"Don't stare too long," Oberon says, having caught up with her. "The roots grew here when the three worlds were one. There's no telling what secrets this tree has drunk."

"I just see vines," she says. A truth, and a lie. Her imagination works to quickly fashion a lady's hair out of the vines. And gnarled, ever-hungry maws from the knots in the wood. She breathes in heavily through her nose, letting the cool air calm her nerves.

Another sneeze near her elbow clears the air. The cat, Pinocchio, perches like a beggar who thinks himself a king.

"Chords," she sighs.

Oberon bends near, his long beard wrapped twice around his left hand. Their eyes meet accidently, with the lamp's light as the broker. Curiosity shines below his set of bushy eyebrows.

"Let's keep going," she swallows.

They walk through the tunnel to the right, which soon turns steep, and her stride shortens to navigate over fallen dirt and rock. Worked stone eventually replaces earthen. Niena reaches out her hand as they pass, for age marks their passage with the signs of flooding. Whatever brought these immense blocks down left no surviving traces of their craft.

The passage again levels. Within a half an hour they are once more on the cusp of a ruined enclosure. Home.

"You could have helped me back there," Oberon says. But Niena walks on.

Graven images, pockmarked by time and conquered by black mold, run the length of the chamber. The root never leaves her.

She stops at the edge of a broken mural where a woman, born in the bough of a tree, looks out from a chiseled seat. At her side is the figure of a man, but half eaten by the root what followed her. Niena lifts the lamp high. Shadows flee as she tilts it this way and that, eventually finding the shriveled old fairy, the lines of his face agitated.

"What's gotten into you, child?"

But when she tries to turn away again, Oberon grabs her arm. The man is old. Decrepit—little more than a heap of bones. He flinches as she sets the light down, and she can almost feel the soreness in every move he makes. Yet, somehow, his grip is like iron.

"Nothing." The lie tastes bitter in her mouth. Niena pulls her attention away from his gnarled hands and shallow breathing.

"You're angry at me," he says. "Why?"

"I'm not angry at you."

"Oh?" Oberon smiles. There is a different warmth there, though. Not like her other grandfather, Marny, who died in Shenan. Oberon's usual smile is mischievous. At times, dangerous.

"What are we doing?" Niena's shoulders and chest slump almost immediately, as if the words themselves were holding her up. "Why are we here?"

He squints. "So you can learn what you need to survive, Niena."

"But what about you?" she asks, slowly. "We can't stay here, underground. Winter is only a couple months away."

"You let me worry about that. You just keep your studies. The best libraries are here, the biggest trade in antiquities is here. There's no better place for you than here."

"I can't work human magic." She blinks. "I thought we established that."

"We established I am a terrible teacher," he says. "I just need to find you a better one. Because there will come a day, when I am gone and—"

"Well, I suppose we had better eat." Again, she reaches into her bag, this time withdrawing from it a wrapped parcel. Oberon, ready to protest the interruption, instead lets his eyes follow her fingers as she peels the linen.

"It's all yours," she says.

Oberon shakes his head weakly. "It's too hard for me, you take it."

"I can soften it, just give me a few moments. "

"Oh?" His left eyebrow curls. "What are you going to do, chew it up and feed it to me like a mama bird?"

"Anything like—" Nena's words are cut short by the sense from earlier, of someone walking around her bedroom chamber. She bends over, cramping as if her lady's day had come. "Sorry, cheese must have been off."

But the solemn look upon Oberon's face in this instant seems to suggest that he, too, shares the sensation. Her eyes fall while his rise, and they meet in the middle.

"Aye," Oberon says. The next few moments seem to escape him, and he pans around to two out of three corners, appearing confused.

"Are you all right, Grandfather?"

"I don't know," he says, and Niena sees doubt cross his temples in pained lines. She reaches out, as if to help him with whatever has struck, but he brushes away the offered hand.

The fragile features of the fairy then harden, and he stands to his full height. "I am fine, but Niena?"

"Yes?"

Only to crack under pressure. "Nothing child, nothing. Just the concerns of the old." A forced smile marches across his fea-

tures, as if reality were the pillory and her face the angry villagers. "We will talk later."

Chapter 15

In Cuiven's Lee stand three thrones
One silver, one gold, and one of bone
There men and fey, and elven fair
Laid the rules of the world they'd share
And fairies would create;
And the men would dream;
And elves would tend those gardens;
In Cuiven's Lee stand three thrones
One silver, one gold, and one of bone.

Niena withdraws from the bard's song. The morning is bright, the air warm as a forge's breath. Hammers ring clear in the background like bells, but her plans are to visit the docks; to hear the birds cry or watch ships. A day of daydreaming.

And a fantasy.

"Oberon," Niena grumbles, remembering he wanted to meet in the library just after noon. A peculiar choice for him, and a first.

"The strange of the fey make the odd normal."

This thought follows her through streets littered with debris, and deep into older parts, where the river and the dock once lingered. The areas around these ancient reminders—still visible in the foundations of newer buildings—wind in peculiar ways. Some follow the remains of buried walls. Others the departed riverbed. Niena's pace is slow and thoughtful; enjoying the history, the peace, and the freedom.

Her fingers trace weathered runes on the side of a former temple turned foundry. *Kimbesh tribe grammar, Vard runes, Aliemann words. First Empire period.* Searching for spells, words of power in the library dug up more history and nuance than magic.

There's so much to learn. Mold covers up a dedication to Aare, an Aliemann river god only remembered in lists of priestly purchase scrolls. *How many people have walked by this without a second thought?*

Historical research would be something. She could also start here; Sunford's records are almost untouched by war. At the very least, it would be a good foundation. *For a book.*

Thoughts she had better keep hidden. Oberon's aversion was only a ghost of Marny's, but still haunting. Who had thought a magical fairy would lack imagination? Niena leaves the ruin behind, and circles around an old watchtower that once guarded a dock. A flash impulse to climb it yields to reason. After all, there's isn't a dragon there.

"Wasn't supposed to be like this, Oberon…"

Alleys widen and narrow, passing from the shadow of stores, warehouses, homes and back again. She stops in an unfamiliar alley where the contents of a bar's chamber pots have been thrown on the cobble to resemble a terrible game of checkers.

Each step brings a fear of making an awful, awful move. Niena removes a lock of hair that had fallen over her mouth.

"He'll kill himself, and for what?" But the "for what" slips away, and Niena wraps herself in a daydream of libraries, books, and nights writing by the fire. Shoulders slump, and she lets out the sigh she'd been holding.

The ground is also slippery beyond the debris and excrement. Storms returned to Sunford sometime during the night, and cooking oils and such have leaked from nearby pans, set out early for the gutter-oil collectors. Fog in the morning has had a word too, slicking the low-lit streets and alleys Niena is now walking.

Finally, at the end of this way, fresh air and light meet.

"I'm going to let him do it. Curse me, I am." She fingers the hooks of her blue coat. "He gets his way, and I get ignored again. Why would he listen, when I always buckle?"

At an old thoroughfare, lost in the sprawl of progress, she dawdles. A broken pillar marks a battle site equally forgotten, and the age of the inscription excavates Marny's death from a wellspring of dark thoughts. Here he was, captain of the local militia, the Bluecoats. He had just led refugees to the city, and with Niena, faced down a dragon. She remembers the ash in the wind. The touch of both chill and flame. The smell of burning flesh. But what will stick with Niena forever was how few had come to his funeral.

"No. No! He will start listening," she says. "I told him this in the castle. And I'll—" Her breath is cut short by a flash decision to jog, as if guilt were nipping at her heels.

Away falls the marker. Away, the smell of death. Hither come wider ways. Streets, and full roads. Soon the rats of the tight places are replaced by the rats of the open space; merchants, peasants. Wealthy and poor mingle along one of the main routes through the city proper. Niena settles down once more, under the yawn of a granary. The mash of red, green, and brown slowly becomes more distinct, as her breathing calms.

Sudden darkness is followed by the pulse of sunbeams in succession, as clouds wander in from the northeast. Niena leans carefully over a crate. Fingers find sawdust, grime, and rust as her thoughts drift. Her heart finds adventure—dreams of days spent in wheat fields, with no more company than the heroes and villains found in the pages of a book. But it is her ears that notice the thread of the song from before.

> *In Cuiven's Lee stand three thrones*
> *One silver, one gold, and one of bone*
> *But the peace of three, broke to pieces of three*
> *Old hate returned to Cuiven's Lee*
> *And spears were sharpened;*
> *And swords were readied;*
> *And hearts were roused to fight;*
> *In Cuiven's Lee stand three thrones*
> *One silver, one gold, and one of bone*

In the crowd, minstrels, beggars, and others freckle the passing throng, but nowhere is the bard from earlier. She steals into a gap between oxen, exchanging pardons and other words of a choicer nature with the drivers. Close by, children play in the street, darting in and out of swatting reach of their parents. Niena, distracted once by their game, nearly stumbles into the bag of a charcoal maker.

"Please," *get out of my way*—though the rest of that is bit into her lower lip. She half-circles the merchant and in doing so accidently jumps in the way of a young couple splitting their clasped hands to get past them. The stream of people sweeps with her, breaking here and there from the jutting boulders—or in this case, buildings—along the path. Around a bakery. And near a round baker where her gaze gets stuck in gooey pastries.

Gulls cry nearby. Just around the corner where the river Semira touches, there will be boats. A ship would mean escape from responsibility. A ship would mean adventure. Niena tears herself from the sweets and follows squawks. One side street leads to a curve, and there two hands of the river open. On each bank are moored the many small craft of the local fishermen.

Though beyond that plain crest of white and tan, a colorful sea bustles. Many foreign banners catch the wind and stream like earth-tethered clouds, touched and illumed by the sun. These draw Niena out from the banks to the bay itself. From the docks, her eyes float over masts that spring up like dead trees from the moor. Her intent settles finally on an outcrop of stone surrounding a peninsula that juts towards the ruin of an eastern pier.

"I want to be heard," she says to no one, which earns her a stare from a gaggle of sailors. Niena, cowers into her coat and angles past their mooring.

"I want a say," she whispers again to herself.

In the distance, a ship's bell rings thrice, and many of the dockworkers along her path pick up their work. Navigating a busy street that has just gotten busier proves challenging, but soon enough she makes her way towards the eastern side where older buildings lean, and there is little commotion. The rocks on the peninsula prove to be worked by hand, forming a strong ring at the bottom then disappearing into the river. *Fortifications.* A castle, or fort. But far from the daydreams such a place might have evoked in her early teens, these stones fill Niena with dread and longing. She pulls herself onto a rough bit of limestone, unteased by the river's tide. Over and over again, the words "I can leave anytime" play in her head, and each time the knot in her stomach grows tighter.

"But I won't just leave him," she whimpers into her sleeve.

Almost noon. Sunlight offers a hand to the western sky, and it, blushing red, accepts. Together they set the horizon on fire in a fierce dance of reds, blues, purples, and oranges.

A red ribbon dangles free on a bonnet of blue, while under it all, the maiden's dirty hair threatens to spring the bundle.

"Glad I didn't go to college, I couldn't read that and keep a straight face," she says. It would be a better metaphor if the water wasn't so brackish, and green from tidewater. That's the fault of older generations and their thirst for hardwood.

"My problems are like an old song," she says. "I want to walk on a foreign beach and wonder at its end. I want to eat strange foods, hear the music of the waves. And dance! I want to be like the Travelers' Stars, always wandering, never staying put. I want to sing a lullaby to the moon in different tongues.

"But like an old song, where elves garden and men dream. I'm not a part of the melody."

Niena's smile dips, and she settles back into her crossed arms with another sigh. "Marny was right about some things. Roads are dangerous. But not in the way he thought. I'll lose my voice before I lose my life.

"Because I am a girl."

Her knuckles flex white. Nearby a haul of fish has taken too much sun. Birds circle and cry out in chorus above, and she is thankful for no turn in the wind. *Because I am a girl.*

"But that's not the song for me." Niena bites her lip. Beyond is a sea of choices. "Oberon will listen, or I will leave."

Chapter 16

White marble. Fresco tiles. Dimly lit corridors. The noon sun waits outside the gabled canopy of the library. This isn't public property, and being bright isn't enough to gain entrance. But shadows provide other ways.

"Why does everyone keep the best stuff in the darkest corners?" Niena asks no one.

The lower areas preserve the oldest documents and tunnels that lead to forgotten places. Like a path where a ritual chamber, dominated by roots, resides. It was how they found their new home in the first place, looking for hidden things in the ancient library.

"Oberon?" A shadow creeps along the stone wall, but the meow that answers back is more likely to be from Pinocchio than the fairy. "Chords. If I were in charge, I'd keep all the creepy stuff in the brightest lit room. Stuff all the books about rabbits down here. But, speaking of creepy things—" *Oberon should be here, somewhere. But where?*

Best to keep quiet for now, she realizes. The threat of staff, or guards wandering down here, is minimal. Though there is always a first time, and enough ruckus might bring worse things.

Monsters.

And it is with this sort of thoughts that Niena preoccupies herself. Stories of underground creatures. Stories of centuries-dead things, refusing the peace of eternity. She's never encountered anything down here to suggest habitation by species more dangerous than rats, but…

Monsters.

Shadows lengthen. Sounds, innocent a moment before, turn in her mind That meow? Perhaps it was a wrapped priest, mimicking the voice of her little friend. Niena's fingers tighten around her clay lantern's handle. She peers around a corner that leads to some of the first arcane texts she discovered. *Would Oberon know to go there?* The flame moves uncomfortably close to her face.

Stop it, she admonishes herself, clutching her right hand to keep it from trembling. *I'm the scariest thing down here.*

Progress towards the chamber is counted in breaths and measured in the length of her small feet; sixty. Each sound earns a quick look back. And each glance is in turn followed by a careful step forward. Until her left hand falls around a rusty iron handle. *Bleeding cold.* Niena shivers, but not from the sudden chill. With a long creak, the door opens.

Empty. Her entrance into the oval-shaped room stirs dust, disturbs cobwebs. *Just as I left it,* she thinks, shifting the flame to her other hand. On a dilapidated table are stacks of books, piled several palms high in places. Niena carefully lifts her hand, letting the light sink over the decayed tomes. An errant beam strikes the door opposite.

The exit stands open, not enough to swallow the light from the clay lantern, but enough to cut the advance in half. *Oberon was here; his* name drags out a small smile. *Good.* Observing the floor nearest this exit, she nods, satisfied both at the print and at the knowledge that fairies made mortal do indeed leave traces.

Out the bloody door, then. A few breaths count the time needed to trespass into a second hallway. She closes door behind more quickly than intended and light from the lantern flees down the dark passage, as it flies from her hand. The flame streaks through the air like a comet Dwindling. Smoking. Then snuffs.

Retrieving takes longer than it should. Relighting, quicker. A chip in the clay is the only damage, but from this vantage she can see Oberon's trail clearly disappear after a left turn. *Right.* She switches the lantern to her other hand and shakes the ache from her arm. That way leads to treatises, maps. Also to histories and memoirs—and if Niena is being romantic, each step she takes is like another back in time. But she is not in that mood. The tunnels under the library are cold and musty. And Niena can never shake the feeling of being unwanted. Now is no different.

After the first twist in the hallway, sounds reach her from a yet unseen cranny ahead. *There should be a double door at this end.* Niena holds her breath and listens intently. *And maybe, Oberon.* Either someone is stomping around, or books are being moved and dropped. She cups flame and wick with both hands, and storms purposely towards where the door should be.

Closer. By this time she has come halfway, and the noise shifts. Scratching replaces the stomping, which she can only hear when remaining still. *But what if it is a guard? Or something else?*

Monsters creeping around the periphery of her mind appear again, and she swallows. Worse. Shadows hover near where the door should be, but every so often the light catches a glint from the iron or a trace of wood. Niena picks up her pace and quickly breaches the distance. With a nervous lunge, she reaches out, wrap her fingers around a ring and pulls.

"Oh, for the love of—" Niena steps back, almost turning the room ablaze with a listing flame. "What are you doing?"

Books, formerly neatly housed in shelves, are now arranged around a rectangular table. *Arranged isn't the right word.* No. While Niena searches for a proper description, the fairy darts behind his construction. "You built a…a bloody fort?"

"Of course, I did," Oberon says. "Now stop being ridiculous and step inside my castle. I have some important things to show you."

"How is it I am related to you?"

"By your mother's bad decisions." Oberon guides her through his makeshift gate. "Let me show you what I've come here for."

"You've been doing a lot of research, I see," Niena says. "Found anything new?

"In a history book?" Oberon's scowl slides right into his usual dotard's expression. "Everything old, nothing new. It's not a horoscope."

"What's a—"

"Never mind." Oberon drops a weathered tome, letting it fall open. Dust scatters and threatens both nose and flame. "It's about…" He pauses, and his lips pucker.

Niena follows his hand as he gives way. The fairy's shadow slides back and gilded pictures emerge. For a moment, the darkness of the chamber, the heat of the torch and the labored breathing of her grandfather disappear, and only these wondrous images remain. She blinks. "Is this a poem?"

"A ballad," Oberon says. "But pay attention to the central figure here, the one holding a lyre."

Niena sighs. "She's beautiful. The script, and the craftwork is just magnificent."

"No, not that." The precious tome gets shunted aside as the fairy pulls another open and slams it down in front of her. A flash of annoyance is quickly replaced with confusion across Niena's brow, as Oberon's crooked form gestures to a faded picture on the book's rightmost page. "Does this not look familiar to you at all?"

"It looks a bit like my old lyre."

"It is that, and more," he whispers. "This is the Evercharm."

"Evercharm," she repeats. A central radiant figure cradles the instrument. *Her instrument,* if Oberon is to be believed. The words are unrecognizable to Niena. They are old. Ancient. *Before the Imperial Epochs. Before Aleimannish.*

"It is the instrument the world spirits used in time immemorial," Oberon says. "To help sing creation into being. It is older than man. It is older than fairy. By legend, with this Lyre worlds can be made. Or unmade."

Niena steps back. "Great, it has a backstory. I assume you are going somewhere with this?"

"Don't you have any sense of drama?" Oberon stammers. "I thought it safe, but it was stolen from me. From us."

"This sounds like your problem," she says. "And if it's gone, there's not much we can do about it anyways, right?"

"We'd better hope so," Oberon says. "Or else you will be murdered for it."

"Murdered?" Niena retakes that step forward. "What do you mean, by murdered?"

"Butchered, exterminated. Massacred? No that usually happens to more than one person. Dispatched! Though that kind of sounds like a package being sent by courier."

Clay bites into her hand. "Explain, and quickly."

"Well first—"

"And no nonsense."

Her grandfather leans across the table. Books topple onto the floor. "You were the last musician, last true fairy to strum its chords. The traces would have echoed across creation, and someone was paying attention. Did you not remember the strange feeling that overtook you yesterday?"

Niena sniffs and pulls the book with the gilded picture closer. She traces the edge of the book from spine to cover and back again. Oberon places his hand over hers.

"Yes, I know, it sounds like tooth fairy. But It takes more than just blood to be able to make that instrument sing," he says. "I should have thought of the implications of you using the Evercharm. In those days, fear ruled me. Between the curse, and the dragon—I had more immediate concerns for you. Do you understand, child? Someone was listening, and they have been killing the last Nephar, the last of the fairy-blood."

She pulls her hands away from Oberon's touch. "How long have you known?"

"A week." Shyly. "Maybe a little more."

"And you are just now telling me?" Niena pushes the book towards him. "Let's say I believe this…this story. Don't you think I should have known?"

"What could I have told you? I'm not as connected to the Fairhome as I once was, and I couldn't be certain it wasn't just a coincidence until the last death and…and I felt her presence. It was strong, enough to reach me from across time and space. From the second world, called Earth. That power, that force—I felt her presence in it all."

And the back of his hand gently strokes the page, lingering upon the gilded picture. "The forebears of the three races. Men upon their silver thrones, fairykind gold. And elves, elves, with their Queen, upon a throne of bone."

"In Cuiven's Lee stand three thrones. One silver, one gold, and one of bone."

"That's it," Oberon says, tilting his head. "The old ballad. There's a version on that paper, right underneath your hand. Did you read it here before?"

"I—may have heard a bard singing it." Niena leans over the book and then looks up, eyes meeting Oberon's. She stares into

them under the torchlight as his expression moves from confusion to curiosity, and lastly, to concern.

A candle on the table is snuffed, and the smoke rising in the
windless air is the last thing she sees. The curtain of darkness
falls over them with the hiss of a dying flame.

Chapter 17

Niena rises, pulling the book to her chest in one fluid motion. Darkness has invaded the space between her and Oberon, and the smell of smoke from the torch tickles the nose. She stumbles backwards, disorientated. "Chords."

Her left hand strikes something, and the crash from a stack of books topples the silence, causing her grandfather to finally say something, "We are not alone."

In a room where each breath echoes, hearing his quivering voice is both cause for comfort and fretting. Niena tucks the still warm lamp away and tries to press the tome into her grandfather's arms, who resists.

"Take it."

"No," Oberon whispers. "Stay still."

And for that moment, she listens. To the sound of his and her breathing. To the rustle of the dress on the stone floor.

"When you see the flash, run home, Niena. Run to the roots. I will be behind you."

Niena cocks her head, but Oberon shoves her away with a force that belies his age. At this same moment a white light fills the room, spilling over book, shelf, faux castle, and floor. The fairy's face, lined and blanketed in a returning darkness, is the last thing she sees before hitting the door and tumbling backwards into the hall.

"Go!"

Thump. The pounding starts. *Thump.* Shaking her. *Thump.* Driving her forward—or back? The darkened tunnels below the library are not easy for Niena to navigate, and she repeatedly crashes into walls where she misjudged the distance to a turn, or where a door was forgotten.

"Where is he?" At the threshold between the arcane and the mundane texts of old, Niena stops to retrieve a torch from a sconce and strikes her flint. The hiss of fire and flame fill the room, and the drumming in her ears quiets down along with her breathing.

"Niena." She snaps to the sound of the voice. *Oberon?* Again, her name is repeated, as soft as a whisper, but loud enough in the silence to be heard clearly. *It can't...*

"They're not with me." Niena hears, loud and shrill from the passages behind. *Oberon.*

"I cannot reach you," he says. "Guard yourself."

Shadows skirt the edge of her torch's light. Niena backs through the door, then spins.

"I hope..." The words of the rest of a song well up from inside. The magic flows from her lips, and her fingers idly tap the wall as she cautiously presses on.

"I hope, more than anything.

To have a way in. A way into the forest, near."

The passage breaks right or continues straight. New brick forward, old stone right. She follows that down, and deeper into the library's bowels.

"I hope..."

Screams in the distance. Harsh laughter follows; she swallows.

"I hope, more than anything.

To find a new day.

A day 'neath the canopy, here.

I hope..."

She half gasps. Are her eyes deceiving her? Or was that a man retreating? The passage snakes down, and down.

"I hope more than anything..."

Around a crumbling cell.

"To meet a new love,
A love of the journey, dear.
And in the clearing, I will dance.
And in sylvan halls, I will chance.
A new world, a world filled with adventure."

Past ancient frescos.

"I hope..."

Through the sudden appearance of gabled halls.

"I hope more than anything,
To see a challenge.
A bright new future, fair."

At the end of a spiraling staircase, there is a well. The rope that hangs over the hole is new, familiar.

"I hope..."

Niena switches the torch to her left hand. Something moves beyond a wall of void. She can't pull her eyes away, even as her right hand grips the rope, and her feet wrap around and clasp it.

"I hope more than anything..." The figure advances to the edge of the torch's reach. *"To discover a new way."* The light swings as she does. *"A way through the darkness, there."*

All her attention is focused on that spot. With each foot down the rope the void advances, as do the sounds of footsteps. Niena swallows. Soon she will be unable to see the top of the rope.

Just a few feet more to the ledge. *"I hope..."* Weakly. Noises filter down from above. *The straining of the rope? Or something else?*

"I hope more than anything..." It's the rope. She's alone now, dangling. But somewhere down is a ledge which leads to their new home. *"To—"* Niena slips, dropping the torch.

One. She grasps the rope with both hands and swings her weight. Two. "Sing a new song." The firelight dwindles, dwindles, and is gone. Neina is alone, in the pitch. "A song for the sky—"

The rope snaps. A second of falling stretches, until it doesn't. Niena strikes the ledge with such force that some of the contents of a pouch, and all her breath, explode outwards and scatter in the black. She paws at the slick edge, pulling herself up and onto it just as the end of the rope falls past.

"Bloody Chords," she says. But there is no time. Something is tempting the walls of the well, and she has no interest in finding out what. Niena flees down another narrow passage, until she is greeted by the dull glow of a ritual chamber, with the remains of Oberon's lunch on her foot, and the murals half eaten by mold and moss.

The drip of water. The flush of air, in some far-off corridor. These are the sounds that welcome Niena home. From the folds of her shirt, she withdraws a dagger.

"Niena."

That voice, again. *It's coming from behind.*

Light from the network of roots glints off the iron blade. Without her torch, the room is revealed only by this.

"Niena," it coos.

And...From the right passage. I can't get out that way now.

"Surrounded," it taunts.

The knife in her hand feels heavier now. The passages darker. With no other option, she continues down the leftmost corridor, the same which brings her here every normal day.

Long and vaguely round tunnels await. The first steps are the hardest; leaving the chamber, the books, the remains of her life.

Oberon. The next few, down makeshift stairs and over debris, are quicker, easier. It is a lonely journey, and every noise, every half-seen shadow threatens. And from the shade, the chiding of her stalker returns: "So quick to leave? But we've only just arrived."

Niena spins. Ahead, there is darkness. Behind, there is darkness. Her grip on the knife slickens with sweat, and the root to her immediate right seems to respond by dimming. She presses on. Sounds of breathing, almost mechanical, echo in the corridor. But the passage inclines.

"You are quick to abandon your friends," the voice says.

Oberon. I did it again, I let you sacrifice yourself for me. Niena's pace doubles, and the tunnel soon ends in the stairs leading up to the warehouse. There are no signs of life at the threshold. The quiet of the corridor ends too, as the noise from the parades and parties happening in the nearby streets wanders down. No shadows or assailants waiting for her above.

"Are you worth it?"

Don't. Just don't. She coughs from the dust and looks for another way out, one that doesn't involve magic. This room is two stories high, but all the windows she sees are boarded up and closed, their lattices removed or long rusted away. Crates make a crude ladder, enough for her to reach the bottom of the sills. Not enough for her to pry a board loose.

"Are you worth his death?"

A table she had been standing on gives way, and Niena tumbles to the ground, landing on her back. The beat of the music outside mixes with the throbbing in her head. She stands up, weakly, vision blurring and pulsing to the sway of her unsteady knees. In her immediate line of sight there is a small, thin figure.

"Oberon?" An errant beam of light crosses her view. Niena shields her eyes. "No—" The figure's outstretched arms seem wrong. She stumbles backwards, right hand falling upon something softer than brick.

The steel-like grip around her wrist loosens the dagger. The metallic ring of metal on tile is swallowed by the *thump* of a drum, just outside. Niena jerks back in time to see the closed fist that soon after sends her to the ground, unconscious.

Chapter 18

Ireland. Specifically, a jail in Trim, Ireland.

Maybe it was the nature of Rein's work: the illegal searches, the time spent in less than respectable establishments. Maybe it was a sign of poor choices, or dodgy laws in countries that had only recently become civilized. Whatever the cause, *I've spent way too much time here,* and in other prisons that can hardly be called "trim." Some more corporeal than others.

"In hindsight," Rein says, "I think it was one pint too many."

Poor choices, then. And this one has cost him nine days. Two wandering Meath county, and seven in this one, Bridewell. Today is the first that he is fully upright, as aside from the hangover he has been battling an illness born from the frigid temperatures in the tub.

Quite adequately cramped, he notes. *Also, typical.* The space has the right dimensions, but it's too near the stereotypes. The staff could be more progressive, too; the conversations he overheard earlier were uninspired, droll. There is no way he could possibly give it good marks. Two stars, at best.

The metal around his wrists chafes. Chills. And he is no longer alone; earlier this morning, the pallet opposite him became occupied. The man's drunken snoring is loud enough to saw the bars. How has he not managed to rouse the guards?

She must still be in Meath, he muses, returning to thought that brought him to Ireland. *The Witch of Tara Hill.* The woman was reclusive though, and likely to be even more so, after the first time he found her.

"She's not still mad at me?" Almost a question at the end. *No.* "That was more than fifty years ago. "A sudden move to scratch his nose takes some of the hair off his arm.

"Pig iron," he concludes, groggily examining his chains. "Well, I'd best make short work of this and get out of here, before Ireland too is cut off—" A cough from the bench alerts him to the fact that he's spoken too loudly. Rein nods his head weakly as the other drunk in this accommodation wakes. *Cut off from the Construct.*

Black marks stain the man's clothes, and his hacking betrays the sort of sickness caused by spending too much time in the wild. Or inhaling smoke. He smells of birch mixed with alcohol. *Charcoal burner.*

"That bank draft might take too long to get here," Rein mumbles to himself.

Metal scratches. Creaks against something hard. Stone. The Inspector tries to peer past a lantern, but it is like looking through a sheet of oiled paper; movement, background, and source light are all indistinct. Sounds, though, tell him much more. He expects the door holding his cell is being unlocked and slowly opened.

"Hello," Rein says. "Jailer? If you hear me, I haven't broken out yet."

The drunk's cough works its way into a laugh, like a rusty squeezebox, but there's no answer from the door. The creaking stops, replaced by metallic clacking. Almost counting down the minutes. The Inspector's mind wanders again.

I could also head to the hill itself. The door to his cell opens. *And investigate the seals.* The lantern rocks on a rusty ring, held by the hairy hand of the man who threw him in here. Rein stares at the ground, and beyond the approaching footsteps, as if the oak floor itself could reveal the world's secrets. *Yes, I think that should be my first stop.*

"How am I supposed to find the witch, anyway? Knock on every door in Meath and ask to borrow some dried newt?"

The jailer, who had been fiddling with his keys, blinks. "Barristers paid you out, and you can get out, thank you."

"Excellent," Rein says, clanking the chains together. "Now I can—" He stops, noticing that he is still not freed, and the jailer has stopped his approach. "What's the remainder after my bill?"

A couple of bank notes are crumpled into his pinned hand. Two pounds; an unusually round number. *Not worth inquiring.* Head down, eyes forward, Rein lifts the shackles for the jailer to reach. The irons come off unceremoniously, and he is led past his fellow prisoner, and out into the narrow streets of Trim.

Freedom comes with the re-introduction to the cold. The clothing he conjured before being captured is not nearly enough. Rein pulls his frock closer to his skin, and the wind cuts right through the poor construction.

"I've lost a lot of time," he considers, scanning past the market stalls of the old medieval town. At least Trim is in the same county as Tara. Though it will take time to make it there, and he has no money. "I'll get a loan from the barrister, and then maybe a coach."

Searching for warmth, Rein's fingers instead find the glass vial holding Higgins' remains. Like a bull, flushed and angry, an idea charges through the Inspector's mind and smashes his previous plans.

"Higgins!" His yelp makes an old woman across the street jump. "I'll draw him back—" He sucks in his chest. It is pure necromancy, this plan. His severance from the Construct would have set his friend's spirit adrift.

Rein clears his throat. "…and put him to work. I will, by God. I will get that lazy oaf to earn his resurrection."

Using the Construct again is out of the question—dangerous, in hindsight. *Those creatures will be looking.* And useless now that Higgins has left the confines of the world. No, the Inspector must do things the old-fashioned way this time. He just needs a few materials, and a reasonable place for the séance. Using the Construct for this wouldn't work quite as well.

Like the schoolhouse, *too busy.* Or the bank—*that's a random thought.* A private home? *Too dangerous, and I don't want to spend the time socializing.*

These thoughts give him energy, company, as he moves through the streets and into the offices of Banewall & Scott, the former a relation of the famous local family. His mumbling and glazed-over look elicit no response—he's not the first to walk in here from the jail, or bar. Nor is he the first to stumble back into the streets soon after, upon procurement of funds.

"A warehouse, the castle, the monastery, the Prince of Wale's undergarments?" *No, no, no, and random, but shouldn't be ruled out. What about an apartment?*

It's a bleak afternoon day when he enters the local pub. The fire is low, owing to the cost of coal, the patrons bundled up so thickly that they resemble rolls of fabric rather than people. Under Rein's right arm are two wrapped packages. *Practicality wins over,* he tells himself when he inquires for a room. What he left off from that sentence is: the practicality of being able to procure a quick, stiff drink.

The patrons try their apparent best to pay him no mind, but a few grunts do manage to saunter his way. He is no longer welcome in Trim. At first there was genuine interest from the locals, thinking him French. Yet the more they spoke to him, the more they moved past his continental clothing. Expressions soured. When he had finished his queer shopping spree, whispers and rumors of his impropriety had passed by every door. Soon enough, even the slowest among them understood that his accent was the "other" type of foreign. More quickly than he could anticipate, they stopped paying polite attention to him entirely. Scowls replaced open faces. Doors closed fast at his appearance.

At least I have warmer clothes now. And pig parts. There was no way to order the *bloedworst*, here. All attempts at translation had left the butcher thinking he was up to something nefarious. *Maybe magic, witchcraft.* That much might be true, but what interested him first was dinner, and nothing Irish. *Which is particularly nefarious.*

Upon the price of the room—expensive—being resolved, and the nature of his lease—poor—being established, Rein climbs a narrow staircase to the loft. The ceiling of the hall is low, but the room, as he enters, private. It is well kept, if modest. A ceramic stove dominates the space.

One package finds a resting spot near this. The other, the bed. Bluebell, hawthorn, and some particularly old lemons. Now, these are the old magic ingredients he needs to summon the dead. The Inspector takes his time unpacking, resting his tired legs. The prison was cramped, cold; his body aches for a full night's sleep.

But rest must wait, even though there is no perfect time for the ritual. Nor are any rare instruments needed. A mirror hanging over a washbasin will be repurposed. Salt shall protect him, and his mental prowess will make the connection. As it is in most magic.

By that evening the mixture for the summoning is complete. His own blood serves as the mortar between the flora. Squeezed lemon juice to smother the smoke from the guiding candle once snuffed. Never in a rush, Rein prepares the first circle—his own, protected by a pentagram, so slowly that by the touch of midnight it is only just performed. And then the second circle —for Higgins, this is left half formed.

At seven, the room is dark. Candles are placed at the outer arcs of a half-circle, and one is elevated in the center diameter. Rein takes the mirror and leans it against the wall, beyond the circle, but catching the face of all three flames. In the middle, he draws a lidless eye with the mixture. The flame of the center candle fills the pupil. This done, he marks a pentagram of protection around his seating place with salt.

"Cenga gucis cird." An errant moonbeam manages to steal through closed shutters. The intrusion doesn't disturb the ritual, and Rein makes a mental link between the three worlds and the beyond. *"Cenga gubas."*

Several moments pass in silence as he watches the dance of the candles' flames. Eventually, in an hour that Rein can't name, a sign comes to him. The Inspector straightens to his knees from a cross-legged position. The candlelight has faded, as if a screen had been placed between them. *It has;* one between the worlds of the living, and those beyond.

"Higgins, can you hear me?"

At once the Inspector feels something akin to a hand on his temple, and a quick sensation paints over the pain in his head, blurring sight. He blinks, staring straight. In the glass of the mirror, the features of a medium-sized man are first etched like an artist's rough study. Next, the background pallet mixes in. Hazy gray. Spots of green. The richness and depth of an ocean-blue waistcoat. More details follow in wide strokes until finally the lines of high cheekbones, brown eyes, and curled hair soften into something alive.

"Your taste in style has worsened," Rein mutters.

The apparition of Higgins flickers. His mouth opens, gestures fly. But no sound comes from his lips. Rein reaches into his pocket and withdraws the vial containing his assistant's remains. The gesticulations stop, and the specter in the mirror takes on the pallor and look of an oil painting.

A whisper from Rein fogs the glass vial, and the contents glow green in the night. Satisfied, the Inspector nods solemnly and replaces it. Though even after confirming Higgins' identity, he doesn't dare to leave the circle. This is different than before in Liverpool. Higgins has traveled beyond the reach of the Construct and the lay of the living. He entered into death, and the dead have no friends.

"I fully plan to bring you back," he says, addressing the air between the phantasm in the mirror and the middle flame. "But I am going to need your help. Unless you enjoy remaining a shade amongst shadows."

A cat in the street yowls, and Rein almost takes his eyes off Higgins. Nervous spittle flecks the Inspector's lips. "Somewhere, close by, there is a witch. And you will find her for me." He leans in, unblinking, staring past the flame. "Allow yourself to be drawn in. The witch's power will be like a flame, and you the moth. Let it guide you."

The air around him chills, chills, until he can see his own breath. The flames writhe to and fro, as if cowering against a phantasm wind. There is the smell of wildflowers at dawn, and laughter in the meadows. Rein clears his throat.

"She calls herself Sofie. A name you cannot mistake, for it lives on the astral winds, thunders beyond the dead mountains." Rein adds, "And I will find her, through you."

The image of Higgins again flickers. Whether or not this is an acquiescence, Rein cannot say. But the candles burn brighter, and the room warms. The Inspector raises his hands and speaks once more. *"Anisdo aguna cur dragair betha."*

When his hands descend, as in prayer, the light falls with. The room is the domain of night, once more, and Higgins is gone. Rein crosses himself and stands, allowing his feet to break the salt-laden circle. He at last blinks and turns once to the bed. Finally, sleep can be contemplated with a smile.

Chapter 19

May 1761, Provence, France, vaguely. The last Rein was on good terms with the witch to be, Sofie.

Their dresses are sumptuous. Their hair powdered and regal as a courtyard in winter. Their mannerisms quite irritating.

I'm not a fan of the cotillion. The dance is much too intimate for my taste, squaring off against only one other couple. I much prefer the classic gavotte, or anything else that allowed him to shift off into anonymity.

And further away from the creature opposite. That Caraco jacket is stylish, and the coral mirroring the flush on her cheeks becoming. Her giggle also reminds me of the last time I was at the zoo.

I think I'll go find something to drink after this.

Rein pulls back the cloth covering the window of the coach. The constant tread of the horses and the rolling of the wheels don't take away from the presentation of the dawn. Light pinks. Tender oranges. They float above and into the rolling hills of Ireland, touched by the browns of dying grass and snow.

A tree they pass in the countryside reminds him of the castle hall's pillars, and the woman he found in their shadow. The seat of the coach is warm, and cracked, and Rein feels every tear as he leans back.

Sofie Van Coeverden.

As if forced, the woman turns her head in his mind. Even in memory, it has the same effect. She wore a low-necked robe over a petticoat, open at the bodice with a stomacher nesting onto the laces and settling into a sky blue. Like her gaze. Rein grows quiet, and the words she said to him then are resurrected.

"Where are your brushes? Where is your easel, your canvas? Come, Christin, do you only work with your eyes?"

"Miss Van Coeverden."

"Mrs., my husband has proven remarkably resilient."

"Yes, I am sure he's endured much, but why are you here?"

One eyebrow arching. Her fan, lightly tapping at the lips. I know what she is going to say, confound her.

"Talking to a fool?"

She's not being completely earnest. Well, I mean, obviously not. She's here to see me.

"You aren't one for small venues." Or the French. "What do you want, Sofie?"

Her attention veers towards an open window, and Rein's, in the present, does as well. The sun is alone in a blue sky. He recalls vividly what she wanted; a small favor. It was always such; something small, something insignificant. At least unimportant by her measure. And it would change his life. It always did.

Woman, your curiosity about the elves will get you—"You know the conditions under which I'm allowed to remain in the Princeps Inspectorum."

"The Birgu affair was a long time ago," she says. "Don't the Curators have something better to argue over, like who has the biggest hat?"

"They do not. Do you not recall the Council's ruling, after?"

She's frowning now. I suppose she had hoped I would forget. "I am watched, and I remain only at their pleasure."

"I know the pleasure of old, stupid men, I—"

"More than two hundred civilians died then. My actions..."

Damn it, how do I explain this to her? The answer, I suppose, is that I can't. Sofie was never one for responsibility.

"But that is beside the point," I continue. "As I mentioned, I would be no of no help. My very connection to the Construct is rationed."

The fan snaps open. But I can still see the curl of her smile. "Did I say anything about modern magic? No, I don't believe I used that adjective. We'll need something old fashioned to get access."

"The devil take it—" Stammering. I know what she's hinting at. Dealing with the old lore of the elves was questionable enough. What she was implying, between that catlike grin and those piercing eyes. Well, it would be heretical.

"Oh, come on Mister De Rein," with eyes reeling me in. "Live, love—" She says this as her hand seizes the lace around my sleeve. "But mostly live. Are you not a master of Primal Magic?"

My own voice, whether by intent or fear, can hardly eek out more than a whisper. "Theoretical knowledge, for me to root out heretics," said this meek person I call myself, a man.

The memory then fades. Broken by the rock of the wagon. The Inspector reaches into his pocket, withdraws a handkerchief, and wipes at his brow.

"No, I was not a man." His stony exterior wavers. Fear and loathing replace resolve, and quickly Rein's hands work in wide gestures, visually pushing aside the threads of the remembered conversation. Patting it down like a naughty dog.

"I was a mouse. And she too similar to—" he coughs. "Time enough for that anew. I will right this."

Trees frame themselves in the window, and the coachman announces Navan. It is still a sunny day, just before noon. A cold yet bright morning, all in all. But Rein is nervous, and the subject continually resurrects shades that manifest in the lines of his temple, and at the edges of his mouth. The Inspector swallows and tries to force through a quivering in his voice. "How much longer?"

"Oh," says the man, with a pregnant pause long enough to give birth to twins. "I'd say about half an hour."

Fittings on the wagon jangle with a jolt. Rein's hands clench the wood of the windowsill. Turning white. Pink. Then relenting, in a sigh. *She will be here. There is so much old magic in this land. I can smell it in the air.*

The Inspector's eyes roll. Over the memory of Sofie. To the grimy window. Speckles of red pop out of the ironwork on the door hinge. How much will she remember? *More than fifty years. Perhaps it is just pride that fills my mind with nonsense. She would be an old lady now. Perchance*—Rein's eyes narrow. "Maybe she has forgotten all about my betrayal."

He cradles his chin in his hands, as if watching a battle between his various concerns. "No, that is wishful thinking."

Beyond, the Blackwater River winds as they approach the town of Navan from the east, along the old Trim road. From this distance, nothing of its features can dutifully be noted. *Best to keep an open mind*—even having read Thomas Bell's remark about "lines of mud cabins, of mean appearance" only six years before.

"There is ancient magic here," he thinks, his back sliding on the seat. "The sort suspected in the year of Our Lord 1666, but known, and feared more readily, in those days of my youth. For her to live in it every day, and be able to see, but not touch..." His voice trails.

"No, she will not have forgotten me, and what I did to her."

Chapter 20

"Good morning."

Rein tips his hat to a young couple near the Market House. Tomorrow is Wednesday, and already butchers from Dublin and farmers from all over Meath are gathering for the weekly market. Everyone is irritatingly cheery.

A man waits for him at the front of a tired-looking building. "Already back?" Pointing at Rein's package.

The door to the Swan Inn remains open. Several men idle in front, and the one who addressed Rein, a carpenter, is busily tending to his pipe. He's on the wall of the rickety building—it's not clear what leans against who—and a grubby window is half open to his left.

"You were right about Eliza, but it looks like I will have dinner while there's still light out." Rein removes his hat. "Saw an undertaker pass us twice."

Both the old man's face and pipe light up. "That's professionalism. Knows the chances she might talk ye to death."

"It was very close." Rein reaches into the crook of his arm and withdraws a small parcel, a slip of tobacco. He passes this to the old man as he climbs one set of stairs and receives a nod. But at the top, just as his new friend settles back, he pauses. A reflection in the mirror stalls his feet, and nearly his heart.

Head down, he barrels into a wall of noise at the front door. News travels quickly among the small folk. Questions ranging from Bonaparte's escape to more local affairs are tossed his way left and right. Apparently, a company of the Longford Militia was overdue from Killock and were reportedly held up in Trim, and many wondered if the French had anything to do with it. But Rein had seen nothing of soldiers in his short stay. Nor did he hear about a wedding, a funeral, or both.

"No can't say that I saw your sister," he says to one man. "Once you've seen one pub, you've seen them all—"and *they all smell, in this country,* to another patron.

The Inspector reels back as a drunkard stumbles his way. The man gestures wildly, and his speech is unintelligible. Mugs are pushed his way, and sadly, three out of four times pushed back. Rein is suddenly weary, and the questions are like grape shot to his rigging. He drags himself past the throng, away from the drunken songs picking up. But though he is tired, the Inspector remains vigilant. Every shadow is scrutinized. Every corner looked upon with caution. The creak of the wood as he climbs to the second floor and the squeak of the iron mechanism are not just glanced over.

The door shuts, and he spills out the contents of his bag onto the bed. There are no windows in this room. Darkness is hastily expulsed with rushlights. Their dull, timid glow is the only thing holding back the terror for Rein, until the embers in the fireplace are stoked and once more alight. He settles into a worn Jacobite chair and rakes over the ashes.

An hour dies, barely attended. Rein's only work is to grow the fire while his mind occupies itself with old fears. The thought of dinner is gone. *They have found me.* He stands and walks over to a chest of drawers where a bowl of water is waiting. *Udur. The chattering madness of the void.*

These demons make themselves first known to their victims in fleeting, forgettable moments. In the corner of your eye. In the blur, upon waking. Or the reflection in a pool of water. Rein splashes his face and then buries himself in the towel provided.

"I need to summon Higgins again." *What good would seeing him do?* "I need to do the full ritual; I need to talk to him."

Too risky, if they are truly here, he would be open to attack. "No, no I can't summon him. Besides, I will pull him from his mission." *If he is doing as told.*

Implements for his original plan find their way into his hand. Almost subconsciously, he works silk thread and suspends the vial of Higgins' remains in an oval, wooden hoop. Rein must tune into his former assistant's energy and hope that he has found the witch, Sofie. And it cannot wait until morning.

The vial glows blue from a whispered spell, then fades to a dull haze. *Higgins is in the area.* He stares at the floating remains for only a second, then rushes to the bed. The contents of the pack are replaced in a hurry, the door thrown open after, and left without locking. Down the stairs, through the revelers and out the door Rein flees, acknowledging neither friendly hello nor curse.

Nothing disrupts the pungent odor of town life this afternoon. The sun hangs high, the refuse lies low. He holds the vial, suspended in the hoop, above his head. Worried looks address him in the corner of one eye. Dark shapes in the other. With a mad, singular focus, he walks through the crowded streets, observing any change. At several points he turns, walks one way, pivots, then walks back.

"Southwest," he says.

A young boy, probably between the ages of eight and ten, stands rigidly just out of arm's length, but in his path. His little squeak pulls Rein away from his contraption. He stoops down, unblinking. "Southwest. Is there a town southwest of here, boy?"

"L-Lismullin."

"Lismullin," Rein repeats, tasting the vowels as they leave his mouth. Then, in a jerk, the Inspector spins on his heels and dashes towards the town center yelling "Lismullin" at the top of his lungs.

Though nowhere in his raving does he scream, "I need a coach" or "I should be locked up." The former is procured, while the latter probably thought by all those in the market square, by the look on their faces. And when Rein closes the door to his wagon, and the freshly painted red coach plods away, he does so without much protest at his leaving.

"Do you know where in Lismullin you'll be boarding?"

Rein, still intent on the vial, leans slightly out of the window. The courthouse slowly disappears as they go around the corner, turning southwest. Someone along main street waves at him.

"Can't say that I do," he says, eyes glancing off the friendly face of the carpenter retreating against the horse's trot. "Is there a house or such I could visit?" The rough cobble forces Rein to grab his hat with his free hand, instead of waving.

"Not much there, I'm afraid," the driver says. "It's an old mill town; old, is all. There's a manor of the Dillons', and Saint Columbia's. It's a church, mind, doubt they'd let you sleep amongst the pews."

"And farmers?"

"There's some nice cottages, yes. Some not so cozy ones too"

The dusty, weak glow of the vial strengthens by a degree of milky whiteness. "Good," Rein says. "If you could indulge me, I may ask at any time to take me closer to one."

"Right, right."

"If Higgins is on point, then I may very well be making an early stop." There is a pause, and a confused whistle from the driver then—as if he thinks Rein is addressing him. The Inspector gestures to the man's turned head, to watch the road. "I will just be knocking on some doors."

With the departure from Navan and away from certain danger, Rein relaxes into his seat. The vial rests placidly in his lap, still only a dull light but growing stronger every mile. Outside and above, clouds and sunlight take turns; a dance cascading into the inside of the cabin in shifting patterns of half light. Back and forth, to and fro, until the play tires, and it becomes late. This is when the gears in the Inspector's mind start grinding again.

Rein withdraws from his sack a particularly small and odd-shaped package. *How am going to deal with the woman, now?* The cork on the bottle of wine pops loudly in the otherwise monotonous wagon voyage. *I must find a way. There's no finer practitioner of the darker parts of the old arts than she.*

A rock thrown by the wagon's wheel strikes the cabin door. *And if I am to regain Higgins and investigate—*

"There's Garlow's Cross," the driver announces. "Might want to look out the window, it is quite pretty.

Passing straight but looking left at Garlow Cross, Rein sees a hill enveloped by a lower, flat-topped ridge. A moraine, deposited, they say, by ice pushing up against the bedrock of Tara. It *is* quite lovely. But Rein's mind yanks him right back to Sofie. *She was lovely when she got mad.* The coach jerks straight, avoiding a cross over a rut and into the field. *And she'll be mad. Very mad. And maybe even mad-mad.*

How much would her mind have faltered in these fifty years? Artisans do not age unless they wish to. Necromancers, cut off from whatever powers they've previously bound themselves to, are not quite so lucky. *I do have one hand I could play; I can remove the curse I placed, blocking her. I'll need to, anyway, if she is to advise on the elves.*

"Best not to tell her that," he says to the vial. Hillocks dot the fields. Rein's gaze lingers away southeast, to stare upon the land before Tara. From here, the castle on Skyrne Hill can be seen.

"There's some farms up, before the river crossing," the driver says. "Then there's your Lismullin not long across."

Rein allows himself a look as farms and cottages approach. Closer to the water, the scattering of houses thins out, as does his interest. It is then that he, upon looking back to the vial, starts. The once vaguely shining contents are now brilliant, but also dimming with each *clop* of the horse's hoof.

"Hold. Stop the wagon," he yells, and the driver obeys, bringing them to a scratchy halt. "I'll get out here." His coachman is on the ground shortly and with a creak and a click, the door of the cabin opens to wide fields.

"Bit of a walk, isn't it?"

A penny makes a short trip from Rein's purse to the driver's hand, replacing words. If the man thought this rude, his smile said otherwise. Without further conversation, Rein turns on his heels towards the wide expanse and the farms that speckle it.

"Kak." He was not looking forward to the meeting. The first steps are easy enough; off the road, and into the field. Tall grass parts and flows around Rein, breaking against his shins like water. The vial is held aloft, and the steady glow would now be noticeable to any onlookers. It's at this time that he realizes there were, obviously, other ways to the farmsteads. A further string of curses in Dutch follow.

Yet, as they day wanes, the sheen of Rein's spell upon the vial waxes—until it is as good as any torch, and he can see the ground beyond his own feet. Above, a sea of reds and purples push, settle, and then retreat, letting the darkness wash over the land. Before the Inspector has come unto the first house, the stars and moon have already taken their places, lighting the horizon.

This house is quiet, though the hue of light—probably rush lights—gently taps at the windows. The vial continues to grow stronger on approach, and then in passing. There is the smell of manure in the fields, and the jingle of bells. Between this house and a barn, Rein finds the road.

It winds, and winds, taking him beyond another set of buildings. Three, in total, each larger and probably newer than the last. But the vial does not brighten here, and instead retreats, as that way took him further left, south. Rein adjusts, moving back and forth several times to catch the right direction. Eventually this takes him again into the field.

Hours are spent sloshing around, as the ground dips low. Rein doesn't immediately see anything. There are no roads, no houses and—*what is in that crop of trees, on that crest?* Hidden in a scraggly canopy is a building, a cottage. The Inspector's pulse quickens. That is the direction the spell seems to suggest, and the protective enclosure is telling. "I've found her."

His pace increases to match his heartbeat. From a walk to a fast shuffle. From that to nearly a jog. And this he maintains, until he is nearly upon the rustic dwelling, and the vial burns as brightly as any torch. He pushes through thick brush and what he assumes are wild plants to arrive at a path before the door.

Raising the vial high, Rein bites his lips, thankful for the dark. "I think I just trampled her garden." Ahead, though, is the door, and he—very carefully now—steps over the verge onto the dirt path before it. There is a light in the one window, but as soon as he steps around a little bend, the glimmer vanishes. Rein, curious, walks forward, forward. The planters at the front are tidy, the grass trim, while the house dull and uncared for. His hand hovers over a worn wooden door.

Wind rustles the branches of the shrubbery behind. *How many years have I dreaded and dreamed of this?* He hesitates. *What the* klere *am I going to say? Sorry for ruining your life, can I borrow a cup of Higgins?* Rein shakes his head. No, he has nothing to apologize for. She was dangerous, *is dangerous.* And this case may present more things at stake than selfish designs.

Something cold touches the back of Rein's neck. "The natural order of things may be at stake. She will listen," he mumbles, pulling his velvet collar close. An audible *click,* however, has a different effect, and the Inspector spins on his heels, expecting to be vis-à-vis a musket.

"Sofie," he says in a whirl. "Please put down—"

But there is no one there. Confused, and fast becoming worried, Rein turns back to the little cottage in time to see the old wooden door slowly open.

She has a very low opinion of my intelligence. A warm light rolls out from beyond the threshold. "You have a low opinion of me, my—" Where he expected to see saws, skulls, and other classic implements of her trade, there was a chair. Rein steps forward, his hand falling over the door's brass knob. The cushion is made from lush, red velvet, which beckons invitingly in the backdrop of a fireplace. On the table, the contents of a faience stein froth.

He licks his lips, eyes peeling themselves from the chair. The rest of the room is just as welcoming. Paintings in the corners and over the fireplace mantle almost seem to move, as if ushering him in. Rein takes a step forward. The room, the chair, the paintings shift. Blur. The inspector opens his mouth, but nothing comes out. He staggers a few more feet further, like he is drunk.

The ceiling, the floor, the walls all swirl together in a hazy mash. The next step Rein takes brings him to his knees. He reaches out, grasping the edge of a tablecloth. There is a crash of plates, and then silence as he falls unconscious to the floor.

Chapter 21

"He's there?" The face in the water ripples, but the Speaker of Teamor does not care. Chancy leans over the puddle, smiling pleasantly. "Good.

"I will arrive shortly as well." He proceeds to answer a question in his usually sing-song manner. "Oh, do not worry about that. I know this man. His personal code ensures that he will do all he must to guarantee the safety of a lady in his presence—and with little other choice, the Fairhome, thus Hearth, will be his next move."

Chancy dashes the water with the tip of his umbrella, breaking the spell. But the action disturbs the tranquility of the night. Muffled moans and cries waft over from a patch of earth, hidden from the road.

"Ah, I was wondering when they'd wake. "

He drops down from the lip of a ditch and into the hollow. There, two travelers, a young couple, lie bound in a clearing. Their personal belongings are neatly stacked to the side, and the captives are arranged perfectly parallel to each other. When they try to squirm away, he winces.

"Well, hello," he says, stretching his arms. "I wouldn't bother doing that, you're just going to soil your coat."

A pile of brush and limbs reveal a stack of firewood when kicked. "One, two. Twelve." Chancy alternates staring at the pile of wood, and the captives. "Forty-seven pieces. Do you think that will be enough for a spot of tea?"

Neither lady nor gentleman attempts an answer, and the Speaker's face contorts. Feelings of amusement, betrayal, hatred, ferocious sadness, and finally a return to amusement flash on it. He stalks closer to the pair's belongings, and never taking his eyes off them, rummages.

"Sometimes I can be quite a brute." Out of one of their satchels comes a pipe, a small pouch of tobacco, and some sewing instruments. "Personally, I'm partial to coffee," he says.

The husband bucks upwards as Chancy bends over. But since the man's feet are bound, he only manages to tip over the pipe with his antics. The lady remains on her side, staring blankly at the needles and thread that lie just beyond the gag.

"Nothing like a cold night with a smoke by the fire, and a little quiet time for sewing." The Speaker stares intensely at the wood pile, his smile dropping into a violent frown. "Of course, as I said, I prefer coffee—" And back again to smiling. "Now what was—ah, fire!"

An owl cries. Chancy cranes his neck to listen. "That's it then, he comes," he says, marking a spot in the ground with the heel of his foot, then taking several wide steps and repeating. Mud clings to his boots in clumps.

He laughs, bending over to inspect the damage. "It's ridiculous how the human mind works," he says, using some leaves to scrape the mud from his heels. "I'm on the side of the road with such lovely young company. Yet, I can't help but think of a song my mother used to sing to me."

He stands, and rubs his fingers together, flaking off the muck. "*Par les chemins creux de la lande, les noirs lutins, les loups-garous. La nuit venue en sarabande...*" The stack of wood contains split logs the size of his arms. It takes a while to separate them into two of equal size. "*...Se poursuivent comme des fous.*"

The husband rocks on his back. The wife remains motionless.

The owl cry is joined by the distant sound of wagon wheels on stone and dirt. Chancy looks to the road. Then, to his prisoners. He shakes his head, and drags his heel along the mud, overturning two long stakes. "*J'entends du bruit près de la porte. Ferme les yeux, mon petit gars...*"

When the man starts screaming and fussing through the gag, the corners of Chancy's mouth pull back. But it is just a dying twitch. "*Le méchant loup-garou emporte...*" His eyes turn to the petrified woman. "*...Les enfants qui ne dorment pas.*"

She moves, squirms now, under his attention, while her husband has taken her place in silence, breathing heavily on the forest floor.   The Speaker walks over to the first previously marked spot, leans and presses one of the stakes into the mud.

"The French sing that to their children, tell them if they don't sleep the werewolf will eat them," he says smoothly. "What they don't say, is the werewolf will eat them anyway."

Upon the road there is the pressing sound of hooves, of wheels clattering on gravel and rock. The air is filled with a foul stench. Chancy cracks his knuckles. The sleeves of his shirt are sticky with sweat, and his head itches. A cloud steals the moon's light, dipping the scene in grim tones. He shivers.

"You can be a good child," he remarks, shoving the second stake into the ground. "Or a good man. An honest man. Still, the wolf eats you."

The wife sobs into her gag. Chancy's jaw clenches.

"I'm afraid I am going to have to kill you both." His words heavy, and quiet.   "Thralls, ghouls, and the other cultist mishaps in imagination don't require anything special. Yet the Udur serve only the Masters. They are a different story."

A black coach approaches. On the road, just over a hill and beyond a small copse of trees he can see the horses when he turns, even as they are, too, dark as night. And black in the night.

"From the fire, smoke. From the smoke, death."

There is fight in the man still. It does him no good. He kicks, he screams. He is still set upon the stake, struggling helplessly as a pungent ointment is smeared over his exposed skin.

"From death comes the song. From the song, vengeance."

Behind, the sound of the rushing wagon slows. Chancy places his hands on the stake and whispers softly. Horses stop meters away on the road. But the crackling of the wood and the cries of the prisoner are louder.

"Fais dodo, mon petit homme."

The woman's gag falls loose before he reaches her. There are tears in her eyes, waiting their turn to be wept. There is desperation in her voice as she begs. Chancy does not stop, but instead lifts her up just as he did the man.

"Car ta maman, près du berceau, veille sur ton léger sommeil."

She says something in response. A plea? Maybe. Perhaps a favor, or a prayer. Only two words escape that are understood by Chancy. He pauses, as if considering. "That won't save you."

Still, Chancy hesitates. The shape of the girl's face, her rapid, panicked breath stalls him. She looks so like the lady that hangs from his neck; the silver miniature. Especially at the moment of her death. *Anna.*

The former Artisan grits his teeth, swearing something into the cuff of his jacket. Then, without further comment, he binds the woman to the stake, hovering close enough that the woman's lips touch his cheek.

"Jusqu'à demain, jusqu'à demain," he mutters more and more loudly. Over the woman's screams.

A figure steps from the coach and onto the lip before the forest, heralded by his beasts' strange whinny. Chancy looks upon the driver, and the driver at him.

"To Lismullin?" the man asks in a scratchy voice.

"Yes," he says. "I have associates to meet."

Back to the woman. The spell to ignite the timbers is harder to spark. Slower to bite. It still comes. Her cries do not quite match his Anna's, but the memory is close enough. And as he looks upon her husband, he can only see Rein.

"Fais dodo," he says, tipping his hat.

The door of the carriage opens, and he, not for the first time, warily steps in. He takes a short look back at the bound couple as the flames threaten and grimaces. "We will need to make a stop in Navan before. I have some shopping to do."

Speaker and driver embark. And as the quaint landscape wheels away, Chancy ponders the moment quietly. The rest of the world seems to do the same. Trees, livestock, even the very wind freezes before the clack of wooden wheels. Cows stop in mid graze. Later, townsfolk remain as still as mannequins, and barley refuses to sway or bend without a wind to tempt it. Everyone, everything waits, hoping that death will pass.

Chapter 22

My feet are cold. Not that her head aches, or anything about the twine binding her. No, the first thought Niena has upon waking as a prisoner is that her feet are cold.

She has been out for hours. *I think.* What happened seems more dream than real. *I wonder if I am still in the library? And* Oberon? *Niena shifts uncomfortably on the cold ground. The rope is tight, and her arms are secured behind her. The gag in her mouth also makes it hard to breathe.*

"You snore. I heard you even through that cloth."

Where, who is that? Niena twists on her stomach, but while she can feel the warmth of a fire and hear the crackle of wood, the room is still featureless. Her squirming ends when a boot pushes her head back down.

"Do you have something to say to me, fairyblood?"

Struggling against him is no use. He presses, rewarding the effort with the taste of blood and the smell of trodden earth. Everything she knows of this man is represented by a dark, rumbly voice and a pair of cloth shoes.

There is a cough. Or was it a gasp? *Someone is in pain— could it be Oberon?* The foot shifts, and a quick exchange in a foreign language ends with her losing sight of the first kidnapper. The voice is familiar, but it is not her grandfather. When the feet slide back into view, they are followed by a low scraping that sounds like someone limping. The floor has only just kissed her cheek when she feels a hand grab her by the hair and lift.

Eyes stare back, needle sharp. The pain from the grip merges with something deeper in her mind, stabbing at all the wrong places. Her own eyes water, and the face comes closer. Through blurred vision she can make out the features and greasy hair of a man who is made uglier by the sheen of his hatred. She looks down. Fresh wounds mark him, black as if he had been put against a torch. When her eyes rise to once more meet his, he squints and throws her back down.

The force of her hitting the floor causes Niena to bite her tongue. Vision hazy, head fuzzy and thick with pain, she struggles to make sense of the situation. But clarity slips through her fingers. Shrill conversation flutters around her, like a robin trying to protect its nest. *That's Hook Nose, I bet*—referring to the wounded one. At the end of every stream of words, there is a short, slower answer. *Soft Shoes.* His responses are lyrical and thick—honey hiding a bitter aftertaste. The argument continues, until cut by the sound of a door being shut. At the end, Hook Nose's voice had eased back into the timbre that taunted her in the tunnels.

"I can't believe you let him treat you like that," she tries to say, forgetting about the rag. What comes out sounds more like a chipmunk with a mouth full of nuts inquiring about the weather.

A swift response, more of a nudge than a true kick, rolls Niena over. She looks up, while he, down. His pants are torn along the cuffs, and there are signs of a past fight with fire, *just like the other.* The once fine tunic he wears is singed, and soot is smeared in places as if he tried to clean it out without water. Over this, he wears a tight-fitting green coat, and there are several buttons missing along the trail to his collar. An unblinking gaze connects with hers, but unlike the other captor, he bears no wounds. It is in this moment that Niena notices his ears are leaf-shaped; pointed.

Just as her mind registers *that's no man,* his eyebrow rises suggestively. "No, I am not the same as you."

Niena, still dazed, mumbles something muffled even before it passes the cloth. Humorless eyes seem to judge her, and his face, once curious, solidifies into a rigid mask.

"I'd worry about other things," he says. The sound of a door opening is quickly followed by the appearance of the other creature. An uncomfortable silence stews, while both captors regard her.

Back-lit by flowers and greenery beyond the threshold, their differences are noticeable. Soft Shoes is much larger and poised, *like a predator*. But there is something about the other that frightens Niena more. When he suddenly turns from her, she can almost feel the hatred bubbling from his spittle-flecked lips. Soft Shoes, for all his violence earlier, remains impassive.

Yet the conversation's tone rises in a crescendo, with Hook Nose's voice nearly reaching the same high pitch as before. Until Soft Shoes utters one word in reply. An explosive tirade flows over him like so much wind. Then, as quickly, quietens down, fading with Hook Nose's departure.

For another moment Niena and Soft Shoes—girl and non-man—share the silence. His action after that is precise; without wasted movement, he grabs her by the hair and drags her far away from the door. She sees the room pass by in pain-heightened vividness, from the mantle of the hearth, white stoned and splashed with the light of a dying fire, to the chairs, tables, and accompaniments of splendor such as she has never seen before. Lastly, to the bloated body of a heavy-set man in the corner—ere another door opens, and she is thrown in.

When this is closed, gently cutting her off from the light of the larger room, she knows which one she truly should fear.

Chapter 23

"We won't be able to break that block."

Culsan paces in front of Sethlan with his hand raised, as if weighing his brother's words. The pain in his leg throbs, but it is the heat from the fireplace that causes him to wince. "You underestimate me as always," he says, clenching his fist.

"You are no fairy lord's equal," Sethlan says. "You are not even mine."

"I defeated that relic, I drove him into the shadows, I—"

"Barely escaped with your—our lives," Sethlan says. "We barely escaped, and now, there is this."

Wood popping in the pit shuts Culsan's mouth just as he is about to speak. He pivots and moves further from the fire, turning his back on Sethlan. "She is just a child. I will have what she knows."

"She is a child," Sethlan says. "And a relation of the King of the Fairies."

The sound of boots spinning on the floor precedes Culsan's growl. Yet, it is Sethlan who speaks first. "You did not know? Why else would she have ever held the Evercharm?"

"She could be the Matriarch's daughter herself, and it would not matter." Finally, there is a reaction from his stoic counterpart, though curiosity was not what Culsan was going for. Even so, the air thickens, heavy with their mutual frustration. Culsan circles around the backside of a chair standing between them.

In the seat is a small, plain leather bag, and as he reaches inside, a smile slithers its way onto his face. "Enchantment is time consuming, and dangerous. Maybe we should try a different tack first."

"Torture?"

He shakes his head. "Talking." As his brother's laughter pops like wood in the fire, Culsan's smile twists. "Make a few promises. Weaken her defenses. Get her to open up."

"I am sure you will become the best of friends—"

"Not me, you," Culsan says. "You always had a way with E'tah women, after all."

"Now—"In the firelight, Sethlan's eyes flash with malice. "Be very careful," he says, breathless.

But his brother does not relent. "Your weaknesses may as well aid your people, for once." His hand withdraws from the bag, but it is not empty. Whatever protest, whatever threat stirring in Sethlan's mind gets snuffs out in that instant. Culsan holds a small orb in his unprotected clutches.

"That is not a trinket," his brother whispers.

The innards of the sphere swirl with smoke and flame, like the heart of a furnace or the eye of Andromeda. It is at once vast and infinitely small, depending on where you look—and for the elves, as Culsan holds it aloft, it swallows the room.

"I'm well aware of what it is." As he unceremoniously drops the orb back into the bag, Culsan shrugs. "Another one of your mistakes." He then slides left, turns and stalks towards his brother, facing the hunter down as if he were twice as tall.

"No other has achieved what you have." As they stand, face to face, Culsan's attention shifts to the fire. "No one has failed as you have, either."

"I have never failed—"

Culsan tilts his head and leans forward. "You gave our secrets to the E'tah," he says, his tone rising. "You told those

Mannelig our stories, taught them the world song. And what did they do? They linked with vile powers and perverted our scripts into a mockery. Sorcerer's tongue? More like blasphemy, used it to seal your own people away in a world devoid of order, birthed in chaos."

Sethlan swats Culsan's hand away as it approaches his jacket. A nearby chair provides a rest for the hunter's hand. Though as he speaks, he shudders. "How could I have known what would happen?"

Sethlan gestures to the now closed bag. "Those men were the first inheritors of the throne of dreams."

The fire is dying, but neither makes a move to stoke the flames. Instead, Culsan takes the chair opposite and sets the pouch down upon a table between them. For once, the hunter is saying something he finds interesting, and he taps at his lips, anxiously.

"We have a mutual enemy, you see," Sethlan continues. "They were betrayed by the same men who imprisoned our people. Those Curators of the Curatorium."

"I have heard. Banished to the void for all of these ages—did you not think they might have changed?" The light from the fire is so low now that it rims Culsan's chin like a demonic beard. "Not even the most depressing humans cloak themselves in shadows just for fashion."

"I will deal with them in time," Sethlan says. And here, somewhere, he finds the energy to sit up. His brother watches as his features change, become more determined. Dangerous. The hunter points to the bag, but it is clear what or whom he truly is addressing. "Until then, that is not to be held unclothed. And never in a naked hand."

"And until you find a way to deal with this mess, it will remain in my possession."

Culsan does not move, sitting rigid, chin down. A storm cloud seems to be building between the two. Hot, cold. Ready to burst. Finally, when it seems as if Sethlan is about to spring from the chair, he falls back.

"Agreed," he says. "For now, we must concern ourselves with the fairyblood, and more so with her master. "We cannot leave these grounds until new wards are set."

"So you expect me to hide in this—"

"Yes." Sethlan stands, glowering. "We cannot risk a fight. Not now. Nor whatever passes for law here discovering us." His jaw straightens once more into that impassive statue Culsan has come to know. The rest of his features, too, relax.

"I will be in the garden house, then." Culsan's right hand sweeps left and right, as if painting the walls twice. Then stops on the door, holding the girl. "I suggest you get acquainted with our guest."

He doesn't wait for Sethlan's acknowledgement, tuning his body away from the hunter. Still, when he walks by his brother's chair, he half expects to be restrained. That doesn't happen. Culsan exits the room in silence and retreats to the garden through the servants' quarters.

A half-moon greets him, smiling crookedly. The relative quiet of the house is left behind, broken by the strings of crickets, and fowl. The air is alive with the odor of what will be an early morning dew. Signs of their original wards hiding their movements towards the manor, tickle the hairs on his arm. But the sensation is noticeably weaker. Culsan rolls his shoulders. The leather bag with the sphere is taut in his right hand, and heavy.

Leaves crunch underneath as Culsan stops next to an oak tree, its branches wandering over the path. *Brother,* he thinks, gaze climbing into the canopy. *You never learn.* This quest. Those mistakes. He can't be the only one to see what will happen, can he? *Or are the beliefs of the E'tah true, that we can't change?*

His fingers tap the bottom of the bag, then cup it.

The door to the garden sways back and forth in a breeze, just ahead. The elf lets the back of his hand slide over a tree branch, then walks in, shutting the way behind. It is a small cottage, once tied to a greenhouse that is long gone. There is little in the way of comforts, but there is a chair and a cabinet where the previous owner stored alcohol. Culsan wastes little time strengthening their original protections, leaving the bag upon the chair.

"In an old burrow nestled in a field of briar, there lived a small family." The elf's eyes touch the corners of the main room, and his fingers follow soon after, feeling the waning power of the earlier spell that his sight missed. "A father, a daughter, and an infant son."

A sense of hot wind passes down his arms, where there is no breeze. Goosebumps mark every inch of exposed skin. His magic weaves itself around the words. "The mother was not there among them. In truth, she was why they were here."

Culsan's attention returns to the chair, or more specifically, to the bag. *I may need a little more privacy.* The edges of his spell fray. He steadies his breathing and returns.

"The children's life was imperiled, ere she finds them—" tying the knots that will continue to hide them. *And Sethlan?*

"When they were hungry, they ate thorns. When they were sad, they looked upon their prison and were pricked."

It's an old story, and like many Elven folktales, it has no ending. The strongest magic is not made to end. *But to be adapted, as needed.* Culsan remembers back to that rendezvous with the Cultists. The shadows in the room seem to thicken with thought. The air becomes harder to breathe.

"The daughter yearned to be free." *From the prison? No, that won't work.* "From her father, if only for a short time. In the briar, she created a hidden nest. Protected by the thorns. So secreted in the thresh of wind and cold that she could be herself."

With the last hiss of his breath, he lets go. The power that had been swelling within like a torrent relents, fades. Until the next time. The effort, however, drained him, and he finds his way to the dusty chair almost too slowly for his legs.

But first he must move the bag. *You.* This sphere, this *tainted thing.* To Culsan, it is a physical representation of why his people are trapped between worlds. *Our naivete.*

"Sethlan will never understand." He sighs, lifting this burden. It is heavier than he remembered. "The Matriach, in trusting him, doesn't either. No, I'm the only one that sees what's coming."

The bag rolls open on his lap. *Men change. That is their nature.* Dark blue shapes bubble deep in the crystal, while he examines the orb. "I must be careful. I must watch Sethlan; I must riddle out this magic and find the Evercharm."

Culsan leans back into the chair. The house is quiet. Night has long since fallen, and morning threatens. This will be the first night sleeping outside their world in literal ages. He slides the orb back into the sack and shakes it to the bottom. Hours pass before he can truly relax, expecting a portal to open at any time and drag them back to their prison. Instead, right before the dawn, the elf falls asleep.

Chapter 24

A constellation leans north, creating a tilt to the Fairhome sky. The sole changeless feature in a malleable world. In situ, like an immense still-life painting.

"Only this place is strange enough to make the Travelers' Stars not travel," Culsan says. Wind flips a page onto his fingers, but it is a sigh what follows his turn from the sky, where eyes shift warily from shoulder to shoulder, as they had star to star. Everywhere an eternity of wood expands. He reaches out and touches the bark of an aged oak. A quick impression of wrongness causes him to shudder. He jerks his hand back.

"I should not be here." The lack of further sound than his own, of wind, has him staring hard into dark places. "Am I, though?"

An attempt to picture a field full of flowers and the warmth of sunshine on his arms succeeds. Where stretches of dismal gray spanned his vision, there is now light—but in the Fairhome, it is always night. Or should be.

Culsan's eyes dart with alarm. Not to flowers, but towards a burst of distant chattering. "This isn't real—" is what he tries to say, yet cannot. Desperation coaxes him unto the crest of a small hill nearby. But the elevation only offers isolation.

The chattering grows louder, surrounds. Leaves dip as if shaking with laughter. Flowers, touched now only by moon-

light, sway back and forth. Branches of haggard-looking trees stretch towards him at impossible angles.

A strand of starlight meanders through an open window, touching Culsan's face, teasing him. He awakens with a jolt, sending the bag flying. The room blurs, throbs, then shrinks. The cracked arm of the chair provides something real to cling to, and he does so like a castaway on a piece of driftwood. Within a moment his pulse settles, as does his vision.

Soft tones, gentle shapes as shown by moon and star emerge out of the blur. There's the cabinet, a few lonely cups from the former owner, and a mirror on the far wall. The fireplace in the corner desperately needs lighting, but there is no ready timber anyway. Most importantly, there doesn't appear to be anything altered.

"A dream? How could I have been dreaming?"

Culsan glances around the room, feeling—as much as look-ing—for the magic. The wards hold, there was no chance he could have been transported. Yet, *I was there.*

It fits what he experienced, but elves do not dream. Culsan rubs his thumb over his palm.

"There are other, far more present problems to consider."

Like politics.

The chair seems more inviting now. As does sleep, again. This mission started out fair enough, and simple; find the Ever-charm, return it to the Queen. Culsan had no delusions that it would be easy, but the first few weeks were pleasant. And in that time, he felt they came to an understanding. *The hunt was exhilarating.* The kills, enlightening.

"We worked well as a team, I thought," Culsan says. It was a remarkably straightforward affair. Until it changed. *Until he ruined everything.*

But their problems were set in motion before their departure. *Politics.* The Matriach chose Sethlan. *But why?* And it was the court that placed Culsan as his partner.

But why his brother in the first place? There were other candidates, though few as powerful. Smarter though, wiser, less prone to temptation. *Like myself.* An unpleasant thought crosses Culsan's mind here: *What if they knew about Sethlan's contacts? What if that was part of the consideration?*

"A foolish risk, or so it may seem," he says. The hour is late. *My presence is an assault on her power, first.* An insult—"all for the old game."

"They might mean to ruin her." *I must protect him.* Sethlan is meant to fail, or worse, betray them. *I must protect myself.*

"My life, too, would be forfeit."

The orb rolls free, past the chair, past the wine cabinet. It stops at the edge of the cold fireplace. Culsan stands. Wood splits in the armchair are worn, broken. There are marks in the soft veneer where his nails entered.

Red light flickers within the sphere like a candle's wick. "It wasn't a dream," he says, staring at and through the fey light. Fear pulls at him, between the chair and the fireplace. But Culsan does not linger, stepping purposefully over.

"So, this is how they choose to make contact," he says, reaching for the orb. Only at the last moment does the elf hesitate, choosing instead to remove a piece of cloth from his pocket and wrap the object. In his hands it grows dull, serene. "I don't find dreams particularly useful. Nor does it make me fear you, if that is your aim."

The word "fear" causes a reaction in the orb. Three lights glow like embers in the swirling core. "How pretty, I—" Culsan stutters and nearly drops the object. *Those voices.* In the fireplace. *Chattering.* At the window. *Moaning.* Even by the door. *Growling.* Just as before.

"Enough."

But the noises, the cacophony does not stop. No, it's *closing in.* Culsan backs against the old chair, for the corners are already taken by the voices. And now, more. For that same dark tide that surrounded them in the Fairhome now oozes forth from every shadow. A desperate growl catches in his throat, and the words of a story to turn back this tide choke him. The elf reflexively holds the orb out against the encroachment. The three flames from before are now merged in its depths, and it looks more like a fireball than anything else.

Feral instinct takes over. Culsan, back still pressed against the chair, removes the glove from his hand. The fires within the sphere pulse as if in anticipation. He grinds his teeth. *You will know your better, E'tah.* The elf stares into the flames, then back to the ring of black that is so close he could touch it. Without a further sound, he grasps the orb and reaches through the swirling mass inside, forcing his will upon it.

His breathing is heavy and the air hot, sticking to the back of his throat. Black coils slither out of the oncoming ring. *No.* The coils birth more lines that stretch across the tiled floor like clawing fingers.

"You will not win!"

Chapter 25

The roll of the wheels is rhythmic, and the scenery scrolls like a slide of engravings sewn together by a mad artist. Evening threatens, alerting Chancy that time is, in fact, unstuck. He still struggles to stay awake.

Not here, never here. As he rolls the twin of the sphere, he gave the elves back into its bag, he sighs. Touching the Masters, even as a nothing more than a witness to their greatness, taxes. Not for the first time the Speaker wonders at the cost of their arrangement. He crosses his arms, pulling his coat more tightly about him. *The power is worth it.* Even if they always make him participate. *Insurance, so I do not think to double-cross them.*

The carriage stops, and before he can react, the door opens. A lone man waits outside. Chancy staggers out, then stares into his face. *An illusion.* The hand offered is turned down.

Noticing the farmhouse behind them, Chancy squints. "What resources do we have in place?"

"Seven ghouls, twenty thralls." The man's voice is altered. *Perhaps, it isn't even a man under the illusion,* Chancy thinks, as the Cultist continues his count. "Three brothers, four sisters. And the Udur; the Udur have come."

"Praise the Masters," Chancy mutters.

"There are many houses between us and him, but they are scattered. The others are waiting, but—" the Cultist's shift is almost out of sync, the spell apparently having difficulties with fast movement. "May I ask what our plan is?"

"Plan?"

"To narrow our path, avoid unnecessary risks and expenses."

Expenses? What it is this man, some sort of evil accountant? Chancy focuses on the form, and the mind beyond. "I want you to organize the rest of our friends. We'll need to start rounding up as many villagers as we can before nightfall."

"That…that will take all night."

"Good," he says. "I find it best if idle cooks aren't left near the pots and pans too long. They end up making a bunch of racket."

"What are we to do with the villagers?"

The wind turns and turns Chancy's attention. Clouds threaten, by afternoon the rain will be here. "How's your sister doing, Levander?"

"I—what?"

"Do you remember summering in Bath? Do you remember how she used to always beg Momma and Poppa for treats? A bit like clockwork, I recall you thinking, though not as politely. Every hour, or every time the horses stopped."

The farmhouse barn door is open, hinting at more of his associates inside. Chancy stalks past Levander towards this. "The Udur are a bit like her," he says as the man struggles with the information. "Only, they need more than a biscuit and are far more likely to drag your soul into the void than kick and scream."

"How, where—with knives?" Levander's voice popping like a hot kernel of corn.

It's a fair question, one which a pragmatic man like Levander would ask. "Fire, always fire." Chancy nods at the farmhouse. "The barn will do."

The Cultist reaches out as if to grab him by the shoulders. But the Speaker stops midway and addresses him directly. "Power comes at a price. Knowledge, with a premium. And yet yours is a task devoid of responsibility. You do not want mine."

His hand hovers over the bag with the sphere, while the Cultist's own drops away. "Don't worry, Levander." Chancy smiles at the nervous back-peddling. "Christaan Dei Rein will soon die, and this conversation will remain between me and you."

Chapter 26

"Wake up."

The door to the closet yawns open and a tide of morning washes over Niena, except one elf-sized cut out is standing at the threshold: Soft Shoes. He wastes no time chatting and apprehends her by the bindings, dragging her through the main room. Finally, after this brief tour as a dust rag, she is deposited near the fireplace. Whispers of last night's fire still speak, here and there, under the soot. The elf makes no effort for her comfort.

"You snore so loudly, I can hear you even through the door," he says.

The answer from Niena is, naturally, muffled, and it appears to take Soft Shoes a moment to understand this. He lets the pregnant pause go into contractions before acting, and whether out of malice or simple indifference, he lifts her head by the knot of the gag.

"We need to talk."

Niena's face slaps the ground as the gag is cut. Her eyes climb the towering elf, but only manage to mount to his chest thanks to the way the ropes hold her. With her back arched, her voice is strained. "What's your name?"

The elf takes his time settling back into a nearby chair. "You may call me Sethlan."

"Sethlan," she says. "I liked your old name better."

"What do you mean?"

By now the elf has leaned back enough that Niena can look him in the eyes. "Nothing." She breathes with effort. *He wants something.* Her grandfather had warned her, in his usual way, about others who were after the lyre. Here was the intangible terror that stalked her. Here was a creature that even Oberon feared. And now? *A day?* A couple of days before this all changed. Sethlan is a physical threat, instead of smoke in the dark. And out of his game. For though powerful in magic, the other elf had been harmed by someone, presumably her grandfather.

"Why should I talk to you anyway, aren't you just going to kill me whenever you get what you want?"

"Yes," he answers. "Culsan will likely wish to do so."

She balks. "Aren't you supposed to lie to me?"

"I do not lie," Sethlan says. "Just know I will take no pleasure in watching you die."

Great, rhymes. Niena muses. *That's going to be stuck in my head.*

But the elf continues, trampling over her thoughts, "If you tell me what I want to know, much can be avoided."

I need to escape. Obvious. *But how?* Not quite so obvious. *Charms, maybe. I'll do that one*—Another thought interrupts: *Where to, even then?* Assuming she is no longer in Sunford, that would mean they are in the High Realm of Almar, which surrounds the city's land. It would still be relatively safe to travel, unless they are on the southern borders. War has come to the Midland, and they would not be safe.

"Or you could convince him not to kill me," she says.

"Perhaps." He leans forward, his tone bouncing between words like a goat climbing a mountainside. "But your aid would have to be extraordinarily valuable. And I not convinced."

"Neither am I," she mutters, letting her cheek fall to the cold ground. "Well, I think I will sit here and just not talk, if you don't mind."

"I understand." He makes to rise. "I will go find Culsan. Though you may not appreciate his methods."

A picture of the other elf, with his piercing, beady little eyes enters her mind. And the hate—the unfiltered hate showing in every one of his lines. Niena shivers. "So where are you from?"

"Some place other than here."

With the aid of a rebellious sunbeam, Niena can study Sethlan. He sits in the chair, regarding her as if she were a recumbent statue. Knifelike ears split his long hair, revealing a face that is both young and alien. She searches her memory, through pages and pages of books for reference, but every time she come close, the image of Marny appears to snatch it up and send Niena outside to play in the sun.

"No, you've never seen my kind before," he says. "I am a but a myth to the E'tah. A myth, talking to another myth."

Sethlan cocks his head, and Niena gets the impression that he's trying to read the expression on her face.

"Yes, fairy daughter," he continues. "I know what you are."

"I guess that gives us something in common, then."

"Does it not? A start? A spark? From whence passion will burn away our differences, and then, in the heat of the moment where your life is held in the balance, I will choose you over Culsan. We'll spend our days in a lonely cottage, and I will again, and again, make you fat with child till you die, withered on the vine." His laughter is cold, and mirthless. "That's how your stories always go, isn't it?" The laughter stops. He leans down to Niena, hands upon his knees. "I'm afraid you wouldn't live any better with me than him."

"Why are you telling me this?"

"I can't abide distractions," he says. "You will tell me what you know about the Evercharm."

Now is a bad time for Oberon's influence. "Evercharm, sounds like something you'd buy at street market," she says, trying to resist the impulse to talk about how cheese is made, or the right way to sew a hem, or another snide comment. "Maybe if you told me what it is?"

"A lyre," he says slowly. "An instrument of terrible importance."

"Mm-hmm. You'll find some terrible instruments at those markets, too."

The sound of a door opening behind Niena interrupts her. The elf's attention follows the creak of wood and the patter of footsteps, like the owner of a porcelain shop might follow a bored cat around his valuables. Words fly over her head, between Sethlan and an unseen figure. Shortly, his feet join the conversation in rushed tones, and she is left alone in the middle of the room.

Unlike the angry discourse earlier, this has a more desperate tone. *They're afraid.* Niena tries to lift herself off the floor, as if by hearing more she might suddenly be able to interpret their speech. Not surprising, neither attempt works.

It is morning, or noon. Niena can't really tell the precise time. The backs of both "men" pace into view. Their movements are deliberate. Quick. From hidden corners, and rooms beyond line of sight, bags are produced. Supplies, by the shape of them. *Whether noon or not,* it's hardly the best for two kidnappers to transport their hostage. Between moving this and packing that, Sethlan stops, and for a moment their eyes meet. A burlap bag that is in his hand gets stretched, and as he approaches he retrieves the cut gag from earlier from the floor. He halts about one foot from her face.

"If you cause problems for us, it will very bad for you," he says, kneeling.

"Like dying? Because that's already pretty bad."

Sethlan holds the gag in front of her eyes. "So far you've been unharmed. Harbor no hope of rescue from any of these E'tah." As Niena's head turns away, he forcefully rights it. His eyes narrow, then soften, as if upon wandering around her face, they found something expected. "No, I can't trust you to behave."

The gag that had been stuffed away is brought out, along with the burlap sack. Fighting either is useless, and her wriggling is a poor delay tactic, but she manages long enough to see the door open and night—night, not morning, frame the threshold.

A sense of the room flipping, as Sethlan throws her over his shoulder, is succeeded by the smell of summer air as it meets them beyond the door.

Chapter 27

Six hours. Dry grass crunches underfoot, and nettles, hidden by night, prick his shins. But on the horizon dawn rises, flush in orange and pink. Sethlan shifts the girl onto his other shoulder, while ahead Culsan scouts an old barn. Six hours have passed since they left the manor, and he is left with no answers.

"We'll make this work," Culsan says, motioning for his brother. "Don't get comfortable, though, we are moving again soon."

"As you say." Warped boards mark the only entrance. Within, there is a distinct smell of rot and neglect. "This is undefendable, but I will work to hide us."

"No. You should be focusing on prying whatever you can from her. Time is not on our side."

It is true, Sethlan's brother knows many stories. *So, do I.* Tales of betrayal. Sagas that will make even the warmest summer snap cold with ice. *None will be written about us,* as the dust clears from the setting down of his baggage. *Unless my people take up the practice of capturing children.*

But the girl is important. "We need to continue our conversation from before." The bag over her head is loosened, the gag discarded. A twitch at the corner of her mouth makes him set his shoulders. "Before you speak, know that my knives bite harder than words."

"They'll still miss the mark," she says quietly. A structural beam behind provides support to push upright, allowing the girl to face him almost eye to eye. At a close instant, the hunter grips Niena by the neck, pushing her down, but can't force her eyes to follow. She struggles to speak, coughing out, "I don't know—" before by force of will finishing: "I don't know where the Evercharm is."

"But you did," he points out, loosening his grip. "And you will find that memory again, or pain will be your muse."

Quiet laughter interrupts, but when he rounds on Culsan, he finds the elf has lost himself again in a story. The tale used to work his wards is uncommon, *rare*. "Silver from a winter's night," Sethlan accidently blurts.

"Maybe I shouldn't make it easy for you," Niena snaps. "Maybe Oberon is out there looking for me, and that's what you are running from."

Oberon? Sethlan's nose twitches. He slowly turns his head back, fixing her with a steady stare. "Oberon," he says coolly. *The King of the Fairies?* "There's as much hope of that as charming bread from an urchin."

"That's colorful, but I don't see—"

"The old fairy may be dead," he says. *One problem, one dosage at a time.* "What disturbed our last rest," the hunter adds as he steals glances at his brother, "is yet unknown, but likely equally dangerous to yourself."

There is a long moment where little passes between them, save stares, and nothing is said. This is broken by the opening of the forward door, tempting both elf and fairyblood to look on, and the hunter to try to hide his confusion when Culsan, muttering to himself about "seeing to the outside," leaves.

Sethlan's mistake with the human sorcerers can be remedied, but only from a position of strength and security. *Which is not the present situation.* And it might have been another mistake in the making, letting Culsan handle the only means of communication with these "Teamor."

Speaking their ancient name out loud was meant to take away the fear creeping up Sethlan's spine. But it fails. No longer were the Teamor synonymous with the faithful, or a token of power. Now, only the name is recognizable across the face of a people he once knew. When the Matriarch affected the breach in their prison and tasked him with this mission, the Teamor were the first potential allies he thought of. After the meeting in the Fairhome, their name sank to his stomach, and has sat there troubling him ever since.

As the door slams shut, Niena speaks: "You're going to kill me anyway, so I'll just take my chances."

Sethlan falls quiet, then says in a whisper, "We may yet come to an accord, but you must tell me what you know." Then, more loudly. "All of it, no matter how small."

"Gad's shift is speckled, freckled," she sings *"Made from the skin of martens."*

"I did not drop you that hard."

Niena, unblinking, inches up the beam, and this time Sethlan makes no move to throw her down. *"We, wee, whistling, we! They call, we call, all eight in chains, when your father took flight to hunt."*

"I hate children," Sethlan says, shaking his head. Six hours, little rest, and now this nonsense. The gag he removed from her tempts him, but his hand is so heavy.

"A spear on his shoulder," she goes on. *"A club in hand, baying, baying, were his dogs."*

Soft tones, like wind rushing through reeds, play. And Sethlan listens intently to them, and they bring memories he thought were lost, but were in truth hidden under a current filled with the long years of his life. The smells of spring touch him once more. The cool taste of water after a long day hunting. He yawns, taken suddenly by a desire to lie down.

"Giff, Gaff. Take, take. Fetch, fetch."

Sethlan drags long fingers down his face, and his head droops. *She's singing.* The room is hazy, and it has nothing to do with the morning light. Like a snake, his left hand flies out and strikes Niena under the jaw, then holds. Her eyes smile back, but his narrow as she is brought down to his level.

"That was unwise," he says. "That was very unwise."

He switches the hand covering her mouth, to the one with the gag. Never blinking. Never taking his eyes off her, Sethlan secures the girl once more, and can't hide the visible wave of relief once it's done. *I should have taken more precautious.* She's dangerous. She has power. *Craft.*

A second binding is produced from a length of cord, and she's in turn secured to the beam. Sethlan deliberates, unsure of leaving the magically capable fairyblood alone. The girl should have the priority, but at this moment being in the same room as she raises his hackles. *Culsan.* Yes, his brother is acting strange. *Culsan needs looking into.* And the hunter needs air.

The door is fast at hand, and Sethlan is too quickly outside. He looks up, shading his eyes. It is early morning, and the summer heat has not fully set, still, there is an oppressive breeze coming from the east, and few clouds. The barn's overhang provides welcome cover.

"I shall put the knives to the girl," he says. No more nonsense. The last location of the Evercharm can be pulled from her. "Then I will deal with Culsan. "

A trickier scenario. His brother is testing his authority. *Dangerous.* Especially with Oberon still running around there.

The wind shifts, bringing the smell of reeds and muddy water. Sethlan licks his lips, tasting the dry grime that has built up.

There can be no more distractions. Culsan will have to be put in line. "Or put down."

A nasty scenario. And one with political and personal consequences. "Trust in the Matriarch, trust—"

Nearby rustling in the grass gains his attention, but it is quickly proven to be only a breeze. "There are hardly any vermin in the field." That includes Culsan. Left or right. Far or close, he sees no traces of his brother. Only the sun, blazing along indifferently, high grass baking in the heat, and a crop of trees near the remains of a house. This forces a second look, as the trees are tall, and he can't remember seeing them when they arrived.

"This whole terrain is too open," he says. They would never see the fairy, should he attack. *If he can.* "Or the Teamor?" Sethlan shakes his head again. "I must find that fool, and we shall move then."

By now his body has turned towards the tree line. There are no other places for the Orator to hide, but it isn't close, and even a veteran like Sethlan has difficulties in the grass. And there are no tracks either. This worries him more, for Culsan is, in all knowing, only a cave dweller. How could he hide his passage so, and in such short a time? Wide fields spread across Sethlan's vision elsewhere. The trees are the only real option.

"Might be a well, or a stream," Sethlan says, squinting. Culsan, so far, had not shown any concern towards the mundane aspects of the mission. But if he were to, now, sourcing water would be a good move. The hunter treads through the grass entertaining this notion, avoiding the nettles where he may. Apart from his own pace, there are no sounds. The dry crush becomes monotonous and the march tiresome long before he comes to the tree line.

Yew trees. *Or willows?* This field is far from the sort of climate where he'd expect to find them. And the water, that rushes just beyond the lip of a small mound? *There is something familiar about this.* Sethlan spins on his heels and looks back towards the farm. *Gone?* Dark forest marches as far as the midday sun will allow him to see. The breeze is chill, and the smell touching upon the memory he—*The girl.* He never left the barn. *I've been enchanted.*

Chapter 28

Summer, 1753. Dates and times flow together, Chancy would get lost if it weren't for certain monuments erected along the way. Like pain, and grief.

The clock strikes twelve. He shifts in the seat, changes the window from which he stares off into nothing. His former lover, Anna, Rein's wife now, continues with her sewing. He can't look that way. Can't bear to think of her as willfully ignorant. The ring on her finger says otherwise, stating plain as day "I don't care that my husband is a philanderer and a philistine, I still love him."

"When will you be leaving for London?" she asks for the fourth time.

Chancy fidgets, his gaze rolling up and over her, to rest on an inlaid cabinet. "Tomorrow morning, God willing."

Another chime in the clock twists his guts out. "Clang," for doom. "Clang," again. Doom. He crosses his arms. Staring at sewing, at needles piercing the muslin silk, in and out, in and out, unstitches the last bit of his composure. But he is still a gentleman in manner, if not in birth.

"Fancy a ride to town?"

She looks up from her work and blinks, as if he had jerked from sleep. Finally, she says: "Poppa has taken the coach."

"But not all of the horses," he says. "Come, it will do us both good to get some fresh air. This house is stodgy." She fidgets, still clinging to the needle, so he adds: "We can take the route by the river, there are some lovely lilies there."

After a few moments Chancy gently takes the needlework from her hand. Together, hers in his—

The sphere rolls from his hand, landing somewhere between the window and the plush chairs of the farmhouse den. The memory too, falls away from his fingers. Drifting. Drifting. Gone. Chancy stands, numb. Another piece of him is gone. Another part given away, as insurance to the Masters.

There's a quick knock at the door. He staggers over, struggles with the lock. On the other side is a Cultist, similarly shrouded in illusion as Levander was before.

"What is it?"

"The hour mi—milord," the man, woman stutters. At least this one isn't bothering to use one of those ridiculous spells to conceal her voice. "It draws near."

"It draws near," he says, sneering. "What are you, some poor man's mock of a Shakespeare character? I know the time is close, you do not need to bother me every hour. I can sense for myself."

She hesitates, and though Chancy doesn't look down, he can hear the creak of the wood beneath well enough to know she's shifting back and forth.

"Was there something else?"

"The villagers are in the barn. We intercepted two wagons trying to pass through as well."

Chancy sighs and wipes his eyes. "Good, it can begin soon, then. Tonight; we strike tonight. The Masters have assured me there is a path open to us now."

Chapter 29

Black. A whistle in an adjacent room startles Rein, and his chin slips underneath his hand. He is just able to catch himself before his face hits a hard, rough—"Table."

The word croaks out of him. His mouth is dry, lips cracked. He raises his hand to his face. Everything is a blur of gray, but slowly blobs of color merge into vague shapes. The taste in his mouth gets an adjective here, too: "Bitter."

Grey-Black. "I need a drink," he says, wiping his eyes. Crust flakes off in large chunks.

"Tea still needs time to steep."

"Very kind of you, Sofie," Reins says. *Sofie?* His head turns too fast, and by the time the rest of him catches up, he's already on the floor. White shoes appear. White shoes, a semi-white dress, only two streaks of red in the form of ribbons breaking the line. The Inspector tries his best to stand, but his legs go one way, his head another, and his eyes end up staring at the floor once more.

Weakly, he asks: "Steep? Tea?"

"Yes," she says. "Steep, cook, brew—" Sofie's voice pipes like a tit that found the sunflower seeds in the birdfeeder. "Boil!"

The hem of her dress cuts the air as she spins, spins, then settles to the ground in front of Rein. A pretty face, scratching at the mid-twenties, looks back. *Young?*

"Double, double toil and trouble," she whispers. "Fire burn and caldron bubble."

"Sofie?"

She's wearing long gloves, white and black. Rein squints, his vision swinging back and forth. Black fingers press against his lips in a quick "Shhh."

"Have you gone mad?".

Her smile straightens. "No, but you're drugged. Of course, you're still boring."

Two of the legs in the chair are loose, and it gives Rein poor support in his effort to stand. "I am a ranking member of the Princeps Inspectorum, and a lead investigator."

Sofie stands, curtseys, and mouths, "boring," with the white glove.

"I've been chased out of Liverpool in a bathtub."

A look of consideration rolls across her features. "Sounds like the Rein I know; stupid, and—" The black hand dips, lowering itself to his face just as he reaches her midriff. "Boring."

"Elves stir, and I fear something worse is about."

"So you decided trespassing was a good idea, after what you tried? And since the former is illegal, I am well within my rights to bury you in my garden."

Rein wrinkles his nose, unsure if that is true of English law. She continues while he ponders.

"You lured me in with the talk of ancient knowledge, then tried to bind my mind. You wanted to make *me* duller than you."

Rein squints. "Well, obviously that did not work, so—"

"So it's the intent," she says. "If I am supposed to appreciate the lousy gifts, then I am within my rights to be peeved over betrayal."

"You were far too concerned with quick progress," Rein says. "And not enough with the dangers of consorting with ruinous powers."

In the center of the room is a large pot. Rein watches Sofie tiptoe up to the edge and peak in. She speaks to him out of the side of her mouth. "That's an excuse. You just didn't like being bettered by a woman."

Every so often she pokes and prods at the contents "Peas pottage hot?" She asks. "Or peas pottage cold?"

Sofie flashes a coy smile. "Peas pottage hot, "shoving a bowl filled with green mash into his hands.

When Rein thought it couldn't get worse, she drops a spoon into the questionable concoction, and talks on and on again.

"Or did you think I was going to make a stew out of you? That'd be a waste; no one to feed except my cats. And I love my cats." Sofie splits a heft of dark bread and pushes it towards him. "So, elves?"

"Yes," he says softly. "I'm investigating the appearance of two, though I am afraid I have lost their trail." Rein then tries to lean in menacingly, but the only thing in danger are his clothes from the bowl. "I was driven from Liverpool before I could plan. The Forum Magicae is overrun."

"By elves?" The sound of her spoon scraping is slightly more annoying than the smell of nine-day-old legumes. "That's nonsense."

"No. Demons—" And when he sees Sofie about to laugh, he adds: "The ancient powers left between Construct and the ruins of creation."

"You're being awful…" Sofie stalls and uses a spoon to spell out the next word. "Open." The utensil bounces around the lip of the bowl as she drops it back in. "Don't you want to know how I broke that curse of yours?"

Before he can answer, she adds: "I'm not going to tell you, of course."

"It doesn't matter," he says with a sigh. "I need to investigate the prison at Tara, if I am to have any hope of tracking these elves." This time the Inspector doesn't embarrass himself as he comes closer. "No one knows their kind better than you. If we combine our skills and link our magics, I think we will have them."

She balks. "You want me to do that with *you?* You're mad."

"There's more," Rein says. "I…well. May need some help recovering my assistant."

"Recover?" Slowly. "Recover—You killed him." Her empty bowl clanks against his full one, as she slides it across the table towards him.

"These things happen in my line of work. Will you help me?"

Sofie pulls off the black glove and tosses it behind her. For a moment, she sits, tapping the table. Then her drumming slows until there are several seconds between taps. One. Two. She stiffens and shifts her shoulders. "No."

"More's at stake than your anger at me," he says.

"England? The world? Your Curators? That stupid hat you still wear?" she says. "Maybe things would be better with the elves in control."

"Elves? You know full well they aren't the little winged sprites that the English like to drool on about, when they aren't chasing their milk maids or their cows. I can never tell the difference. But elves—" He is feeling the rant building in his bones and beating it down with a shimmy of his jowls. "They are a rigid people, with traditions and rules for every bit of nonsense that make the French court seem quaint. They are absolutely boring."

Sofie smiles curtly. "What about wars? The diseases, the poverty?"

"We'd still have them," he says. "Elves are a wondrous race. Their cruelty, their alien minds, are all wonders to behold. We'd be no more, or in fact less than blades of grass in their world." Rein tries to lift his head here, to meet her gaze, but he is still too weak. "On a more practical side, they aren't known to consort with greater spirits. They do not like to ally with beings of equal status either. Anything that they cannot control invites trouble, or chaos. Chaos goes against their nature."

Sofie leans back into her chair, and Rein takes this as a cue to continue talking. "Therefore, It would be more likely that men are involved, somehow."

"Who?" she asks. "And why?"

"Cultists?" Rein makes a movement with his hand, as if measuring the thought. "Most are nothing more than little twits who could never challenge the Curatorium, much less overrun it. Who then? Someone I don't know? Or maybe someone we have merely forgotten about."

"There are powers that have lived a long time in the void," he adds. "And ancient exiles. I need to figure out what is at play here—who is working with whom, or this series of unfortunate events can be considered coincidence."

"Not my circus," she says. "Not my monkey."

The woman's raised eyebrow loads a memory into Rein's pistol-like mind. And as most weapons of the time, it takes a while to prime. In these moments, he manages to stand, turn ninety degrees to one side, then look back at her dramatically. "Whatever knowledge you have scraped from the muck of your garden cannot compare to the library available to Artisans. You are just rummaging through the garbage left for the hogs."

"Does this have a point, or is this a lead-up to get me to read Radcliffe?"

"I know how to pass between worlds," he says. "I know the song needed to enter the Fairhome, and from there, any door can be opened."

There is a glint in her eyes. And Rein reaches for it. "I will give this to you, and more if you help me."

"You are desperate," she says in a quick exhale. "You drop promises like my brother does shoes. Why should I listen to you?"

"Because I will teach it to you, here," he says, pushing the bowls to the side. "Now."

Even in his weakened state, his mastery of the occult shows. Each word, each piece of the song rolls with power and force. But this is more than a simple spell. Here is a song, woven by the three races, that endures with them. There is no traditional *Étincelle,* a physical component touched by the mage's understanding of magic, and connection with the immaterial. The *Forme* twists in the practitioner's mind and requires more than Rein can summon. It is the barrier to entry; the life force needed for men to cross over was meant to protect against random incursion. One aspect of the classical magical structure is present, and the *Mort* relieves the stress upon the Inspector, allowing him to crumple back into the chair.

All the while, Sofie looks upon down on him with one quizzical eyebrow. He can't help but to search her features. Looking for a bit of familiarity. Friendliness. This leads to some mistakes in his retelling; which he is sure she catches. For his purposes, though, Rein is unsuccessful. The inspector collapses in mid repeat.

"It's done, I'm done," Rein whispers. "Do you have any brandy?"

"No. Do you have your assistant's remains?"

Slowly, and with a fragility that for once hints at the Inspector's true age, he passes the vial to Sofie. "Then our bargain—"

"I never agreed to anything," she says.

The vial glows an unhealthy green between her fingers, and the light shining over her face makes Rein quail. He reaches, weakly, out to her hand, but is pushed away like a small child.

"Do you really think throwing a few mouldy phrases at me will do it?" Undertones of anger shatter an almost statuesque performance. "You're still the same pompous, ignorant, selfish fool." Her hands tremble as they reach out towards Rein, as if to strangle him, then withdraw halfway. "You abandoned me. You can't mend that with a few words. I'll decide when and if I trust you."

"They are here," he gasps. "The demons have followed me to Meath."

"Good for you." Then, softly: "I will think on it." She moves towards the Inspector and places her hand upon his brow. "But tonight, sleep. *Cadal nis.*"

Rein leans back, eyebrow inching up quizzically. "What did you hope that would do?"

A serious glare from Sofie peels off into a laughter that seems to roll out in waves. She steps back and tilts her head. "Never can get the precise dosage right."

"Dosage?" Rein wavers, wipes the sweat from his brow. "The peas?"

"Maybe," she says.

Rein's stomach twists, and clenches. His face and arms are now sticky with sweat. Sofie ignores his following howl of pain and pushes him aside, letting the Artisan to fall to the floor.

"Peas pottage puts you on the pot. For nine days long."

Chapter 30

Morning. Awful, bright, and *Klere,* arrives at the appropriate time; too damn early for Rein. The vagabond rays reach him under the table, playing off the colours of his last meal, as if such could be poetic. It's not. And no inner narration can make what the Inspector did to his pants heroic.

There are spells, hacked together, for cleanliness. Incantations for health. Many of these are used by the orderly Cultist, to varying degrees of success. Yet these take life force to work the *Forme*, and the Inspector is rather dehydrated.

"Clean yourself up," Sofie says, laying a bowl of water at his head. "I'm putting you and the cats out."

"You are just going to cast me aside?" He looks to the door instinctively, seeing a trio of felines there pawing, rubbing on the trim. When they notice him, their mewing becomes a chorus, giving Rein a triumphant melody for his attempts at standing.

"Do you want your lackey back or not?" Sofi shifts her hips and walks towards the cats.

The front door swings open and the mewing stops, leaving Rein midway to standing without any accompaniment. His shoulders relax from relief, which nearly topples him. After a moment, he succeeds in lifting his head. She moves, and returns to rest against a windowsill with an eyebrow raised as if expecting what the Inspector may say next. But he remains quiet. This is the first time he has seen her, fully, in over fifty years. Like he, Sofie has not aged a day. Between the awe of seeing his former lover standing there ageless, and the fear of what this represents, he forgets where and when he is. "Would you care to dance?"

Sofie bounces forward in a laugh that is half scoffing and half surprise. "There's a basket outside," she says, amusement draining out of her face. "It's a long walk to Teaghmorreagh."

"Do not repeat that name," he chides. "Call it Liathdruim, or Tara."

Beyond the door, birds and a warm day preen, and as he makes his way past the threshold, the Inspector turns to Sofie only to have her look away. On the doorstep there is a basket, partially harassed by the cats. When he bends down to pick it up, the door closes behind him. Locks bolt when he stands. Before him, the garden obscures the countryside like an open fan, but Rein is certain he has a full morning, and afternoon of walking. *Southeast from here, and a castle marks the ascent.* The same he saw from the road upon arriving near Lismullin.

Wind picks up after crossing over a narrow mound that separates Sofie's land from another's. The Inspector scratches his chin, searching the terrain now that there is plenty of light. Homegrown paths lead out and away. *A few are promising.*

Grass ripples, the smell of barley touches him, and he looks up and west to trace the direction of the wind. There, as he pauses, he can hear horses neighing. From the commotion he would say they are close, but he can see no stable or barn. Only Sofie's cottage marks the land between here and perhaps the next mile.

Rein closes his eyes. Unseasonably warm air from the west caresses his hair, blowing a single strand across his nose. *I need a haircut,* he thinks, breaking his concentration. The Inspector huffs and blows the lock away from his face, then tries again.

The quiet this time takes him. Smells of the fields, of tilled earth, of beats of labour, fade. The sound of horses, the whip of long grass and wheat, dies. A hum encroaches upon him. The Inspector pivots towards where he thinks the neighing might have come. The hum also retreats, replaced by a splash of colour against the background of his shut eyelids. Rein reaches out, pushing in that direction with his will, his mind. The colours form a pattern, then a shape. He frowns.

"She's cast an obscura," he says. *She's etched it on the land itself.* The significance hits him in the gut, so that the next statement, "and made it a permanent scar," is hoarse, and lost.

He swallows. *But she has not learned to hide everything.*

It is hard for him to leave the shadow of the spell work. To abandon his assistant to her. But he does, even though this concern follows him to the next field and beyond, where he finally joins the path instead of trampling through a farmer's livelihood.

"She's grown," he says. The ground is much firmer than the muddy hell it was the night before, but in the lower places there is still some treachery to be found. One such hole nearly takes his shoe. Rein shimmies his leg from the sting.

"Though if I had studied only the old ways, and not spent so much time traveling and hunting Cultists, I would be just as knowledgeable." Rein sighs. "I'll note in my journal the time and place. It will be interesting to see how long it takes me to believe that."

Rich farmland swallows the hill of Tara, and the approach is slow because of this. Within another two hours of navigating property lines, and other obstacles, Rein manages to ascend to the primary hill from which the area receives its name. Beyond, the land is flat, and on a clear day it would be easy to see all the way to Navan. Today is not such a day. The westward wind has shifted and blows from the opposite side. Rain threatens, but for now the sky is resigned to remain veiled and angry. Thunder bays in the distance.

To verify elves have broken free, he will need to find the signs of their passage. *To and from, if the rumors are correct.* And he doesn't have to search far. The fruits of the craft are present everywhere. Rein kneels close to the ruins of an old church. "It's so complex," he says, referring to the spells woven by the Curators. *I can feel the Construct's power touching every blade of grass.* He staggers. The influence of the ancient Artisans works on his nerves, as if trying to push him away.

Rein rolls and pops his neck. The power of the prison needles at his senses. And in this edge, where the instinct to leave is painful, he takes a deep breath and closes his eyes. The rush of forms, of lines, and the strength of this land's connection to the Construct hits him like ice water. He gasps and forces in another hard breath, shutting his eyelids tighter.

Under an aura of power, thick and swirling with currents more dangerous than any tidal flow, he plunges mentally. Lines —and a leyline—ancient and skillfully made begat this sea of magic. And the approach is treacherous. Sweat rolls down his face, and the taste of blood is upon his lips. Rein breathes in slow, rhythmic huffs, hoping to ready himself for another push. But his body trembles, his bones ache, and there is a sound from outside that yanks him from his meditation.

"Horse," he says weakly. A similar visual distortion as before, back in Sofie's cottage, takes effect. He leans and looks towards the main road just as a blur of movement crests. There is a flash of light, a trail of vivid splotches, and a shape writhing like an oncoming thundercloud. Rein wipes his eyes, but even before she speaks, he recognizes Sofie. She rides sidesaddle, and splendidly so.

"Fool," she says, the whip of her dress hiding and then revealing sunlight in a game of make-Rein-blink as she dismounts. "I'd ask if you could be any more reckless, but halfwits like you take that as a challenge."

The Inspector spits on the end of his undershirt sleeve, and dabs again at his eyes. "My inspection requires haste."

A lock of Sofie's long black hair breaks free as she shakes her head. Rein can now see she is wearing a gray riding dress —the thundercloud from earlier—with a short jacket of military cut. Soft, rosy cheeks play against a muslin chemisette, and the edges of a man's undershirt poke out. On her head is a top hat, and here he sees the storm touching her movements, as if she has ridden in with it.

"You could easily have been killed," she growls. "Rushing in without knowing a damn thing about anything? So typical."

A black strap hits him, which he can only guess are the reins. The Inspector steps back, narrowly missing a bell from the swinging leather. He opens his mouth to speak, but Sofie's voice knifes his.

"I've been studying this area for nearly all my life. And you think you can just start digging without protection, or even a plan?"

A memory of an equally angry, younger Sofie surfaces. She had been his second choice for a dance that night, and it didn't sit well. Rein temples his fingers. "There is no time for—"

"Choose your distraction: this, or a funeral. Even the lesser works of your Curators are protected," she says. "What idiot would think their greatest wouldn't be? The traps here will split your soul like an apricot."

"If they yet function."

She pushes past him, horse following. The look she throws at him as she does is contemptuous. Rein follows, and they move away from the church ruins and many of the other monuments, stopping only to tie the horse. Sofie takes them to a small patch of grassy land. There is nothing distinct about the area, and the signs Miss Van Couraden sees are not clear to Rein. But he waits, and in time she turns and addresses him in her usual manner.

"The Curators did not route every leyline directly to the Construct," she says. "One remains here, and their spell work is lashed to it. I am told it touches the bigger work, so that if it is broken, they would know immediately. The flow of true magic is greatest here, and their control the weakest."

"And you plan for me to use it how—as some sort of canal, or river?"

"Sometimes you prove to be less dim than I give you credit for," she says. "Yes, you are going to sail around the battlements and hope for an easier landing."

"But you don't have a boat, so I fail to—"

"And then you go and say things like that." A small bag that he missed earlier appears from under her arm. She tosses it down to the ground, near Rein's feet. "I am going to armor you with protections and provide directions that even you can follow. With luck, you'll get past the first defenses. It's all up to you, after."

"Wait," Rein says. "Unless something's changed, you have no connection to the Construct. How did you manage this?"

"You aren't the only Artisan, you know?" The coy, disarming smile that stole his heart so long ago returns. "There have been other collaborations. Jealous?"

"No." *Yes.* Fear and doubt unsettle him. He swallows. "I think I can manage my own protections well enough."

"Like you did before? Another moment and you would have been feeding the grass."

Rein crosses his arms. "You lack any sense of tact; that has always been your failing." The Inspector straightens and picks at hairs on his jacket. "Your help has been most welcome, but I will take over."

"And being a stubborn, obstinate mule every time you get your feelings hurt is yours. You asked for my help."

"And you have provided it," he says forcefully. Rein turns, as if to inspect the clearing. He nods, absently, then makes to craft a ward in the ground. Sofie, though, is quicker—and every time he bends over, she is there with her own implements.

"What are we, children?" he asks.

Yet she ignores the comment and continues her own work. Rein watches her move from *Étincelle* to *Mort* skillfully and can't help but feel admiration for the breadth of her knowledge. *And jealousy* of her skill.

With the first set of wards in place, she curtseys to Rein and says: "The keel of your boat is laid, milord," then cocks her head while rising. "But there's more to do to make it sea-worthy. Why don't you return to my house and get your friend? I will keep working here."

"Higgins? He's alive?"

She smiles. "By the time you get back, he should be fully brewed."

There is a bounce in Rein's step that wasn't there a moment earlier. "Magnificent, I will just fetch the horse and—"

"No." Her face and tone return to the stone she is apparently made of. "You will walk."

"It will be evening then before I am back."

And just as quickly as they came, the stony features leave. Again, there is an almost joyful pulse to her voice. "Till this evening, then, Mister De Rein."

"I—" Rein, mouth open like a seal waiting for a fish, turns and storms away. Between the mound where the Stone of Destiny was moved after the 1798 Insurrection and the lip of land leading to the main road, a crash of thunder makes him lift his head to the sky.

"You better jesting." One. He grimaces. Two, three, four drops of rain hit his face in quickening fashion.

"Oh, and Rein?"

He spins on his heels in a slow, grinding arc.

"There should be some parsnips I prepared earlier, bread, cheese—and can you be so kind as to bring brandy from the cellar? You and Higgins can carry it in a basket, you'll find it near the fireplace."

Rein snorts, then turns his attention back to the road. One foot in front of the other. One, two drops of rain against a dampening forehead. The ground travels by without notice while the droplets splatter. And the Inspector this time forgets the count of meters, or even miles. Or the unnatural length of the shadows that pass around him.

He also forgets that he can make an umbrella.

Chapter 31

Of all the wonders in the halls of the Forum Magicae, few were greater, to Rein's mind, than the knowledge kept in its archives. It was a place frequented by him and the other members of the Inspectorum Princeps. His lot had free rein—because to catch the enemy, you had to know their ways and magic. Upon reflection, this might now include him. Things change.

In reflection, specifically in the window of Sofie's cottage, he sees a tired young face: his own. A lamp spell gleams just behind him, illuminating the way, and sets his jaw and high cheekbones in eerie contrasting light.

Rein tilts his head, considering, hesitating. All those years tracking down the worst of the Cultists and *I've never had a look at any of them. They were just jobs, challenges to overcome.* Nor had he even spoken to the Necromancers who brought others, like Higgins on many occasions, back to life. They were a strange lot, and heretical.

Maybe the other Artisans thought the same of me. The door to her house is unlocked. At his feet a trio of cats wait expectantly, their meows the only sound other than his pacing. Rein pats his chest, where he keeps the few remaining pages of his grimoire. *So, I am a heretic.* The door to Sofie's cottage creaks, opening. Night has made its home in the room, deep and unsettling.

"Am I even doing this for the Curatorium anymore?"

A thousand questions burble around in the back of his head. Stirring, bumbling—accompanied by many adverbs—but the eager cries of the felines and their obnoxious pacing dominate.

"All right, all right." He throws his hands up. "House cats, fi. Where does she keep your dinner?"

On the table? *No.* On the stove, in the pantry? *In the cupboards.* Fish. He heard somewhere that cats like fish, and as luck would have it, Sofie was soaking some salted cod. Rein tosses the pan and its contents onto a counter top and returns to scour a cabinet.

The Teamor must be stopped, he thinks with a slam of the cupboard door. "I will deal with the rest later." Pots rattle back an answer as Rein paws through the kitchen. "No, first —"*Dishes, dishes, dishes, oh.*

He made the mistake of leaving the fish unattended.

"And at least I'll be left alone for a while." Rein moves, then stops at a cellar door. "Probably bother me again when I'm on the chamber pot."

He exhales. The kitchen is full of fragrance from the flowers Sofie must have cut from her garden earlier. Lavender, roses, flowering sweet peas. Though it is not yet full spring and nowhere near summer. "How did she grow them?" The answer is clearly: more magic.

Everywhere in this place she has woven spells, he suspects. The Inspector falls quiet, listening to the house groan, moan, and—*Stumble?*

Higgins. She must have prepared him, down in her cellar. Grizzly daydreams of witches, their brews, and the awful experiments tied to them in legend prick his mind, causing him to shiver. Rein places his hand on the iron latch of the cellar door. It opens with little effort, revealing a set of wooden stairs.

Shadows cascade on the stairwell walls unnaturally. Rein jerks back, laying his hand upon the door behind. He finds nothing, save the way open, which he promptly closes. Below, he can hear a moaning

"Hello," Rein says shakily. "Higgins?"

After several moments a hoarse voice answers, and Rein's chest heaves forward in a gasp. Twelve steps are conquered in a second and he is smacked with the view of an open laboratory. Light blast him in the face like a shot from a blunderbuss as it reflects off every vial, beaker and other glass instruments. The Inspector reels and rubs his eyes. When his sight adjusts, he is almost blinded a second time.

"Rotzak," he cries. "Put some damn clothes on, will you?"

Upon an apparatus that looks more like a mold for lead sits a confused Higgins. He is wearing a lady's bonnet and a scarf, but nothing else. There is a pair of pants in his left hand which he seems to be pondering over intensely. When Rein addresses him, he stands up and mumbles something intelligible.

"I have to do everything, naturally," the Inspector sighs. Clothes in Higgins' sizes are willed into being, as he taps the power of the Construct. In this moment, Higgins' dreamlike stupor sharpens, and he leaps off the strange device where he'd been sitting. At first Rein takes it as recognition of the clothing he'd crafted, and a good, decent, Englishman's—and his assistant is the only one he will admit to liking—preference for general modesty.

But then Higgins speaks: "You fool, they'll see, they'll know!"

Rein squints. "Who?"

The answer comes in a series of screams and screeches from upstairs. Higgins rushes past the Inspector to shut the door. His face is white, paler than pall, and he shrinks from Rein and contact.

"You've brought them here," he says, taking the clothing offered. "This will be our tomb."

Prowling noises from above join in with a haunting tone that envelops the cellar. The Inspector grabs Higgins by the shoulder but the assistant flinches from the touch and pushes him towards a desk.

"Put that chair against the door," Rein says. The sounds of nails on tile, as if a large dog is walking on the floor above with unclipped nails, begins.

"Good, good," Rein adds distractedly. "Now the sack of potatoes. And, Higgins? Could you—"

Cracking wood at the door gets them to quickly barricade it with an assortment of vegetables and small furniture. Higgins, his weight against the stacks, adds his howl to the chaos.

"Quick man, think. Can you still see to the other side? How many of them are there?"

The assistant bites his thumb as potatoes thump the floor. One. Two. "Enough."

With his hand against the door, the Inspector can feel the tremble and bulging of the wood. His words flow between spell crafting and conversation. Finally, a mishmash of wards is linked together, and the door stops shaking. Rein looks to his assistant. "They will hold," he says, his timbre rising. "The barrier must hold."

"We can't guard the walls, door, and the roof."

"No," Rein wheezes. The tone circling the cellar grows clearer, louder. Both recognize it for what it is: a chant. Higgins shimmies off the table to grab a small rod from a batch of hazel in the corner.

"Lord, should I fight or—?"

A clawed hand reaches through a gap in the door. The ground trembles, jostling both, but sending the Inspector to one knee.

"Keep quiet," Higgins says.

Or is escape still an option? He doesn't have a bucket. There are no windows here.

"Solna—"

The start of a spell tears the Inspector's attention from the door. He stares at his assistant as if a walrus just waddled up to him and asked for a cup of tea.

"Solna nea, Oran cruchaid, an beath."

Blood drips from a puncture wound on Higgins' hand, onto the hazel rod. And wherever the ichor touches, a brilliant white light erupts. "Stand back."

The door shatters. Chairs scrape and scuff as a terrible force pushes inward.

"Have you gone mad?" Rein barks. "I've never heard of this spell."

"It is remembered only by the dead."

Arms now crawl over the refuse. Things that pass for hands, and hands that are so shriveled they might as well be claws, threaten to overrun them. A solitary potato sack still lying on the side is rent open.

"Solna nea, Oran cruchaid, an beath."

The hand movements, the repeated intervals of foot positioning. The strange, primitive words. They all come together to make Higgins look as if he is practicing some new sort of interpretive dance, instead of a spell. Even as vegetables spill out one by one.

"Solna nea, Oran cruchaid, an beath." The flames brighten, swirl in deadly arcs ahead of his wand.

Yet the terrors barely relent, keeping only out of range of the light's tendrils. The Inspector is forced to huddle against his friend, as their boots crunch over broken refuse. Up. Echoing on wooden stairs. Up, through the door. Even as the unearthly chanting seeks to wrap around them like a blanket. Up, up. As glints of teeth and appendages alternate between smoke and solid form.

"This spell won't last forever, and then what?" Higgins whispers and turns his head only slightly. "Will our souls be devoured right as we reach the commons of Lismullin?"

"We'll make for Tara," Rein says, taking control. "Sofie is there, and she can aid us."

A hoarse laugh is the response, but the Inspector continues, pressing his face close to the right ear of his assistant. "We'll make for her stable and steal a horse or two. That should give us time."

"We're relying on the charity of your former lovers to save our skins?" Higgins' guts growl, as if he's summoning something other than courage.

"Let's press forward to the stables, by God," Higgins bellows.

Up the last of the stairs, Rein's friend pushes bravely, fiercely. Through the threshold, into the main hall where the stars can reach him. Higgins' nerves appear to waver with each step.

"What would your Sir Author Wellesley do?" Rein says. "Think of him."

"He'd run off to his tent and drink coffee," Higgins answers. "And let you die for him."

"Maybe you should think of Lord Nelson."

Night air, and the moon lies behind a twisting line of smoke and terror. Higgins drives into it, at times growling, at times screaming. The chanting is joined now with a mad sort of chattering that threatens to swallow them whole. Trees, flowers, and shrubbery all look alike in the gloom. And feel so. Every scrape of a branch, each tickle from a leaf, invokes shouting and cursing from the two. Until it seems like there is little more of either to give.

Rein strays too far from the protective light, and one of the shriveled beings takes a swipe at his exposed leg. He cries out, calling for his friend, who reaches back. Together, moving as one, they enter the garden's middle yard.

"Hold!" The Inspector kneels. Blisters mark the wound. Rein leans on his assistant, searching for the path to the stables, returning to the light each time.

"Damn," he gasps. He lowers his head, and whispers into his friend's ear. "The path is here; I will steer us."

The aura holding the tide back buckles. Higgins shrinks further as Rein grits his teeth. But the creatures are still testing the barrier. And the creatures now are testing both their spirits. Using his assistant like a crutch, Rein urges his assistant along.

Demonic things leer from an oak's branches. Eyes, lighting up like twisted stars amidst the foliage. The two partners pass warily, the glow from Higgins' makeshift wand flooding the lower leaves, making the whole thing appear alien. From here Rein pushes his friend right, left. To a wall. Against a small iron gate, and beyond. The creatures chant, the creatures chatter. Yet no attempts are made against the spell again. Together they inch towards the stable.

"They'll be upon us as soon as we mount," Higgins says.

"That can be taken so many ways," Rein says in a pained laugh, reaching for where the door should be. *Wood. Wood. Wood. Aha.* A slight smile teases his lips, as he lays his hand on an iron latch. "Take it slowly."

"The spell is nearly out," Higgins retorts.

Double wide doors open, and their light floods. Four stalls, three of them empty. Panicked neighs come from the fourth, but luckily none of the creatures have made a move for it.

Rein shuts the way quickly, letting the shadow of his assistant disappear towards the stall with the horse, while he ponders the fragile boards that mark their only egress from this place. "Those things could move through the door, I'd wager, without taking it down."

A grunt from behind could be acknowledgement, or Higgins' attempts to calm the beast. Rein turns in time to see him struggle with a saddle. "Why do they wait?"

"Might be tactical," Higgins says. "Testing our defenses, waiting for us to weaken. They have time, all the time of eternity."

"Or maybe…" Rein cuts himself short. A heroic image of him staying behind to allow Higgins to escape rises, them fast sinks to the pit of his stomach. He grimaces.

"Or maybe what?"

"Nothing." His friend mounts the horse in one fluid motion, and Rein can't help looking on, impressed. Higgins leans over, offering him his hand. Shame thickens Rein's Dutch accent and slows "Just a foolish idea," into a slough.

Wood bends and cracks, mixing with the otherworldly chaos of voices outside, as the Inspector swings up behind his friend. The horse fights the reins, refusing to leave the stall.

"Get us to the door," Rein says. "When I throw the latch, sally forth."

Higgins leans to the side, pressing with his legs and putting the horse on the bit. The ears of the creature swivel rapidly, but he moves. Rein reaches back and snags the handle of a broken pitchfork from the side, watching the tail of the clamp down.

"The beast is tense," he says. "Should I say a word to call him?"

The door looms. Hay and excrement are tossed in the air by nervous pawing, but Higgins presses, "Don't you dare. You just throw the latch and hook the door. Take the rod from me."

Rein leans forward, pressing both the rod and the broken half together in precarious balance. "Well, on my count."

"One." He struggles to loosen the lock as the wood buckles. "Two—"

With a heave that almost throws him, the lock is loosened. Rein reaches forward once more as the count passes beyond three. He wiggles the wood between the cracks of the two doors, but it's the demonic creatures, batting, driving inward, that really help open the way further. And with a shrill cry of "three" at his back, Higgins urges the horse forward.

"Watch your hat!"

Rein lurches as the horse charges into the night. The terrors part as if hit by an unseen wind. *Thralls, human slaves.* Surrounded by the formless creatures. *Spirits, wanton things.*

As the horse gallops past, a queasy feeling stirs the Inspector's stomach, and it has nothing to do with the jerky movement of their ride through the country. *They could have us, yet don't.*

A fence appears out of the night, and Rein falls forward during the lunge, pushing Higgins against the beast's head. "What the devil? I don't remember there—" Stars. *Wait, is that Cepheus?* "We're going north! Change to south by southwest."

Their turn is wide, and laborious. Yet in the arc the Inspector can see the twisted forms of these demons, these spirits, waiting. "They're just—" The last spark of the spell's light glints off a row of steel buttons in the crowd. *Fine lines. Tall hat, but —no, it can't be. Chancy?*

"We're being herded."

Chapter 32

"Ride hard," he says, and they do, into wheel-rutted paths and through fields of sleeping wildflowers.   Onwards to the hill, ascending, ascending when the main road is met, on a path as if to reach the stars. Or touch heaven. Onwards towards the crossroads of the known and unknown. Onwards, and back to Sofie.

When the hill is crested, Rein points out a small campfire to Higgins. Smells of earth and hay permeate the air. Then both regard the woman nearest, and the Inspector wonders aloud, between her glare and the fire, which would burn them more.

"Sofie," Rein says, arms outstretched. He nearly falls off. "We must hurry, the enemy is not far."

"What right do you have to steal my horse?" she asks.

The beast whinnies, shifting right as Higgins dismounts in one move. The Inspector, on the other hand, is not so quick, and his right foot remains caught in the stirrups while the horse backpedals. His friend helps him, and together they take the reins and pass them to Sofie.

Rein, wheezing and out of breath, looks her in the eye as the heat from the campfire whisks him. "The right of the desperate, we—"

But his sentence is never completed. Chanting, dark, and rattling grows louder as something marches up that lonely hill. Higgins mutters a curse in Welsh, and Sofie stares off past the

Inspector into the darkness. Rein touches her arm, and by the look on her face, is close to being slapped for it.

"Wards, woman," he says quickly.

"The ones I know will be useless."

"Higgins has a spell we can bind them to. Did you prepare the protections?"

"There," she says, pointing towards a bald spot on the grass. "But if I need to put up wards, I won't be able to guide you."

Her craft is skillful, he can sense the power without searching for it. "I will be fine, but you will have to pull me out," he says, sitting down. The grass slickens his trousers. *Quickly, look inward.* Darkness threatens in the form of thunder clouds, and wind whips his hat off his head. Rein closes his eyes. "Necessity precludes caution. I hope your wards will protect me from the shock."

No time for safety. *No time for distrust.* Slowly, the Inspector visualizes the intermixing of two lights: one, a dark, earth-based form, swirling and snaking through his body from below. The second, a heavenly light flowing down from his temple. Where the two meet, Rein keys in, slowly losing himself in their dance, and in his rhythmic breathing.

The four corners of her spell light up in his mind's eye, *and yes, in the form of a ship.* He focuses on their lines, perfect and symmetrical. Forgetting the storm outside, *and the fifing chanting.* This time however, when he plunges into the flush of power surrounding the prison, the protections fill his mind, buffeting and keeping it from overwhelming him. He leaves his body, sinking into the magic of the Curator's creation and the powers of the ancient landscape.

It is a little like swimming. The pressure, the sensation of being a moment from drowning. Yet with Sofie's help, he can endure, gaze upon the ancient prison. Under the aura of power, their work shines like veins of silver in a dark mine. Rein stretches for one of these, while simultaneously holding the impression of the elves from the murder scene. The threads glow menacingly, hinting at the power behind, and the Inspector is forced to pull back.

No shortcuts, then, and instead his eyes trace the vein as it crosses more like it, covering a throbbing expanse of black matter. From this, the threads—as much as they can be called that—pulse in one direction, towards a single, powerful cord. *A leyline.*

The individual threads of power flow inwards, puckering the middle of the prison like an orange with the center removed, only here, the leyline meandering through. *Where is the weak spot?* The current pulls inward, and Rein drifts with it.

Closer. The veins cross one another in regular lines, many directions. *There are patterns, but I can't tell their purpose.* Closer, and the flow of power here alternates between push and pull, with more of the former so that each second he's brought *closer.* Until everywhere he looks, except forward, is illuminated by the silver light.

Words, their crossings form words. Spells. The leyline crackles with energy to his right, dominating. And below, and thus forward, where the orange puckers, the parade of spell craft ends in an impossibly dark hole. *Absence.* For there appears to be nothing beyond. *Yet that is where the current is taking me.*

Panic grips his mind as he looks deeper, deeper into the void. Rein pushes hard against the impulse to turn back, stuffing it down into the dark, just as the dark from outside threatens to swallow him. And here, with the powers of the ancient leyline ending and the abyss threatening, a thought occurs to him: *How did the Artisan of Sofie navigate this?*

He, almost alone amongst sorcerers, can also sense the primal—the Chords of creation. It is the reason why he became an

Inspector. The number of others like him can be counted on one hand.

How many? An Indian lady, a minor relation to the current Raja. *Missing for five years.* The second, a farmer in the English penal colony, New South Wales. His name escapes him. The third? *A chap from Belgium I—*

Oh. His mind had strayed. Only the darkness, only the void remains before him. Rein struggles against the flow, vainly.

Rot! The light of the prison's spellwork exists at the periphery. For the Inspector, the pit looms and cannot pull back.

Aanhouden doet gedaan.

Spirals of light warp and ripple around him like stars on a black flag. Left. Right. Up, down, and in between, the former orientation is lost to him. Rein feels outward with his emotions, butting against Sofie's wards and something else. He has no physical eyes to open, but the effort lightens the burden of darkness. He can sense a wall between him and whatever lies on the opposite side.

Open, his inner voice echoing. Rein digs deep, throwing anything, and every feeling at this invisible barrier. The blockage bends, warping inwards like a bubble, and his mind claws into the thin film, spreading a tear that yanks the rest of him through.

A sheen of wet drenches his clothing as he passes. *Clothing?* Rein wipes his forehead, dragging the soaked end of his sleeve over and not making a bit of difference. "What the bloody hell?"

Louis XIV-style architecture peeks at him from the downpour. Rain biting and cold deluges. Dutch weather. Christiaan looks up and into the night sky, letting the storm pass over him in a part-troubling, and part-refreshing sensation. "I shouldn't be able to feel any of this."

Or talk. Before, emotions and his connection to the Construct were the tools he used to perceive the prison. "Why would they go through the trouble of creating an illusion like this?"

Lightning flashes in the distance, and the white-washed face of a palace opens fully before him. Two large floor-to-ceiling windows keep company to a sizeable entry door. Three more mark the second story, and there are two flanking sides that fold towards this frontage, as if in some frozen half-hug.

"Kneuterdijk Palace. Why?" The night sky, however, has no answer for him, only more rain, splattering on his forehead.

Whatever this is, it is vivid and dreary. The building looks as if it had been pulled straight from his memories, along with the wonderful Flanders weather. Marble lines the front way, and already he can hear laughter and a harpsichord.

"I remember this," he says. The door is open. Snippets of a quatrain greet him at the door, sprinkled with muted conversation. Rein strains to listen, but the voices retreat further inside.

"She called on me, well, through her friends." He lays his hands flat upon the door, feeling the music through the lacquered wood. "Neither her nor I are the same as we were, then. Too much has changed between us."

Or not enough. He pushes gently on the door, hearing it squeak, measuring the sensation of the oiled hinges giving way to its opening. The desire to walk in and see some of his old friends pulls at him, but a little voice in his head tells him, "It's a trap."

"That harpsichord," he sighs. "I was so confident. All right, cocksure. Until I felt the whirl of that virginal through the wall. I didn't hear better music until that child in Vienna, 68." *It's a trap.* "Oh God, who was that? I vaguely remember her father's name. Leo something."

It's a trap. "I was worried about sweating through the silk then, I was so nervous. But my friends from the consulate were there, and, no, I remember that didn't help."

Even as the memories of dancing with Sofie, of her smile, twirl between his ears… *It's a trap.* "She still has that smile, though." There is a gap now between the doors. Enough for more of the music, and some of the smell of sweet, sticky pastries to rush him.

Rein takes his hands off the panel. "No," he says. "Sofie warned me there would be dangers." His fingers linger on the wood and then drift as he turns.

"I must be inside, but not fully," he says, walking away. "Where they created the spells of containment, or for all I know I'm in the parlor." He stops, concentrating on the night. The illusion shimmers, as if it were a pool and a pebble had been tossed in the center. "If the elves snuck through, I would be able to tell here."

Simultaneously, Rein holds onto his perception of self and pushes against the illusion, like a man trying to load a potato into an over-large sling. The matter is difficult. *I see what they did.*

At once, the material. The sounds of merrymaking, the crash of thunder. The chill of a late November rain. Then back to the disembodied "reality," in a space between the threads woven into spells and the great leyline in the center, as his mind perceives it. Flipping between, over and over.

"The sky is—" *full of salad.* "No," *no.* Rein's laughter echoes across the firmament. "The Chords, I must listen," *listen.* And this reverberates in his own head. "My mind is tearing—" *lettuce?*

From the depths rise hidden things. Old bullies from his childhood live again to torture him. Awkward meetings and missed opportunities galumph on his self-worth. Every little idiotic comment he had made, every time he hurt someone accidentally surfaces. Or purposely. *The wellspring of experience is overflowing with regret.*

Then there is a name. A first name, and last. A set of initials—they all stand for the same thing. The flowery phrases of a budding love, secreted away, read between the lines. A first kiss, a first night in her arms. The second, longer spent. Songs, sung in the meadows after a spring rain. Curses spoken after a merciless tickle. Signs of something wrong; more days spent in darkness than light. The worried looks of her parents after the doctor's diagnosis. And last, searching her eyes for the familiar—recognition, and love—before saying goodbye. All of this bundled into one, the name of his wife. *Anna.* The pain almost breaks him. The pain is also what focuses him.

"Sofie," he whispers. *Anna,* he thinks. The illusion of the palace falls away, and only the disembodied realm of the spell work remains. *I always lose those I care about.*

Rein stretches out with his remaining emotion—love—and listens for the remnants of the Chords. He listens and observes. There are several threads, like the pieces of cloth a child might leave while running through a briar-patch, scattered about the latticework of the prison. On each impression is the hint of the Chords, and the trace of the elves. They had indeed left the prison, several times in fact, but each excursion ended in a violent return. Except one. The desire to investigate the older escapes haunts him, but as much as scouting those scenes might tell him about his hunt, they would also put him further behind what is quickly becoming a chase.

So he pulls closer to the latest one, a strong mark, recent. Pieces of the event flail about in the mindscape, tattered like scraps. The music calls, and he investigates. A wave of the remnant's primordial magic touches him. Images shoot across his perception in rapid fire. These are different from what he saw at the crime scene; more like ruts in a road, as opposed to full-fledged memories.

With haste he goes to another one, flying through the space, his mind pressed further by the power of the Curators' craft. This thread is old, but the lines of are clear enough.

They were pulled back almost immediately. They somehow managed to leave the world, I, Oh. The willpower Rein had been using to hold on to this view collapses, yanking him back into the false reality. Thunder crackles overhead, and he is filled with the sensation of his last strength draining from his body, as if from an open vein. The Inspector reaches up to the sky, and croaks: "Fairway, come again."

The stars disappear from the sky, the sound of rain fades. It takes a moment for him to realize that he can no longer see, or that the spells of the Curators are no longer forcing the vision upon him. He tries to stand, but the room spins. There is only the feeling of wet grass and the sensation of *a hand in my own?*

Something is holding him, keeping him from falling to the ground. "Higgins?"

"I'm right here, old timer," Higgins says. "Did you have a good nap?"

"I was not napping," Rein says. The stout men underneath his arm become two, then one as his vision steadies. "I've told you this before."

"Well, you were dead to the world," Sofie says. "But you are back just in time to be dead to all three of them."

"Good Lord," Rein says. "The chanting."

Far beyond their wards is nothing. Nothing—in that every-thing, light and sound trying to escape die. But there *is* some-thing near; between the trio and this wall there are creatures. Gangly, emancipated and twisted, they almost look human, as much as a corpse that has been reshaped could. Rein knows them as thralls, creations of Necromancers who've stepped beyond the limits of common decency. From these comes a song. It is different from before, and from the chanting of the wraiths. The words are almost pronounceable, and their song starts low, and gravely, as if escaping from the mouths of the dead. Choked with dirt and decay. At their backs are the shades, and darker things whence the chants once came. From this wellspring of cloud and shadow emerges a man.

The Inspector attempts to push his assistant away, and moves to cross the ward-line, but is stopped by Higgins' vice-like grip. "You."

"So, this is where you choose to die, Inspector? I would have thought you'd have better taste," Chancy says. "Caught dead in Ireland? What would your dear Anna say?"

Higgins snorts. "You can ask her yourself soon enough." A finger on the side of the Inspector's nose silences his assistant, and he retreats.

"Bad form," Rein says with a sigh.

The chanting increases, ending each stanza with four high pitched screeches. Chancy briefly gestures behind, then looks down his nose at the Inspector. "Lovely isn't it? I taught them that. I always feel that every situation is made so much better with ominous Latin. Try it next time you have a bad turn on the toilet. Then again," he continues. "I think you are…how do they say? Already deep in the shit? Your hackneyed wards won't keep out the thralls of the Teamor."

The attacks come even before he is finished speaking. Those thralls milling closest to the protecting light slash and claw tentatively at the barrier. Their actions are met with an equally violent reaction from the barrier. The sound of oil being thrown on a hot pan meets the smell of sizzling flesh, and the thralls make as if to return to the protective darkness. Until Chancy makes a strange sign in the air.

First one by one, then in twos, and lastly in a throng, the monsters throw themselves against the light. The air fills quickly with smoke and flame, and the trio is forced to back pedal to the center of their formation and protect their faces from both smell and heat.

"It cannot hold under this," Higgin says, pulling at Rein's sleeves. "Our spells *were* hacked together, and even if they don't get through—" The frantic pace of his chatter slows, as he chews the words. "We'll choke."

"If you have any ideas," says Sofie, to his other side. "Now's the time."

Moonlight teases them, as clouds pass by in celestial fury. A quick wind from the storm spins the smoke around them in a cyclone. And Rein, in the middle, sings.

"And the skies flow gray—as the sea, and the night till morn." He closes his eyes, and touches an image of a flickering, malleable world. A jewel of pearly obsolescence touched by an ever living night. *"Light carries the days—like leaves, lost in the wind."*

Rain, cold and slick, starts in a drizzle, drowning the smoke nearest them. *"Fairway, come again."*

Higgins starts. "What the bloody hell are you doing, singing? Have you gone mad?" he asks, reaching for his master; but Sofie intervenes, and thunder rolls in the background.

"Fairway, come again."

Rein's eyes open, and he looks for the Travelers' Stars, impressing upon them an image of the world from before, with a shining path leading to them.

"And the waves crash—against shores, heaven bred." As he sings, Higgins gasps, and the sound of Sofie taking control almost interrupts. But where he points, a vortex opens amidst that shining path. Smoke and shadow flow into it, as if being

swallowed by a siren's pool. *"Where time is born—and remains a rare guest."*

"Fairway, come again."

The crackling of the barriers is replaced by silence and the quick expulsion of light. Sofie grabs Rein and his friend by the arms, and together, bumbling and dazed, they dash into the portal. At their backs, the Teamor's creatures start a terrible howl, and the shrill commands of their master follow.

Chapter 33

Books have their own voices. The script, the writer's rhythm. These things Culsan understands, but the words on a page can be tuned out. Mostly.

This, this is different.

The skin on his arm itches. *No, not the skin.* Those things from the orb are still here, with him, inside him. He drops the book he was holding, the *Seventy-Night Campaign*, by Grey Um Kimbesh. The spine hits the dirt, pointing exactly where he thought it might. His stomach churns as he faces mountains.

"Sethlan," he attempts to say to the approaching dawn. But the wind whispers "east," the trees rattle "north," and a third element, using his own voice, repeats "northeast." So, northeast it is.

Chapter 34

Loose pebbles roll inside Niena's shoe, jabbing her as she ducks into a shed. Spiders scurry at her intrusion, and the logs are covered with cobwebs—those that are not yet in her hair. Naturally. Outside, a cloudless sky hints at another hot day. She checks the sack she stole from her kidnappers.

"Hard bread," she says. There's nothing wrong with that, but she has no water, and *that* is hard. *Maybe I can double back to that stream, or the fountain in town.* And this farmer's stock, for something to fill.

"Or." *The woods.* The forest that lurks beyond this farm is wild, and unknowable. The stream wound that way, but so do other dangers. *Would the elves expect it?*

"Maybe, maybe not," she whispers. "I don't know if that will help me. They found me from…from who knows where."

A gap in the shed's planks allow for a glimpse. Coppiced wood ascends just beyond line of sight, but even still, she can tell that as the land rises, the forest thickens. "I'd get lost, like, really easily. But Marny always said I was a lost cause."

Though if they are not expecting her to risk it, *they also might not expect traps.* And if both follow, she might be able to catch them in an enchantment together, and then—Rustling in the stack of logs makes Niena nervous, and she throws herself against an opposite wall. After a few moments, a rodent pokes its head out of a crevice, and as quickly, back.

"Me or them," she says. "Or is it them or me? I need to write this stuff down." *For now, though, I can keep moving.*

Her feet agree, and as she leaves the shade of the farmhouse, she smirks. *There will be adventure there,* joining a trail, past the first of the tended groves. *Lots of spiders too, literally tons more.* Her smirk falls away.

About face, and to the town.

The edges of the woodland hill leave her view, and potatoes and a garden of other root vegetables return. She grumbles, doubling her pace to rejoin the road. Here, alongside the stream, the ground is low, a remembrance of a time when this was a marsh. A thing which Niena is thankful for, as her bare feet grow weary of the badly maintained road. The side, however, is filled with soft grass and spongy mud. It doesn't make for a lovely sight, but the walk is more pleasant.

She passes farm and day-laborer huts. Cattle, and wheat. She leaves behind the muddy trail and is merged into a worse affair at a fork. This continues south, and north, and from the latter it curves to reveal a small town hiding in a southern finger of the Alemann Mountain range. Ahead a covered bridge crosses a larger river, of which her own stream joins at its own fork, north.

"Chords," she says. The bridge is not high, and the water is swift. But the slope to the shore is gentle, and the water at the edge shallow. "I'm an idiot. I forgot to get a cup, or a stupid bucket."

Wind whispers through the planks of the bridge. Niena peers into the rafters, and cringes. *That's a lot of cobwebs.* One step in, and the shadow of the roof—patchy in places—covers her. It is warm outside, cool here, but the air is also musty.

She closes her eyes and takes another step. Wood creaks. It is no longer noon in Niena's imagination but dusk, and the bridge covers a stream in the heart of an old forest. The sound of frogs and crickets overtake the gush of water. She sets her hand against the wall and gasps; the wood in this daydream trembles.

"It's the Alemann Mercenary." Her voice mimics the croaking. "Bar the doors, pray that he passes quickly in the night."

Over the sounds of settling planks, over her own footsteps, she can hear the rush of horse hoofs. Niena moves away from the wall and wanders into the center of the path.

"His steed is the storm of the north."

A horn sounds: "His lance, terrible lightning." There is a second sounding, and this time it thrills in three urgent blasts.

"His path, straight into the heart of men."

The gallop is like thunder on packed dirt. She stretches out her arms, feeling the air for something. Balance? A taste of the old magic?

"His aim, death."

"Out of the way," a man cries out.

Niena opens her eyes in time to see the horse's head rise as it breaches the threshold of the bridge. All the air leaves her lungs, and her stomach sinks like an anchor. But the girl's feet —loyal and steady—launch her away in time to avoid being trampled. She hits the northern wall with a hard thump.

Steed and rider disappear, leaving her to listen to the retreating gallop. She sucks her teeth. "Chords," half laughing, half choking. "Only a day away from Oberon, and I am already acting like a little girl again."

After the fairy lord kidnapped her—though he claims it was to save her life—she has known little else but danger. Bandits. Woods, like the one she avoided. A dragon. Perhaps the scariest of them all was the Fairhome; Oberon's home. Now Niena's inheritance. Daydreams were left behind. As were stories, and just plain regular dreams.

"He's still my grandfather," she says as the sun emerges on the other side. Two emotions, fear and shame, vie against a third for room—relief. Fear, because outside of her daydream she can see it is clearly past noon. Shame, for the relief she feels at no longer having another person's needs to consider. Or his ideas about her future.

Her slow walk becomes a fast trot, and then a jog. More of the little town peels back, away from a craggy outreach whose furthest edges come to the curve of the road itself. Hereafter she can see that the town is divided by a controlled stream that splits the street, all the way unto a bare rock face, where it was first born as a waterfall. Squat buildings, made of the same white stone as the cliff, populate both sides of the road, many making use of the water. There is no city wall, and hammers ring in regular intervals. When Niena arrives, breathless, at the bend where the stream and path separate, there is a gaggle of women knee deep in the water, taking turns beating laundry against a boulder.

Opening her mouth to ask a question produces only a cough, then another, but between these she discerns the sign for an inn, and it is by chance the closest building to the brook. Niena feels under her dress belt for a pouch, where her purse is sewn in. A quad of large coins, mixed in with double the number of smaller ones, stirs up a sigh. Previously, the cost of a night in an inn would be an extravagance, but times change. Still, she never thought it might be the price of freedom. Or more.

There are other costs first. The rhythm of the smithy tolls a bell in Niena's mind. She swallows, and despite an aversion that would empty her stomach, walks in that direction. Thoughts of murder darken an otherwise bright day. The building is easy to find. A wide stone base, open to the elements, supports a second story of cruder stuff. The green shutters and flowers on the windowsills seem to be hardly a recompense to anyone unfortunate enough to live above. But that is probably the blacksmith's family. He, and several helpers are in the open space below, with all the machinery and trappings of their craft. Especially the heat.

"Hello," she says, a little too loudly and a little too cheerfully. An older man, who she presumes to be the master, barely moves his head away from his work—which appears to be arranging, rearranging, and cursing over the arrangement of completed wares.

"I would like to see about getting something made," she says.

The blacksmith stands, stretches his hands over the table. "I don't make shoes," he says. "Not for people, least, and you're not ugly enough to be a horse."

"Thank you." *I think.* "I was looking for something else, though."

"What sort of something else?" he asks, craning his neck.

"A knife."

"A knife." Even with the incessant hammering, she can almost hear his gears turning. "A knife for eating, or for cutting threads? Wouldn't you rather have scissors?"

He's starting straight at her now, and although old, his silver eyes make her want to say something, anything. The rest of the man is dirty, blackened by his craft, but those eyes are like gems in a dark mine.

"No," meekly at first, then overly strong. "For something else."

His eyes say "Ah," even while his voice uses something more guttural. "Where are you from, miss?"

"I come from a little town called Maidenhill."

"Well, maiden of Maidenhill," he says. "Where's your father?"

"My husband will be arriving shortly."

"Well, then your husband can provide," he says. "Unless the knife is for your husband."

"He sent me ahead to—"she stops. Not for the ringing, or for lack of words, but because of the laughter bursting from the old man like a broken bellow. Everyone milling around the smithy turns to look at her.

"Sure, I believe that," he says. "He sent a waif to fetch him a knife, when he's not bothered to buy her shoes or clothing that ain't threadbare. Pull the other one, girl, it has bells on."

Niena straightens the creases on her blouse, but the master speaks first. "I don't sell weapons to strange barefoot girls wandering in from that road." And then more quietly, directly to her: "Just away from here, across from the temple is a seamstress. She's always looking for more hands."

"I—thanks," she says. "I am not staying."

At her answer, those silver eyes seem to deepen. "Fine, he says. "But I am not selling you a weapon."

I'll just find one somewhere else. She curtseys and leaves, crossing back over a small bridge on the way to the tavern. In the temple, a real set of bells chime the time.

She glowers in the smithy's general direction, but with each tone her shoulders relax. "I don't have the time," she says finally, and storms off.

Green shutters adorn this building as well, and a similar work of flowers appears on every windowsill, as if the townsfolk had a meeting and decided that everyone would conform to the same measure of dullness. This time, however, there is a proper welcome at the door. There are very few patrons at this hour, and the owner, upon seeing little Niena enter, acts as if she was a long-lost cousin. His gestures sweep her in, his voice almost pulls up the chair. And when she produces the right currency and enquires about a room and a meal, why, his face lights into such a sunny countenance that Niena feels a need for shade.

At length, a room is provided and shown. It is not the most spacious of rooms. But already a secret, devious part of her mind wonders if she would have been better off finding a barn or a cave to lay a trap. Yet *it might still work.*

"That Sethlan, he's clever," she says. "He knows he is, too. How the Chords am I going to trick someone that has probably seen every trick there is? I fooled him last time because he underestimated me. I can't hope for that again." *I'm not lucky enough for him to still be stuck in my enchantment either.*

Which is unfortunate; after a night spent bound and on the cold, wooden floor, the bed calls. "I have to assume he already has an idea of where I am. He'll probably try to strike at night, thinking he has me figured out." She needs only to catch him off-guard. She needs a weapon. The temple's bells ring again; it is now one-thirty.

"He doesn't know me."

Chapter 35

Evening brings cold weather, and more people to the tavern bundled against it. They gather around the fireplace, or as close as can be managed; Niena has been squatting there for most of the day. Elsewhere, the smell of toil enters with every new patron, and the stomping of feet on the doorstep adds percussion to the harmony of cheers and chatter. It almost makes her homesick. Almost.

Dinner comes and goes. Her meal is meager, but still takes the last of her small change. The rest of her funds are tied up in two full pennies and a silver farthing. Trying to spend the silver would bring too much attention, and possibly even imprisonment for theft. She's no thief—at least in this city, yet—but small folk need little evidence for their lynch mobs.

"Everything should be set," she whispers. A trapper throws his bag on a table to her right, toppling it. Space is finite. Still, the firelight is charming and its warmth inviting, tempting her to stay amongst the company and relative safety of the crowd.

I'd never sleep again, though. There is no guarantee that the elf couldn't or wouldn't try to kill his way through a group of farmers. Sethlan was tall, muscular. He had the grace of a hunter, *a killer.* Fighting him is an act of desperation.

"Stew," a cook yells. "Who had the mutton stew?"

Stew sounds delicious. Also, expensive. This doesn't stop her stomach from growling, even if she already ate. The old man elbows and shoves his way through the throng.

Maybe in a few years I will come back here, when they've forgotten what I look like.

Niena absentmindedly rubs the coins under her belt. One of the pennies will need to go towards supplies. The other to find Oberon. Freedom or not, she needs to know he is all right. Assuming she survives tonight.

As the last rays of day grow old, and falter, the little tavern fills, and spills out; into the stairwell, out to the street. Niena can't remember seeing this many people around the town earlier. Gossip spreads, worse than the plague. By eight o'clock, she knows the business of every seamstress, and the reputation of every husband. Her own story is the worst of all of them.

"Tomorrow I'm spending that silver on some shoes and a new dress," she says. *Or,* another idea crosses her mind when a farmer stumbles past: *I could spend their money instead.*

Both thoughts she chases away. Fast as things get around in this little town, the mob would be knocking on her door before morning. Even if she robbed no one. *Knives on the other hand,* watching that same farmer stumble into his chair. *They can get misplaced.* Every man has one, these long-handled, curved blades that are neither sword nor dagger. *Peasants' defense.*

The door swings open again, and a bear of a man tromps through. Several others rush to greet him, crushing him in a wave of cheer and smiles. Niena leans against her table.

"Berne," one patron yells, then others join in chorus: "Big Berne!"

On his brow sags a wolf-head pelt, and the rest of the giant is similarly clothed. In one of his hands is a long rod with interlinking markings, forming a continuous flow of knots. And if it weren't for the barkeep, both hands would be used to hold it. Bits of metal dangling from the crook jingle like dinner bells.

"Sunufatarun," someone yells. "Segenhort," another. The gathering turns into a procession, and Berne is coaxed towards the fire. Chairs scuff the floor when pulled. Tables get thrown. Her own is shoved away, a neighbor, a fellow's with a blade she has her eye on. Niena disappears into the background, as more and more people fight to be within earshot. Finally, Berne sits down in a large, plush chair—hers before the ruckus—and with a raise of his hand, the crowd falls quiet. As if by magic, the missing bar wench appears with a pint of ale. This disappears within his meaty paw.

The man's hood comes off, exposing soot-blackened eyes and a grizzled, bearded face. He raises the stave, shakes it in a wide arc at the crowd. It disappears into a boy's hand at the end of its journey. The Segenhort's coat is then taken away too, and the stave eventually reappears over the hearth's mantle. Berne opens his hands to reveal the mug of ale, like a thief displaying his latest prize.

"Have you heard the story of the Sigun and the great worm?"

The tavern erupts in cheers. Niena retreats to the stairs as the onlookers throw up their arms, letting her own sink low, low, to brush over the hilts of a few famers' knives in passing.

"The sagas tell us of heroes of wonder, of splendid feasts, and times of mourning. And I shall share these tales, if you can stomach the sorrow of your folk."

He leans back in his chair, everyone else forward. Niena too, so that her hand is resting on the back of a man's spoiled tunic.

"In old Tuimil, later Toimil, and now taken by the Shaenites and called Shenan, there was a maiden. A noble lady, fairer than the fields that birthed her, but still a pale, jealous image of the great mountain range we call the Suevo. We remember her as Kriemhild today in the tongues of the invaders, but her true name is forgotten."

Niena's groan is met by a dirty stare, and a sum of other undesired attention. She lowers her head.

"Three noble kings watched over her: Maldras, Massila, and Malaricus. Maldras the younger, made his home in the southernmost peak, guarding the way to the barbarian east and the southern holdings. Malaricus, the middle child, held the northern passes, closest to rich flax fields and trade lands, for he was a studious knight and new the value of things. But Massila, eldest and most renowned, dwelled in their father's castle, on a great outreach of rock nestled between these peaks. For the three kings were Kriemhild's brothers, and her care fell to them."

A knife hangs low from a triple frog. The sheath, however, is fitted so that the weapon can be quickly loosed when needed. *A double-edged problem, on a single-edged blade. For once, luck smiles on me.*

"Now it came to pass that this pure maid had a queer dream: that she was holding her beloved falcon, only to have it stolen by eagles, for which she shed unnumbered tears thereafter."

I bet this is where her mother—

"She told this to her mother, Uta, who being wise divined the meaning as such: The falcon is most surely a nobleman, whom the gods will lead to you and steal away."

Knew it. The weight of the knife is substantial, as its length. Briefly, she reconsiders taking this one; could the man who would risk owning a weapon so close to a sword be more than just a peasant? This thought falters as the man's own momentum pulls the blade free.

"For which Kriemhild looks upon her mother, 'Why do you speak to me of a man? I would do well without suffering their love,' and after saying such, she earns a piteous smile."

The weapon is too big to disappear down Niena's dress. And too conspicuous on her own belt. No, she instead wraps it in the burlap sack stolen from the elves.

"To which Uta tells her to not be so certain, for 'If you are ever to have happiness here, it will come from the love of a man,' as mothers are wont to say to their wayward daughters."

Wayward daughters? It's as if these people never watched their mothers pick up their father's stockings from the middle of the floor, again and again.

Berne exposes the palms of his hands placatingly and is answered by a burst of laughter. "They would argue over the mead of love and its nature and relation to sorrow. And long did this maid keep chaste. Mothers, though, usually have the right of things." This earns him another laugh, which he shuts down with one raised eyebrow.

The stairs creek with Niena's weight, but no one notices. She steps back and up, and scans over the heads of the gathering. Red caps, blue hoods. Gray and brown. All eyes, though, locked on the Segenhort. A twinge of desire creeps its way up her spine until it finds a memory. As a child she had spent many nights in taverns in and around Shenan, with her father playing the bard's game on the stage. He never had the respect this man possesses, and just as often spent the night outside as in. This was something, as a young girl, she had deeply wanted.

"One day she wed a man, and this was the falcon foretold. Her vengeance upon the kinsfolk that slew him was great, but that is another story. The name of this knight was Sigun. This is his saga."

"And this is my cue to leave," Niena whispers. The flow of the evening's stories dwindles as her room comes into view and departs, save the random cheer. There is a safe pattern Niena must walk, else she would be caught in her own enchantments.

This takes her to each door in the hallway in a crisscrossing fashion until, finally, she lays her hand on the latch of her own room.

Here's the stage for my own little saga, she thinks as she unlocks the door, and it swings open with little effort. The room is just as she left it; the bed without sheets or covers, the sole cabinet empty. Curtains for the one window are drawn, but are still free enough for a sliver of the moon to peek in. The place smells of straw and sawdust. There is no fireplace. All the warmth in this room lies on the floor, behind the bed—that is where she will sleep tonight. Anyone else walking into this room will see her, with covers, asleep in the bed. If they mean her harm, it will be their undoing. Before she trespasses, Niena checks her right arm. *No red ribbon. The spell hasn't been tripped.*

After entering, she settles down upon the hard floor, under the window. "*Red ribbon on her right arm.* If my name started with 'R,' it'd make a nice limerick."

Sleep does not come easy, but it does come.

Chapter 36

Stars, the moon, all appear in Niena's dreams as caricatures. They sit around a table smoking pipes, discussing the plumage of a bird in the center. At one moment a star transforms into an eagle, another a falcon. The moon changes too. First, it takes the form of a nude, blonde-haired woman. Then a giant bear, patchy haired, with a wolf's head and black, coal-like eyes. As she listens to its explanation on how to fill the barkeep's head with ale, its own falls off its shoulders.

From the wolf's ears sprout arms and legs, and it stumbles off the table into a silvery light. When it turns back and opens its mouth as if to answer a question, Niena can see a familiar head peering back at her from among the yellowed teeth.

She awakes with a jump, throwing the cover to the floor, and instinctively withdraws the knife from the bag. The night, or morning, is still young; starlight lingers around the windowsill above. There is a pleasant draft, and—*the window is open!*

The smell of the street pinches her nose. Niena, shaking, lifts her head above the straw mattress. At first, she sees nothing, but just as she turns against the window's light, a shape comes into focus. Beams of light reveal the outline of a tall, mannish build. But what he holds in his hands is far more interesting; here, star and moon come together to play along the edges of a silver clad dagger. It is long, wicked—and most worriedly thrust, deep, deep into the middle of the mattress.

The man does not move. She stands, her own knife slashing the air in the little motions that come from nervous hands. The man does not move. Her grip steadies. She breaches the little space between them. The man still does not move. She can see his face.

"Sethlan," whispering. The man does not move. Niena's eyes fall to his knife, a gleaming twin to her own. She swallows and breathes in hurried gasps. The knife shakes once more as she raises it, making a path of marred threads up his cloak. The man does not move. She can smell the street, the straw, her own sweat.

The point is raised, placed squarely in the center of his back. It takes two hands to hold it steady. Her spit is thick in her throat. *O Chords,* closing her eyes. In one quick motion she pushes the blade into the back of the elf.

Fabric tears, the knife sinks first into the wool, then straw. The edge of the blade slices both neatly, and Niena drops to her knees, confused. Where Sethlan's body should be stands a pile of clothing. She struggles to her feet, using the mattress to steady herself. The darkness retreats. Black shapes spin, fold along the corners of the room. She stiffens and pulls the knife from the straw.

The room grows. Walls lengthen and lean, the floor groans as more and more of it is needed to fit.

"I'm dreaming," she says, looking at her right arm.

"No," another says. Niena scours the room for the speaker, from the bed to the window. From the window to the looming cabinet, the place is empty—empty, except for the shadows.

Thin lines become legs. Shades of the bed, of a chair and of the cabinet slide and join these. Niena's throat tightens as they all, together, flow into a familiar form. *Sethlan.*

The elf's shadow leaps from the wall to the floor, and immediately where he was not, he is, appearing out of the air as if immaterial. In his hands is the returned dagger.

"Fairy. Child. You are not the only one who is capable of making traps," he says, spreading his arms.

"You stay right there," she says, raising the blade to meet his eyes. "I'm not coming with you."

"No, you're not," he agrees. The elf does not stop moving forward. "Interrogation is not my way. You have played the Evercharm. In here, your mind will reveal more than your lips ever could."

"I'm not—"

The elf's blade sings in the air, darting forward, forward, driving her back, and back. His movements are fluid. His aim precise, striking at lengths of her dress each time. Niena retreats, putting too much weight upon her back leg. A shredded length of sleeve rustles in the wind as she tries to threaten him with the knife.

"Your enchantment was crude," he says. "A child could have found it; a child would have easily broken it."

The point of his blade dances around Niena's, flying high, then sinking low to cut a strip into her blouse. She reflexively grabs for it, which leaves her open to another cut, which this time removes a lock of hair.

"This is not your creation any longer. You will feel my blade." Sethlan smiles, lunging again, effortlessly batting away her strike. She lurches backwards after his missed cut, and crashes into the cabinet.

"As knights ravage the land," she says. "At dusk their swords hang to their sides."

The elf's smile flips, and he strikes her again, pinning the girl against the wall. Her back arches over the cabinet.

The girl does not scream in pain. Nor cry or beg. And now Niena in turn smiles as his lips mouth "how," before understanding glints in his eyes. She reaches over, ignoring the blade as if it wasn't there, and tugs at the red ribbon on her right arm.

"You—"

She pushes him, laughing as the elf stumbles backwards, confused. "I'm the granddaughter of the Lord of the Fairies, who are you?"

His answering growl is wild, and fierce. "I am the hunter, the first song of the Hohfolc. I taught magic to your pitiable race, I —"

"Am trapped," she adds. "By a fairy child."

Wherever his gaze lands, Niena can almost feel it. Probing, testing. Back is the arrogance and the impassiveness of a hunter stalking his prey.

"Yes." Sethlan's eyes narrow. "Why are you still here?"

The dagger disappears behind her back. "Beca—" She steps back, making herself small against the wall. "Because I need answers."

"At first I thought you were delaying. But I see you, child. You did not create a way to escape." Sethlan inhales. "Of course not."

When this fight started the elf was dangerous.

"That means you are stuck," he adds.

She was afraid of him then. Even as he toyed with her.

"Inside the cage, with the wolf."

Sethlan is cornered. Trapped. His face unreadable, manner no longer playful but cold and calculating. Deadly.

"But which one of us is the wolf?" she squeaks.

"If you are in control—" he says in mid prowl. And he then freezes, like a statue, with only his eyes following her. "Do something. Change the color of the sheets."

"I'm not taking my eyes off you."

"Wise."

"Can we, can—" Words catch in her throat. She moves from the wall, widens her stance. "Maybe we can talk about this Evercharm thing. Why do you want it in the first place? Not your Matriarch. What would you, Sethlan, do with it?"

"From the home that hid me, I traveled," he says. "I saw a passage with many ways. A way beneath, a way above, and a way on all sides. Name me."

Niena pinches her arm, quietly behind her back. "Is that a riddle?"

The elf recovers the distance he lost when she pushed him. But the girl slides along the cabinet, then leaves the edges of the room entirely, seeking the middle.

"It's a bridge," she says. "You came by a bridge, there was a river under it, and birds flew above and on either side of you."

"I only desire my people to be free, though I would cast down the Curators and their Construct."

There is a different feel to this rhythm of question and answer. At first, she thinks to focus more on his eyes, perchance to catch him lying. Seconds fall into moments of silence as they circle one another. On a hunch, Niena steals a glance away. To the walls. To the ceiling. To the details. It is not just his intensity that is causing unease. *He's working a spell.*

The workings are familiar. *It must be like my singing.* His movements are lithe. His features, predatory. *Distractions so I don't pay attention.*

Careful. There must be some way to turn this on him. "And humans, what would happen to us?"

"What is the great one, that crawls over the soil? He swallows both waters and woods, yet the wind he fears."

"Fog," she says.

He glides along the wall, while she takes the middle. The room is vast now, like an ancient theater with low ceilings. "The Hohfolc and Men cannot live together. Men must abide in Hearth. If it were my choice, I would choose so."

"I don't know anything about the Curators," Niena says. "Are they good men, evil? Are—"

"Four do hang, and four do gang. Two show the way, two ward off dogs. One drags after."

"I—" Niena steps back from the table. "What happens if I get one of these wrong?"

His smile is telling. "That would require another riddle."

"It is a cow," almost strung together. "Four teats, four feet. Two horns, and two eyes. She drags her tail after."

"They broke their vows and imprisoned my people in a land where roots can hold to the sky, or ground. There is no order, but that which you are born with."

A table almost corners her. A quick move is all that saves her, and she manages to put it between. *Can I do the same as he? If I were to picture this room as my stronghold.* "I protect my hearth, my hoard and my home. Surrounded I am and filled with excellent treasures. By day, I stave off the terror of spears. My success is greater, the more I am filled. What am I?"

The elf's features sharpen. "A fortified town." There is now nothing separating them, but the wide-open space of the hall. "Clever girl."

The room brightens, details fill in on the periphery. Niena sighs, as she can feel her bond with the enchantment strengthen. "I can keep at this as long as you."

He nods, and withdraws from his pursuit to find a chair which he drags close. "Do you play dice?"

No. "Yes, I do."

Chapter 37

Grasp it. Sweat beads upon his temple. *Force it.* A solitary drop trails down his face. *Picture it.* The Fairhome is not only a place, but a state of mind. Smells of winter, of a frozen spring hit him. The texts say it is a dark place, like evening on the cusp of dusk. As too, the fey who once lived there, and now have dwindled into shade. Sofie and Higgins fly past him, further into the vortex, the unknowable swirling around them. The way behind has already been sealed.

Rein arches his back and stabs with his cane. The path must be strengthened. What he is doing here will be felt. And not only by the Curators.

"Slije kothroma aritist," he utters.

The wall of smoke and shadow before them melts with the force, like boiling water hitting sugar. What's left is a tunnel that leads into darkness, where black is the end, and void is the way through. Higgins hesitates in front of Rein, with the former measuring his head against the distant end.

"Be aware of the danger," Rein says. "This place reacts to your thoughts, much like the Earth construct for an Artisan. But while the Earth has rules, the Fairhome is wild. We are entering the jungle of creation."

"A wonder," Sofie says. "A treasure, then."

"Bollocks to that," Higgins yells. And in one motion—quicker than Rein had ever seen the man move before—he disappears into the tunnel.

"Bravery is for the young," the Inspector whispers.

The first step is simple; the second, another matter. With each foot gained Rein bounces between feelings of relief and of new burdens. The pressure of the investigation leaves and is replaced with a sense of loss. Sofie passes him, disappearing ahead, while his connection to the Construct strains, strains, until broken. In contrast to liberation, the severance makes his palms sweat.

And then he is through. There are no fireworks. No strange, mind-bending tunnels. He was in the black corridor and now is not.

"Hell of a thing, if I might say." That's Higgins, he's sure. Direction and placement are difficult, as the dull features of a forest emerge—because there is light. Stars roll away their thick sheets to peek.

"It's the Little Dipper," Rein says.

"Is this the time for stargazing?"

"N-no," the Inspector stutters. Rein's head tilts up dreamily to the sky once more. "Of course not. But it is strange. The stars here are nearly the same as our own."

"They are called the Traveler's Stars," Sofie says. "They are the same in all worlds."

"Well, I suppose I should try to make some light," Higgins says.

She knows this, but I do not? "I'm happy for your enthusiasm, but you will fail," says Rein.

Higgins snorts in a wet sort of half-laughing way. He's here now, next to the Inspector, and thanks to the starlight can be seen. "Bugger your opinion. I've progressed, just watch."

"Can you not feel it?" Sofie interjects.

The same stare his assistant has given him on numerous occasions is now shared with Sofie.

"You will fail, not because of lack of talent," Rein says. "The Fairhome will not abide any other light. Not so long as its King fades."

"George may be a little mad but—"

The violence in the Inspector's glare drives Higgins back. "The King of the Fey," he growls. "You are not in your glorious empire any longer, Harold. No." Rein's fingers grace a sapling. "A different power rules in this world."

"World," Higgins laughs. But there is no accompanying smile from his master. "What did you mean by that?"

"The Fairhome is a separate place. A reserve of sorts, just as Earth is, but not constructed per se." Rein walks past, as if in a dream. "Every apprentice will eventually learn the truth of it. I wasn't much older than you now when my Master told me."

"Much?" Higgins huffs. "You have to be only twenty or so years my senior."

"Appearances are always deceiving," Sofie says. "For the other matter…"

That tree thickens, its bark roughening in the Inspector's hands. Her gaze flows past several more, meandering around the rise and fall in the land like a stream over its course. "Once, there was only the one world."

Higgins looks from Sofie to Rein, as if they have just sprouted potatoes from their ears.

"No one really knows how it began," Rein says, interrupting. "But amongst the many peoples, three rose to the mastery of Edinnae. Elves, the fey, and men. Each had their own ideas on how to rule. The Edinnae supposedly was a place much nearer to this…to this Fairhome. "

But Sofie takes over the thought, halfway mocking Rein's phrasing in a sing-song voice: "…elves had an innate need for rules, and rigid order. Fairy kind preferred things as they were, wild and chaotic. Men—men desired to create, and to have the control. Specifically, a few wanted control over the many."

Bird calls in the night divert Rein's attention back towards Higgins. And he, as if feeling the weight of his master's eyes, turns aside. "Was just thinking about nightingales."

"I see that," Rein says. There is a hint of admiration in the Inspector's voice. "Sometimes those creations can be wondrous; at others, terrible."

"Explains how the French came to be, if nothing else," Higgins says. "And why there's some much savagery everywhere."

"Something like that, I suppose, but think bigger," Rein says.

"I see where this is going," Higgins says. "A more pressing concern is where do we go from here?"

"We?" At once, both are again made aware of Sofie's presence. "Your little adventure does not concern me."

Rein is taken aback; somehow, he just assumed. "Then where will you go. How will you manage?"

"Better than you," she says. "There is so much I can learn here, so much I can do." She puts her hand against her chest, and breaths in slower. "It seems your work again separates us, Inspector."

His smile is genuine; for her it brightens with a familiar spirit. "I believe it always has. Until next we meet, my lady, you have my most heartfelt thanks and good wishes."

"You are overdramatic," she says, and then to Higgins. "He used to say the same thing before he went out to the coffee house."

Willows sway around her. Back and forth. Their branches and leaves, covering and revealing Sofie with each turn. Like a theater curtain that just won't stay closed. Finally, after a few silent goodbyes, the foliage sweeps around in a green embrace, and she is gone.

Mixed emotions for Rein follow in her wake. His assistant comes around, as if to offer some advice, but another worry gnaws at Rein's stomach. He turns inwards to his own thoughts and the Fairhome. The air is neither warm nor cold, and the forest that reveals itself smells and feels like any other. He looks from tree to tree, hoping to see a pattern, before realizes his mistake.

"There will be a house, less than one of your miles north." He points. "We can talk there."

Higgins: "How do you know?"

Rein smiles. "Because I do."

Dusk reigns. The way there is slow, for there are many snags in the brush—just as the Inspector expected—which elicit plenty of grumbles and complaints from his friend. But ahead in a clearing, just as he said, is a house. Rein marvels at it, taking hold of a small sapling.

"A fine cottage. White fences, thatch roof," Higgin says, squinting. "Riverstone walls too—and look, bless me. There's smoke, maybe a fire waiting for us. I wonder who built it?"

"My father did," Rein says. Wood bends and snaps in his hand. "It has been years since…" He grimaces. The thatch seems to sag in the darkness. The smoke from the chimney dwindles. "I have not been there since I was a boy." He regards his apprentice. "Your nightingales, my family home. All begin their journey towards creation in the mind. Come, let us rest next to a fire. I feel a chill coming."

There are no flowers in the garden. There is no one waiting for him, at the front door. One twist of the latch and another solid push is all that it takes for the warmth of the cabin to introduce itself. Night reigns here as well. The door closes behind them without a sound.

"It's darker in here than outside," Higgins says.

"And it will get darker." Despite the pitch, Rein finds a set of chairs from memory. The sound of wood scraping over wood fills the hovel. "You are surprisingly resilient to this place. But the longer we stay, the more your thoughts will turn on you."

"I'm rather fond of the dark," Higgins says. "When I was a boy, I would leave my bed in the earliest hours, and sit upon the grass to stare at the stars. I can still smell the wet daffodils."

Almost as his friend speaks, the sweet odor of dew-touched meadows visits. There are no gaps in the walls, that can be seen, or open windows. Rein's mind turns to the lesson from before. "The three races chose to split Edinnae among them. One land would stay as it were forever linked to the people and its king. Another would be a place of order and idyllic nature. A third would fall in the middle. The mistake of the elves was leaving the keys to the triad's creation with men."

"In Cuiven's Lee stand three thrones. One silver, one gold, and one of bone. There men and fey, and elven fair, laid the rules of the world they'd share." The ferrule of Rein's cane taps out the rhythm until the end, and he leans in closer to his friend. "But the inevitable happened. War. The elves did not fare well. Where they would have ruled, instead there are now men."

"You mean?"

"Earth," Rein says. "Yes, in effect our world belonged to the elves once. Men imprisoned their kind within its fabric. Men had the mastery. Artisans, those who through their bloodline can manipulate the rules of Earth, reign here. And once upon a time, an offshoot-controlled Hearth too, but by older means."

"So, this Fairhome," Higgins says. "The Curators must manage this place as well."

"I see what you are implying, but no," he says. "Not much is said about the fey, and they never give reasons as to why, but they left them be. Fairy land, fairy rules."

In a passing moment, the air becomes stale, acrid, while Rein stares at a wall. He then returns to the conversation, regarding Higgins with a short gesture, as if patting dough. "There is more. The Teamor—these are not just some Cultists as you must be thinking. They are in truth the rightful rulers of men; they sat upon the Throne of Dreams during the first era. The Curators, the current keepers of the Construct, wrested control from them. It was the spark that ignited the greater war.

"As for current news, we may be here for a little while. Getting to the Fairhome is one thing, but leaving? I know over seven hundred phrases in the old arcana that have various effects on the material," Rein continues. "I've no idea what they will do here." But he quickly adds: "I will find the answer, though."

"Bugger me," Higgins says.

"It gets a touch worse." *Is honesty really the best policy?* "We are after all quite literally in uncharted and uncharitable territory. Or, at best, moving from the latter to the former, should we find a way out. I will need to again discover a trace of these elves, which will be difficult."

Before Higgins can add anything, he illuminates: "I've never been to Hearth. Neither has any Artisan since Roman times. I don't know if my special senses will work the same there, or if we shall be blind. Either way, our work continues. We must track the elves, capture them if we can, and find a way to save the Curatorium from the Teamor."

"Bugger us all."

"Well said again, my friend."

Chapter 38

Feels like ants on the back of my neck, Rein thinks as he scratches himself.

"Did you hear that?"

Higgins' question was superfluous, since both turned towards the shout. *Better manners require me to say something,* Rein notes. But forests are as tricky for social etiquette; check that limb, roll that rock. You never know what may be hiding up a sleeve, or underfoot.

"Are we going to do anything?" That's his apprentice again, always prodding. It's a wonder he hasn't strangled the man yet.

"Could. Never mind." Rein sinks into his coat. Decisions normally come easy. Charge in here. Delay there. He had always worn his mortality in the same manner a vagabond might a pair of shoes; until it was on that last thread. Yet today was different. If his life were indeed such a pair, the soul would be flapping. *Might I be setting a bad example?*

More looks of consternation from his friend, too, while Rein loses himself in the gloom. There are powers, here—he felt them. Feels them. Sights, eyes that flash yellow then fade into the empty sockets of trees and the knots of roots. These are more than imagination. Glimpses of ancient fairies? Or had he stumbled upon something worse? By coming to this place, he may have let his quarry know they are being hunted. *And what happens when the squirrel turns on the hunter?*

"Things go nuts," he says, right pleased with himself for that.

"Are you feeling all right?"

No. But the answer given is mixed; a shrug, and "Yes, I am fine." Rein stands abruptly and cocks his head. *There is a melody here.* The Inspector's hands caress his calluses. *An enchantment. A trap. Were they aware of me?* "Higgins, what do you know about elves?"

"Elves?" The word clogs the man's throat.

The inspector sighs, wiping his hand down his chin.

"Elves," Higgins repeats. "Related to the fey, fairy kind, and men."

The apprentice's arms cross, as the Inspector's shoulders lift. "They are imprisoned, by the Artisans," he says, waggling his head. "Their tomb is sealed on Tara Hill."

"They are living souls," Rein adds "Elves can manipulate the Chords, because they are very close to them. Thus their magic can affect this place."

"What gave it away, was it all the screaming?"

"Higgins—"

The fuzzy-lipped man smiles at him. "You're not going to lose the moment with weird portents and rambling stories. Now, what's your plan? Should I follow from behind or flank?"

The heavy breathing of his apprentice replaces the sounds of life, of birds, and of wind in the tree tops. Rein looks past him, into a canopy unloved by the light of star or moon. He waits then, expectantly. Listening for crickets, wrapped in the smell of moss and leaf mold. *If I have caught the rhythm, then*—the screams return, and he motions with the end of his cane at his friend. *Yes, the elves are slaves to it.*

"The best thing is not to run head-on into danger," Rein says. Unfortunately, his calm and casual tone doesn't settle the matter. For some reason, Higgins stirs, and Rein is forced to get his attention with the tip of his cane. "I know what you are thinking, but that leads into a moor of bad choices."

"You are saying it is a trap."

Yet it is what he doesn't say that changes Rein's tone. And as the stout man's stance widens, and his hands try to find peace within his pockets, the Inspector rises to stare him down.

"That is not Sofie." He immediately regrets speaking, as the whole of Higgins' body turns towards the tree line.

His friend balls his tiny fists, and the Inspector raises his eyebrows as a spout of curses erupts out of Higgins as if he were a broken kettle. Yet Rein's calm demeanor never changes. Curse after curse. Growl after growl. And when the man scrapes the bottom of the barrel and finds only shit, the Inspector speaks up again.

"They expect our kind to run after the shouts of a woman, like beasts. No, they do not know I can sense their music. One moment."

Rein sets his feet firmly on the alien ground, and peers intently at the direction of the screams. *"Fìar shellad."*

True Sight. A basic phrase, long relegated to the dustbin of the Inspectorem's archives. Supposed to work in the land of Hearth and Earth, but would it have an effect here? Rein's focus on Higgins reveals little. He is no changeling, illusion or other oddity. But what of the rest of this forest?"

His attention swings from branches, darts around floating leaves. And buzzes a hornet's nest, just where he knew to find it. *Damn.* They are marooned in a changing scape. *Damn this all.* With his friend looking on, Rein instead listens for the Chords. It doesn't take him long, and he grabs Higgins' hand and places it firmly upon his own shoulder.

"I will be your hunting dog," he says.

Into the woods. Into uncertainty. The Inspector's footsteps are measured. He is as much hunting as *envisioning* this hunt.

Over hill. Under bough. Leaves rake the top of his hat, and branches bend to harass. All around him, the smell of decay strikes. But he remains intent on his path.

A path that is equally interested in eluding him. Briar and brush link wherever possible, denying a straight track. Thick patches of trees block his way further, even going so far as to hide the sound of Higgins' crashing through its undergrowth behind him. Rein pulls another thorn from his beaten legs and grimaces.

"Lord," he says, stumbling into a small clearing. "What have I dropped us into?"

"More of your usual, seems."

"That wasn't meant for commentary."

Shapes in the periphery flicker with the tension of the Inspector's voice. The True Sight spell is working in a unique way; plying to draw his attention to hidden movements. He sees the tree move, paths change. Shifting with furious intent.

"I was right," Rein says. He stops near a boulder, wedged in mud, and lets his hand climb the moss nestled into the crannies of the stone's side. His eyes seek the canopy. "The elves were here; this was meant to ensnare us, and hide their passage. But I have found how, or should I say, where they left."

"Good," Higgins says. "I'm happy you found something you could dribble on about. Now, let can we continue?"

Two fingers from Rein's left hand squeeze a patch of the moss, then rise and touch his lips. His eyes widen at the taste, then narrow. "I wonder." The Inspector reaches out with his mind, feeling the edge of the forest.

Bird calls replace the last of the infernal shouting. Rein wipes his mouth and stubble scratches the back of his hand. He looks east. Then north.

"Fis agad deta a tigin."

The trees to his right lean over the brush menacingly. And when a breeze catches them, their long limbs rake. Rein clasps his coat close. It isn't cold, but still he feels a chill. This world is strange. Over this chaos the chords thunder in symphony. The music is like wind through your hair; touching you, even as it goes unappreciated by others.

The Inspector pulls Higgins up and over a hillock. Rein grimaces. The forest has closed rank to his right, and ahead. *That way will be difficult.* And right? *That way will be dangerous, but if the spell works, I might see more.*

"What is it you see?"

The spell will work, ignoring his assistant. A sapling refuses to give way to his will. Then another. *I must believe that.*

Higgins puffs. "Tell me, goddamn."

Noise and movement at the edge of his sight alert Rein. He again looks north, eyes searching for the source of a rustling. But when the noise circles him twice, he raises himself to a small hill overlooking a bog.

"Seial dinead," Rein says.

The birdsong stops. The rustling dies. The Inspector lowers himself to one knee. *Fools rush in where angels dare to tread.* "Reveal yourself, you damn—"

Rein wrenches and tears the grass around his feet. Phantasmal fire ripples along the nerves down his spine, and his scream is chased by the sound of wood splitting overhead, then joined by Higgins'. The cane drops to the ground; his fingers reach and find only hair. He looks ahead, as if any moment—

The spell! Oblivious to the mortal danger he is in, Rein stares hard at the flames. He rolls onto his stomach, with the pain, with the anguish. Black flames enshrouding his body flash, then shrink. Wind extinguishes the remains.

Rein crawls over his friend and touches his shoulder, taking the flames from him as well. Again, the Inspector, sensing the end of his hunt, reaches out for the Chords. Everything is amplified. Sound, sight—and pain. Mostly pain, lingering from the attack.

Mud smears the Inspector's clothes from crawling, stains his cravat and fills his nails. The earthy smell of peat hits him when he raises his hand. The taste of his ruined lip is on his tongue. Rein stretches forward, leaning into the music. He pokes and pries with all his emotion at the traces the elves left. Unable to resist his prodding, a path opens in the forest.

The road, that's it. "Slije kothroma aritist."

As before, the magic touches the remains of their portal. Ferns and brush ripple with the force. Rein then drops the spell, reaching out instead with sheer willpower, imagining his own hands holding open a collapsing tunnel.

Higgins mutters something close by. The Inspector stares hard, picking further at the memory of the elves' passing. There is the sound of fast whispers. The smell of fear. The feeling of tenseness, drawn tight as the bow. And then, the release. Rein stands.

"You have been lucky to evade me," he says. "But all luck must end."

One. Each footstep feels like ants dancing around the hairs on the back of his neck. Two. Rein swallows hard and wraps his fingers tightly around his cane. Higgins joins him nearby. He can feel the man's hand against his neck, as the forest path changes. From a tree lined road. *Three.* To a dirt road, and the promise of fields and sun, behind a ripple in the air. Flowers bloom along the edges of a widening tunnel. A portal, a portal opens like a bloom.

"Make your way through," he says to Higgins. "Our hunt continues, from home to Hearth."

Chapter 39

Morning blushes red, finally loosening the sheets that wrapped it so thickly a moment ago. A smile visits the Inspector's face, finds it a comely place to stay. Yes, smiles enjoy climbing high cheekbones, or dipping their toes into deep blue eyes. And his oft-broken nose was a pleasant spot to rest, or if a tune might be caught, slide down into a whistle.

"You are terribly happy," Higgins says. "I find it awful."

"It is a beautiful day, and I have the scent of our prey," Rein says. "Just ahead, they must have spent a good deal of time and effort upon protection. It is a very strong trail. Good God, Higgins, we may very well have them."

"So, happy like a dog with its head out the window of the carriage, then," Higgins says. "Just please don't start singing."

"Quiet, now."

A stately farmhouse looms on an incline. Fields of wheat batter the edges of it, and three buildings make the fortified manor look a little like a castle in a hostile sea. Higgins, as he had moments before, again expresses his discomfort at approaching the place in the heat of the day. "Elves are nocturnal," is the Inspector's response.

"An hour ago, you were willing to take on the world for the sake of a lady," Rein adds, skulking around the bend of an outbuilding. He tries to open an iron gate quietly, but the squeal of the rusted metal is deafening. "Where has the hero gone?"

"Cremated in black fires."

A spartan garden separates this building from the manor. Rein cranes his neck, looking for any sign of life. Huge oaks obscure sight into the upper floors. "It is very quiet."

"Where are the servants?" His assistant asks. "Hmm? It's rather empty for such a posh and well-situated estate."

"Long dead." As he takes a tentative step into the garden, Rein looks around. Sneaking is, however, not his best skill set. After a moment of stepping on twigs and crunching gravel, he motions for Higgins to follow. "Elves are said not to regard any life as different from another. So they are as callous, or covetous, as a gardener."

"Shouldn't we not walk right up to their front door like this?"

Rein sweeps his head towards Higgins, then back to the manor, regarding it with a wave of his hand. "They were, but are not now. That is to say, the place is empty. Could you get the door?"

"If you are certain." Higgins hesitates. The wooden frame is set into a thicker, stone arch. It is smaller than one would think for such a building, but the oak of the door is thick and stately. When the assistant lifts the latch and pushes inward, the morning sun is the first to enter. After this comes a breath of fresh air, which is well needed, for the escaping smell causes both master and apprentice to cover their faces. "Good God, did they die in here?"

"No." Rein is already searching for the lingering presence of the elves. Here, it is strong. *They drip with the Chords, as if they were a sheep that's crossed a river and now steps out to dry.* "They stayed here long, much longer than the other haunts. The building remembers."

His hands feel the air, like a conductor searching for rhythm. "They separated." Rein walks in, pushing past his friend. "There were three here."

"Three? Three! How?"

"One of them is similar, but different," Rein says. "The music takes her as a glove, or better, a piece of its own. I don't think she is with them." A thought then occurs to him, or rather a name, from before. "Niena," he says. "They found her."

The sound of Higgins' footsteps is only a touch louder than the creaking of the old floor. "Then we are too late."

"I don't think so," Rein says. "There is something else, a taint."

Goosebumps pop their heads up and down the Inspector's arms. The touch of this memory is the coldest he has ever felt since—"Tara. Liverpool. The Teamor have been here." At once Rein opens his eyes and pulls a cloth to his mouth. *I should have known.* "I am a fool."

"Good, good. Acceptance is the first step towards healing."

"Bite your tongue," Rein says, then after, more softly, "I don't believe it. I can't—but it must be true. These elves and Teamor are working together. It is too close to be a coincidence." The Inspector turns back to the room, letting the cloth drop. "What is it they are seeking? What does this girl have, that they want?"

"Maybe—" A look from Rein makes Higgins backpedal. His timbre is first low, rising as the vowels do. "That is, when all of evil is aligned, the heavens are threatened."

"Elves are not evil," Rein says. "No more than a lion is, or a wolf. They are just alien."

"That's enough," Higgins says. "Bloody foreign types. Present company excluded, naturally."

"They left in a hurry." The Inspector scans the room, looking from floor to chair, then to the space to the right of the door.

Higgins watches him, confused, seeing his friend stalk in his funny heel-to-toe fashion over to the entrance. There the Inspector kneels, and picks up a small, black sack.

Pages turn in the Inspector's mind. Flip, flip. Then, like the monster he is, references are dog-tagged. Collected. He closes his eyes, sifting deeper into the impression left on the bag. What is there is more than a few nights of memory.

Dull pain. Terror. Black—a choking darkness that snakes like tendrils from every corner. But most, *most are born in an orb.* Not in. *From.* He peels back this layer, shivering as the face of what he assumes to be one of the elves stretches and thins in a look of pure horror, fighting his movement even as it folds like paper. The next memory is equally powerful, but less terrible. Two faces emerge; the one from before, and then another, taller, some distance away.

Rein pushes back the urge to retch, as he reveals more. Another page, another memory. The orb is center, always key. The faces of many ensnared men and women look back at him from the ages. A hundred years. Two hundred. A thousand. Until what is left is only smoke in the wind, but enough to form the impression of antiquity. He pulls back, but not before one last image surfaces.

It is of a small gathering. Two men, and a woman. They gaze his direction while his point of view rests in the center of a table. *I'm the orb now, I'm the orb and*—there are three thrones. *Bone, silver...* Recognition causes his knees to shake. The hopeful faces of these kings and queens enthroned therein are more hurtful than the terror of a thousand others that follow.

"This held something very dangerous, and very old," he says, sniffing it like a dog. "We must hurry as well. To me, Higgins! Let us save as much daylight as possible."

Evening threatens by the time the Inspector halts. The count of the hours is six, but they have been telling time by a different method: Higgins' sneezing. Between the manor and the distance to a dilapidated barn, they have passed through several fields, over a small stream, and around a few dairy farms, though the Inspector's assistant insisted there were chickens. Rein didn't argue, after all what would know better than his friend's nose?

At the barn, Rein is tired, sweaty, and worried. The traces of the elves, the trail their magic left, diverts into two paths. It would only make sense to him if their prey knew someone was hunting them. But Rein does not think this is the case.

"From here they split," he says dreamily. The sun has hounded them every bit of the way, and though it is ungentlemanly to do so, he sheds his frock coat and the inner mock waistcoat. His friend however, endures, and from the smell of it has ruined his silk. "One travelled mostly west, with another following after. The third wandered northwest, I believe. That one left first."

"So, we will go after the two then," Higgins says. "As it is, I find it unlikely they would just let the girl leave. I think it is fair to say she escaped, and the others split up to find her."

Rein smiles. "Good deduction. Though I wish I were as sure." Day retreats from the inside of the barn, and soon it will withdraw from the rest. "I am of two minds here. One part of me agrees with your summation. . The other, that this may be a trick. I will have to think on it. We will need to set wards for the night."

"Here? I'd rather have stayed in the manor. There are no beds, only moldy hay."

"You'd think for someone who has been dead all these times a little discomfort would not be so unmanageable," Rein says.

The threads of the elves' own protective spells still linger. Briefly the Inspector dreams of repurposing them, but his own ability with the Chords is non-existent. Instead, he observes his friend work the conjunction of a spell from the previous night, wondering all the while where Sofie might have learned it.

The girl is the key. I must get to her before they do, or free her if she is imprisoned. The shuffle of hay tells him that Higgins is settling in. *There will be a fight. Can we defeat them?*

His friend shuffles, grunting as he tries to get comfortable. The Inspector stares at a stack of hay nearby. *How many times have I put him in danger?*

"Too many," he whispers. Night is not far away now, and should they survive it, morning will come with a new set of problems. "I can't ask anymore of him. The Curators—"

Higgins turns over, and curses. Lately, whenever Rein's thoughts have strayed to his superiors, he can't help but feel angry. And when thinking out loud, these misgivings become "quite loud," until they can even disturb the sleep of his friend.

Would the world be better off with someone else in charge? His hands fiddle with the papers in his inner jacket, then search for something else. *Yes.* Though throwing mankind to the elves doesn't rank high on his list of good ideas, the Inspector is hard pressed to find any love for the order.

They let wars happen. "And natural disasters." *People starve, suffer.* "I will never find those shoes, damn that cancer-ridden ship, the *Worley*. Captain probably stole them, the monkey."

Orangutan. At the end of the word, he finds himself gazing down upon Higgins, who twitches to some unseen night terror. "I don't think I can win a fight against two elves without him." There are no more vials. *No more chances.*

"*Edrom Aitenna,*" whispering into his hand. A soft glow swirls around his fingertips, and this he takes, and cups it over the end of his cane. Again, his eyes return to Higgins. The cane is taken up, and quietly, as his assistant pounces on an imaginary foe, he makes one last spell: "*Fagdo Chu'Eile.*"

The heavy slump is the sound of Higgins relaxing into sleep. The terrible, awful noise that comes after is his snore. Rein stands up, dusts some hay from his jacket and nods. "On second thought, maybe I should do this alone."

The air is chill, for summer. The breeze, nonexistent. The Inspector looks back at the barn as he leaves, nodding satisfactorily at his assistant's work. "He's going to be very angry whether I am successful or not. Better to be marooned here, though."

"No." Rein thinks with his hands on the barn door. "He will be fine in the end."

And, at last, he continues onward.

Chapter 40

The moon leers, yellow and angry, but the stars—*the Travelers' Stars, as Sofie calls them* —still glow like a lover reclining on velvet sheets. Rein shakes his head. Getting her involved in all this was not his plan.

"Maybe she is safe," he says. "Safe in—"

There is a tingle in his ear, followed by the sense that he is not alone. The Inspector starts and readjusts his boots. The Fairhome. *Yes, that place.* The one location he would personally not want to be stranded in. Wild and primal, there are ways from which one can enter all the worlds of creation. Or, into the void.

"Where the Teamor skulk," he says.

Ahead is the moon, lighting his path. The road will be a long one. Quiet and introspection are his companions. Night rules. Morning is but a dream. Rein settles into the monotonous sound of his footsteps. During this time, a stranger reaches out and touches his mind.

So, what was your plan again?

"Who said that?" Crickets answer. He swivels around to the other side of the road and back, peering over a fence and into a dried-up stream bed.

Nothing. Rein chuckles, then balks, feeling a touch of fever. He stiffens, his arms sticky with cold sweat. "There isn't a plan, no."

A frog joins his croaking harmony, to the melody of the cricket's strings. Otherwise there is little noise, save the crunching of the Inspector's footsteps. Over the lowlands this dirge of nature plays. Always in rhythm, always just out of sight.

Tomorrow? "I haven't thought much beyond this morning." The night air is humid. Rein lingers under an oak, its branches spanning half the road. "Find the girl, fight the elves. Try not to die, that's my plan."

So, you are looking for the girl? Good. This is said nasally, almost shrilly. But a sudden queasiness strikes Rein, and he continues, as if he were talking to his own consciousness, or otherwise.

"I don't know if that's good," he says to a knot in the tree. His stomach churns. "Two elves—"
A wrong step brings his trousers against the leg wound. Rein winces. "No one has even seen their kind in a thousand years. I've no idea about how to fight them."

It may not be necessary.
More creatures join the symphony. A buzzing fly. The owl. But they are all soloists. The Inspector pulls at his collar. "I'm going mad, I'm—" A step forward reveals a gap in the tree's canopy, enough to show the full moon. "Is someone there? Are you a vagrant?"

Who would answer yes?
"No, I'm not mad. I am under assault. Elves. Demons!" The owl's screech turns his head, then the rest of him. "Is that you, watching me from afar?"

Demons, elves. Humans and fairies. What are they? Just names. Just names.
Rein grips the barbed iron of a fence, then shrinks back with pain. "Who are you? How did you find me?"

I am the spider, my web is in the shadow of the great tree, whose roots touch all. I felt your presence as soon as you entered this world. Those who are marked stand out. You, another.

"Marked?" The Inspector rubs his palms, wipes the sweat away on his coat. "The wound. The Udur. You *are* a demon."

All creatures born before the sun share the same parents.

"Where are you?"

Look around the bend. Should be a small pool of water.

Rein leaves, nursing his hand. The road does curve, and dip. But there is no water here, at least on this side of the fence. Out there, in the brush? The starlight doesn't penetrate.

Over here. Is it coming from a tree, opposite? *No, dummy.* A rock? Why would it be coming from a rock? *You are about as dumb as one, look over the fence again.*

"I can't see—"

Your spell? Or did you forget it was still going?

"I..." The light on the tip of his cane was useful once to avoid stepping into cow manure, but for the last mile or so he had ignored it. Rein hefts the end up, and carefully pokes it over the fence.

Just over the edge, in a hollow between the dried stream and the road, is a muddy pond. And in that pond, a face, not his own, stares back at him. Rein squints, trying to make out the features in the murk. "A long beard. Hooked nose and glasses?"

Hello, handsome.

The image is pulled together by the odd conical hat, wavy and indistinct in the mud. When Rein rubs his chin, the face does as well. When he opens his mouth to speak, the owl from before calls again.

You and I need to talk business.

"Business, with a devil? I've seen you before," Rein says. "In the memory of the orb. Good God, I should have known not to do that without protection."

Many men have said this before. Your father, for example.

"I—what do you mean?"

Listen, Christaan, I didn't come here to torment you, as fun as that sounds. And speaking on names, you may call me Oberon.

"Oberon." Both his and the alien reflection's lips curl back. And the words spoken in his head? They are being mimicked in the water too.

You are on a dangerous road.

"I tend to agree."

The reflection yawns, and Rein catches it after, yawning in solidarity.

You aren't as afraid as you should be.

Demons. Fairies. "Just names," according to the new intruder. But words, names. Stories, and songs—they all have ancient lineages. Far from innocent, these works of art and creation have secret connections, and powers. Powers beyond the purvey of mortal kin. This one seems to want him to forget that. Rein fears the Teamor. He is also wary of this creature.

You can sense beyond your dapper little rival, and his abominations.

Yes, he can. The Cultists were never innocent. The Curators were right about this much. And Chancy is a pleasant face on a hideous enemy. Is a story only scary when there are pictures, when we can see the danger before us? Or is the implied threat, the gnawing madness beyond the public image, far more dangerous?

Where is the end, what is the true face? the fairy adds, as if reading his mind.

The owl cry is joined by a far-off wolf, then a cow.

Ah, the sounds of nature.

Then a cat, and finally a donkey. That they are all baying in unison is a bit odd. That the cat, cow and donkey all sound as if they, too, are trying to howl is even stranger.

Rein turns his head from the pond to consider the moon. "So, you've read Radcliffe?"

West of here, there is a town. And in this town, is a tavern. Ask for Niena, they will point you to her room. There, she is sleeping with an elf.

The wood post Rein had been leaning on shifts, and he is forced to steady himself on his cane.

Not in that way. They have absolutely—what's the English phrase for it? Ah, yes, buggered themselves.

"So, the elf is alone, is what you are telling me. I like my chances."

The elves aren't your true enemy, remember? But yes, he is alone.

"And the girl is there with him?" If what this interloper says is true, this is information he can use. "What should I do?"

You will need to wake them, feed them, clothe them. Call them pet names. I think the elf is partial to "Mittens."

"As you say," Rein says with a sigh. "Will you be staying for tea?"

Focus. They've spent three days in enchantment. Time flows differently. Kill the elf, protect the girl. It's that simple. I will meet up with you—

"Wonderful. Madness is a thing that crosses languages. I will be locked up, surely. Or burned at the stake, depending on what the savages here do."

In the flesh, completing the thought. Rein gets a vague sense of dread, like the last of the sherry is gone and they only have bourbon to put in the pudding.

Do you have any idea, Christaan, what this is all about?

"That I must have kicked a puppy in a former life?"

One word: the Evercharm.

"The Evercharm," Rein says, but the word has no meaning to him, and saying it out loud doesn't help. "I assume this is more than a little trinket?"

What if you could re-order creation? Or even unmake it? All with the aid of an elegant yet unremarkable lyre?

"I once thought a violinist on Kirchstrasse in Munich would be the death of me," Rein says. "A cat died for his sins, and here I am thinking that screeching was bad enough. Then I am told a lyre out there will ruin my whole weekend. Must be awfully out of tune."

This is no jest, though I am over simplifying things for sake of time.

"I have all night ahead of me. So, this girl, she has the lyre, I suppose?"

My time. No, yet she might give them what they need to find it, unknowingly. Niena is tied to the Evercharm, she's the musician, the catalyst. The Teamor should never have it. I am sure we agree here. Will you help me?

Rein laughs and adjusts a bandage over his leg wound. The result draws a grimace, and he reminds himself to boil some water later to clean it, then walks on. The brisk night is welcome after a hot day. He can still feel the presence of Oberon. The Inspector, clinging to the fence line, taps the drum cadence to the *Defileermars der Koniklijke*. Oberon hums along. Finally, in a sigh, he says: "Agreed."

Oh, how I love it when your kind says that. I will leave you to it, then. Protect her now, Christaan, and she will save you all.

"Omnius," Christaan says. *Tedius,* he thinks. For a second he waits, expecting a snarky reply. When it doesn't come, he exhales. "I'm going to have to prepare something so he can't do that again, I—"

The quiet and the return of normal night sounds unhorse his train of thought. Rein picks at a scab on his lips, and quietly considers a rotten piece of timber on the fence. "The wound," he whispers. "It's the cause, isn't it? Must I amputate my leg, must I…"

The timbre of his voice slowly dies, dwindling as he says, "I must be careful," and ending in unintelligible muttering. He looks from the moon to the Travelers' Stars and continues west. Always west.

Chapter 41

Oberon wakes from his trance, alone and secluded in a forest near the Alemann Mountains. He coughs and lifts his head. Ancient standing stones come into focus, bare on the side facing him but otherwise hidden by the same moss that was his bed. The grass between his fingers is cool and wet. The sun, forgotten.

"It is—" The cough returns with friends. He pushes off the forest floor and falls back to the ground. Gnarled hands clutch at his throat, then jaw. The fit leaves him shaking violently in the dirt.

"Chords," he says, wiping blood-specked hands upon his vest. "That was much easier before I had a body."

A magpie cries nearby, and the fairy rolls over. "Not yet," he says. Other birdsong returns, distracting him from the appearance of a flock of crows. From a sack on his hip he retrieves a piece of bread, eyes them again, then devours the stale meal. No crumbs are left for the birds.

Oberon leans to his left and retrieves a sapling he cut earlier. With this, and a lot of groaning, he rises to his feet. The stones, the woods, all sway with him. The piece of bread he ate moments earlier threatens to come back up.

The fairy sniffs. "Almost time, time to go…" His normally crooked neck dips so low, he risks toppling over. It remains this way, hanging as if in prayer, until a strong wind threatens. Then fairy, his wild hair splayed out and teased by the wind, sweeps his head left and right.

Between the third and second pillar is a gap, untouched by brush or tree. The surrounding forest is hardly bright, but here the gloom lengthens. The way beyond is touched by a perpetual night. "Home."

Using the makeshift staff for balance, he plots his path. The stones still tower. The canopy remains impenetrable. And there are no other visible trails out.

"Fairhome," he says, tasting the word and not liking the bitterness. He lays his head over his hands. "Heh," he sobs. Birds scatter, and Oberon leaves the center of the circle. His shoulders slump. "I must go home."

He is the Lord of the Fairies and needs nothing special to return. *But everything to leave again.* Oberon clears his throat. With a few steps, his schemes will be undone. His physical form will not endure Fairhome long. The black will deepen. The few areas of persistence will fade. With his death, fairy kind will dwindle and fade, he and his home will be nothing more than a dream. And dreams are fast forgotten upon waking.

"I'm sorry, Granddaughter."

Oberon walks through the passage.

The Fairhome reacts almost instantly. Always it had maintained a position; before dusk, but at his entrance the gloom darkens, becomes hungry. Shortly therein, it has devoured the pale face of the moon.

"There is much to do," he says with a raised hand.

Brush retreats, revealing a path that only he knows—because it exists only in the fairy's mind. The trees here are tall, old. There is a mustiness, an odor of dead ages. As he walks along a trail, branches lift.

The sound of birds is the first marker to tease Oberon's ear, and it follows him for another hour. At a stream, the canopy of the forest breaks. Here, on the verge, he looks up and through a patch of maple. Sunlight returns triumphantly in this instant, a thing long forgotten here. The warm rays stir his bones, get him moving. Oberon shades his eyes, and nods.

He fords soon after, closing his eyes as the cold water rushes past his ankles. Memories of days, long, long in the past slip around the periphery. Flashes of fairy children playing in the water. A smile from a maiden. The song of his youngest. Oberon thrusts his staff far ahead, into a current speeding around a boulder, quick as death. He groans as he vaults himself up onto the rock. Then over and onto the opposite shore. The path continues onwards, fast sealing him in a tunnel of green.

More time is lost. The dirt trail gives way to patchy grass and hints of ancient passage; a bent tree, undergrowth thinner than the rest. He crests a boulder and cups his ear. *Stream, I must turn north.* So he does, treading through brush and over hill. At a small clearing, where the woods turn from maple to greater oaks, he again halts.

Leaves shiver and shake, loosening patterns of light on the floor, setting the ground in mock blaze. The fairy tilts his head, sharing his attention with the ground, sky. "Here?"

A sapling clings to the side of an elder. Beyond this point there is, to the untrained eye, only wilderness. Oberon pokes at brush here, there, and around this one stop. "Mmm, memory is hazy."

A rock is rolled. Log, overturned. Oberon closes his eyes and leans into the staff. Nearby, there used to be a house. *A burrow, men call it.* Nestled into the surrounding hill side, bordered by a swift stream to the west and the foothills of mountains to the north. One of many, but as his people died, their places of abode disappeared. He hasn't bothered to remember home in an age.

There will be music. And there is; a swift but soft tune wades along the stream bed. *Singing.* Her voice is reed-like, whisper thin. Oberon opens his eyes, only to bury them again in his sleeve. The voice is distant, faded. *She is close.* The clearing now is better maintained. A path opens, just where the leaves first danced.

"Ariah," Oberon yells. Branches hang over the path, whipping him when he moves too fast, biting him with thorns if too slow. But signs of habitation appear at his approach. Specifically, so. Where a second before there was a trace of saplings, now a shallow pool bristles with fish. Earthworks that used to feed it shift at once from a low thicket to a small canal. The sound of water is everywhere.

With the twist of his head and the turn of the path, Oberon comes to another clearing. The trees here are still wild at first glance, but closer inspection shows the care with which they are tended. There are flowers, gardens—edible—and bushels of nuts between the narrow spaces separating garden from grove. Sunk into a hill at the far end is a burrow.

His footsteps trigger more of the scenery. Like a pop-up book, people, things, and animals segue back into life. Oberon moves past these, paying little attention. Instead, the song from before guides him. It is stronger now, closer. He can hear the distinct notes of a lyre. It lures him along a little trail that is narrow, too, and low—too low in places, where the briar threatens the old fairy's head and hat.

Far behind the burrow, beyond his proper home and the memory of life, there is a pocket. A hollow. Here, the children of his affairs dwelled in holes dug into another such hill. Even in this remembering of them, most of these are overgrown. All except one.

Her door is open. It has worn green stripes, a contrast to the bevy of flowers and shrubbery blooming all around in randomness, as if a gardener had a hole in his seed pouch and had suddenly taken to dancing. On a stump there is a little girl. Short hair, freshly cut to be a dream of the long locks that were there, shines golden in the afternoon sun. In her lap is a lyre.

Ariah. "Little one, what is that you are playing?"

My mother's father's heart song, before the vale of green shadows, he remembers.

"Mother's heart song, from the vale of green, a lay of shadows and sunshine," she says, and lies. It is some human dirge from the village they stole her playmates from.

What did I say after? The memory fades.

She tilts her head. "Where have you been, father?"

"Before, and after. Sometimes during, if that is the will of the wind," Oberon says. "Has my wife visited you today?"

"No," she says. "My hair has not grown back."

Oberon smiles, and moves to sit on a log nearby, but he is not as young as he was then. The shade of his daughter, however, does not see. Her eyes are black, her face drifting between pale and flush. There is no recognition here, and the fairy's smile is quickly gone.

"Do not worry," he says gently. The desire to reach out and hold her seeps into his arms, but it is a poison he can do without. "When it grows back, she will want to see you again."

The girl's smile is practiced, almost too perfect. *I'm losing the very memory of her. Losing. Always losing, and almost now* —her manner is also stiff, like a puppet. *Dead, gone.* The fairy's chest heaves as he puffs up, then deflates.

Up, from his sleeve. Down, to the girl. "I'm afraid I'm going to need your lyre for a time, child."

She holds it for him. He can't recall what was spoken, so the girl's shadow remains silent upon taking. "You are so strong," he says. For his arms shake from the weight of it. Or so he tells himself.

"Will you let me play it again?" she asks.

"Perhaps," Oberon says. "Either tomorrow, or yesterday, I shall."

"She says I'm not very good."

"Who?" The silver lyre is unremarkable, dull, except two small pantomime faces along the bow. "Oh yes, my wife. Your daughter will be a true musician."

There is an unmistakable rustling behind him. The sound of a dress, passing through brush. And footsteps. Oberon pivots on the log, and all the feeling drains from his face as he sees who approaches.

"My daughter." Ariah's nose wrinkles. "Why her?"

"Because she is the melody of three," Sofie says. "Is she not? Why I am not surprised you hid the Evercharm in this place."

Titania. "Wife," hoarsely.

"*You* have no right to call me that. I am Titania. I am Sofie, but not your wife. Never that. Never again."

Oberon leans forward, head down. "Never before in truth either. How are you here?"

"Are you asking how I am still alive?" Her laughter is cold, without mirth. "Grief is a poison that I never took to. Look what it has done to you, my husband."

"I didn't think—" he says, then clears his throat. "No, that's wrong. You were banished from here, Titania. We barred your dream from joining us."

"We? They," Titania, formerly Sofie, says. "They are all dead, and you are weak. I had only to wait until a path was opened. One can always count on the sentimentality of humankind."

Oberon makes to stand, but she effortlessly pushes him back to his seat. "She was very pretty," his wife says. "I liked her the most of your children. Shame you had to poison her with lies, make her believe she was mortal."

This time the old fairy stands, and Titania makes no move to push him back. She looks at him, as young as the day they met. There is that same twinkle in her eye. The same cruelty. Her voice speaks with power.

"You did it for the greater good," she says. "Is that the lie you are going to tell me? You did it because you are a broken old goat and thought that the Evercharm would return your children to you."

"What do you plan to do with it? Turn the world into your simpering harem? You always required too much attention."

Titania steps forward; he back, more slowly. She grasps the lyre in Oberon's hands, and he holds on, clutching the instrument to his chest. "I still to this day don't know how you seduced the elf witch into having your child," she says, inches away from his face.

"Wit," he says. But in the effort to disarm her, he has the Evercharm snatched from him.

"You betrayed me," she says, shaking her head. "You lied to me. It is all you male creatures know how to do: lie, cheat, and then cry over your mistakes. Humans, fairies, elves? Does not matter."

"Did you not lie to me?" Oberon's voice is shaky, weak with strain. "You told me you wanted children? Where are they? What happened to your promise?"

"I never promised anything. You dreamed that, along with everything else. Creating the picture of what you thought our marriage should be."

"Well, you won't leave with that," Oberon says. "This is the Fairhome, and I am still lord here."

The hollow falls away. The girl slips back into death. Everywhere, between the forest, the sky, along the ground, and radiant in Titania, there is light. The fairy lord looks around, bewildered, searching for his gloom, seeking for the nightfall. He perceives little beyond the triumphant face of his wife and her victorious laughter.

Titania steps forward. "Spent all of your power fighting elves?"

The ground shakes, sending Oberon to the ground where he flails, helpless.

"I think it was gone long before that," she says. "Else you wouldn't have so desperately sought out my Artisan."

From the ground: "The human from Earth?"

"Mine," she says. "Rein is weak, pompous, but still more of a gentleman than you. I see why you thought he could be an ally, but I am afraid that neither he nor the elves are a match for the Teamor."

"Your dogs."

"An alliance of opportunity," she says. "We've chatted enough." Titania tilts her head and smiles at the bend of a willow. "I must hurry. The boy is marked, and at any moment their agents will be upon him and my granddaughter."

"How—*your* granddaughter?" Oberon thrusts the staff into the ground and rises. Briefly, there is a flicker of power about him that makes Titania step back. "Lies upon lies."

But like smoke in the wind, his power quickly disappears. "I —" He crumbles again to the ground. "You cannot leave. If I can't, they you, too, are stuck."

Titania laughs, but not unkindly. "You forget, the decree you made is still alive," she says, kneeling. "Weak, but alive. Like you. I am mostly severed from this place, and your grief. Let this serve as your prison," she adds. "I will gain her confidence. She will learn to love me and forget you."

And with the last word a gust roars through the trees, throwing him back to the ground. When he climbs back, both his wife and the Evercharm are gone. He is left in a Fairhome, dimming with each passing moment. Shortly, it will be night again.

Chapter 42

"You are bad at this," says Sethlan.

Dice clatter. Niena looks to the window, and not for the first time wonders if he is cheating. "You say that a lot."

"It is true, a lot."

"How long do you think we will be in here?"

"Our craft has intermingled." His eyes seem to latch onto a corner. "Until we wake or die."

"All because of you." The words hang between them, but the elf shows no sign of acknowledging them. Neina continues, "You see this—" She gestures around. "*You're* bad at this."

"Your people once called us the fair folk. Fair in mind," he says, cocking his head. "Fair in judgement. But 'fair' leaves a lot of ground for terrible deeds."

"Mostly terrible riddles." Niena's face reddens in a flash, then—like oil in a pan—simmers. The cause isn't the elf's change in demeanor. A feeling overtakes hers. *There is something, a sensation of otherness.* As if she is in a dream, and about to—*wake*.

"Did you feel that?" she whispers.

But the elf has no time to answer. He disappears, melting into the ground, and leaving Niena alone. Fear cries out in the back of her head, urging: "Wake up, wake up."

In the preceding moments, each story Sethlan told her is replayed. Analyzed. She wonders over the placement of a word here, the tone of a reply there. "I don't think he wants to harm me. He did tell me about his race, the Hohfolc. Even how he thought the Queen might remake the Earth with the Evercharm. He wouldn't tell me all of that, then"—the floor blurs, and shrivels as she finishes—"kill me."

The walls shred before her eyes like curtains to a mad Tabby.

"Sethlan also said I'm too dangerous." Niena's attention is swallowed by a hole in the center of the floor. Her arms tense, then relax into limpness. *Chords, like this?*

Time is soon counted by Niena's pulse. From the point where the hole widens and the edge touches her feet to the emergence of buzzing. Two, at least. Onwards from here, with the fall of the last wall and the loss of the ceiling to oblivion. Three more heartbeats. Blackness is next. An overwhelming dark that devours the remaining of the room, sinking Niena deeper than the pit in her stomach. Taking her breath, voice, and a string of thoughts—thoughts that had spiraled into fear and confusion already.

This is followed by a dull, throbbing pain. She opens her mouth, forgets what was on her mind and all the worries that came with. Loses the words to express either. There are sounds, though, words and thoughts that are not her own. They surround Niena like a blanket. Float in the air, which is hard to breathe—she is breathing. Finally, the noise coalesces into something familiar, talking, but bearing an unfamiliar voice.

My name? She ponders. "My name," she understands. Niena opens her eyes and tries to move. Colors swirl in with questions, one after another. *What words?* Her head is fuzzy, nothing he says makes sense. Nothing she thinks makes that much sense either. Language in this moment of waking is as foreign to her as the ability to talk, but somehow Niena gathers the wits to say: "Sethlan. Where is Sethlan?"

The same voice answers: "Who is that, your father? A friend?"

Friend? "No." The name and the noun don't seem to go together, but one word does: "Elf, he's an elf."

A hand worms under her own and helps Niena to stand. She coughs, heaves, but there is nothing to retch. A man leans over her like a towering willow.

"Who are you?" she asks.

"Ah, good, you can understand me. My name is Christaan Dei Rein. It is a pleasure to make your acquaintance. I assume you must be Niena."

"Yes," she says. *Chords, my head feels like someone has been sitting on it for days.*

"The elf is not here," Rein adds. "I was told he would be here, but—"

He blinks, then turns as if to listen. The window is dark, and the draft chill behind. *Not the elf, but where is he?* Niena notes, joining him at threshold. "What is that?"

"Panic," he answers.

Her eyes trail from his stiff collar to his head, shiny with sweat. She follows him into the corridor. The night is cool, and he is breathless. She moves to the top of the stairs, while he lingers behind. "People are screaming, I can't make out what they are saying."

"I can wait here."

Wait here? The stranger shoves her away and disappears down the stairwell, crashing into the railing, walls, and what sounds like some decorations as he does. Niena stiffens, letting her head adjust to the waking world. A breeze sways in from an open window.

"Bugger that," she says. "I am getting the bleeding Chords out of here."

Chapter 43

Panic greets Sethlan in the streets of the village. Calls for the town guard mingle with screams of fear, and the wailing of children is ever close no matter the direction.

The moon uncovers him at the tavern's side of the bridge. Him, and another on the opposite shore. *Culsan.* It wasn't any human who woke Sethlan. Culsan had touched his mind — *touched and fouled it with strange thoughts, voices.*

"Where have you been—" Sethlan swallows. "My brother. I have followed the girl from field, to mountain. Perhaps togeth-er—"

"No."

Culsan's answer strikes Sethlan and knocks whatever questions had been brewing off his tongue. He walks onto the bridge.

No. "I don't understand." *He told me no.* "Clarify for me." *Betrayal?*   Sethlan widens his stance, bracing one leg against the left railing. "Do you say no because you have another plan?"

His brother's face is hidden, shrouded by the folds of a makeshift hood. He lowers his shoulder and makes what sounds like an attempt to clear his throat. "Goodbye."

"Goodbye?" Sethlan snaps. "No, we have a mission to fulfil. You do not get to say—"

Culsan's levels his head so that his eyes are to the sky, and chin parallel to the ground.

"I know who had the Evercharm last," says Sethlan, moving closer. "I know where it must be."

Several humans mill around the edges of his sight, but it is not this that shows him the cause of their fear. The moon, the stars, these lights are not strong enough to reveal what has taken Culsan at a distance. Yet his ears are forest trained. Whispers flow under the current of panic. Whispers, chanting, and more. Sethlan's head keens. Terrors walk among them. *Udur.*

"Patience and skill rewarded me. I took the information from her mind unnoticed," he says, adding his own to the rest of the whispers. "Brother, our hunt can continue, away from this place." *Betrayal.* "The fairy took it from her before his bargain was finished." *He's betrayed me, betrayed the Matriarch.* "It could be in only one place."

Out of Culsan's mouth comes a metallic groan, like a spoon rolled around a copper bowl. Those whispers, that chanting joins with this awful cry. Rising, until Sethlan can take no more. He strikes out into a run.

The railing shatters. Boards buckle underneath. Sethlan gains the near end of the bridge in a breath, but it is still not quick enough to avoid stumbling from the collapse. He falls on one hand, shifts weight, and again finds his footing in the darkness. Looking up at this last instance grants him a clear view of his former partner.

Mist swirls at his brother's middle, or more truly, *out of him.* A streetlamp shows the impossible as thin seams of blackness undulate through flesh and air alike. In Culsan's hand is the orb.

"Have you no pride?" says Sethlan, as a dark line whips just over his head.

The tendrils don't move with the wind, and his twitches are not natural. One such causes the orb to fall to the ground with a terrible thump, as if all the temple bells from every town were tossed down the mountain at once. It shakes the tavern. The hunter staggers to his knees.

When he looks up, his brother is gone.

Chapter 44

The tavern shakes.

Yet this is not what has the wenches cowering behind the bar. Or the barkeep trying to arm himself with a sword-no-longer-sword-but-decoration. Rein stands with a few other men, staring at the black mist seeping in through the windows.

Why is everyone just standing around? The Inspector tries for the door, but one of the patrons stops him. His was one of the many faces in the revelry before, though sober. Fear has replaced the man's drunken leer with something equally twisted. Worn hands trembled with the latch. And they tremble now, just holding onto the chair. *What did they see?*

A man nearest to the window backs into a table. Mugs tumble to the floor, and uneaten food and drink spill.

"Get away from the windows," Rein yells, but too late. A black torrent rushes into the tavern, drowning the lights and separating the shouts and screams from one another in the panic. He climbs up, over something. Tables are tossed aside. Chairs are thrown in the mad dash.

Seconds flee, in time with the pounding of his heart. His is not the only body pressed together in the jumble of furniture. A man and a woman whisper words of encouragement to each other just above Rein's ear, and another man challenges the darkness. This last voice weakens, grows distant, even though Rein knows the fellow is no further than an arm's length away.

The building shudders. Beams and timbers topple onto table, chair, and patrons, stirring up howls of pain and fear. The couple above Rein panic, pushing him face down into the rubble in their attempt to get away. It is a lucky chance, as a second impact against the front of the building sprays glass and wood, cutting some of the shouting short.

For a moment, silence settles in with the dust.

Pain is informative. It tells you when a pan is too hot, water too cold. Or that, simply, you are alive.

"Alive," Rein coughs. "With a dislocated shoulder." The spell for heaven's light comes to mind, but more slowly to his lips. And it is weak, like threatening a blizzard with rush lights. Pain tells him the rest. Rein crawls from under the wreckage, spitting sawdust and wiping glass from his eyebrows. Moans surround him. *Wounded patrons.* But the sounds move too fast and never utter an intelligible word.

"Back," he says. *Back*—pushing with his will. The spell brightens from needle thin to a small candle. Shapes flit across half-covered walls and debris.

Ghouls, he thinks, readying his cane. Their long nails click on the rubble. *At least one.* Their wails fill him with dread. *Two.* The Inspector feels around in the darkness and listens to their wild, testing movements.

One wall still stands. Rein scrambles to put his back against it. Stone that should be cold is instead warm to the touch, though there is no visible fire or the sound of timbers being devoured. He angles himself. *Bloody*—"Shit cancer," screaming as he slams into the wall and sets the shoulder.

There is a shriek in the near distance, and an answering two inside. *Three. Kak me.* Rein raises the cane like a fencer as the two, now three, ghouls click their way over. He takes a breath.

One. Approaching from his right, over the remains of the bar, over the remains of something soft, where their nails do not tell. *Two.* Straight ahead. The wind catches this one, bringing the stench of death to his nose. Rein avoids an involuntary cringe and presses harder against the wall. *The third is coming from outside.*

Two. He twists right. "Dorntrom." Claws slash and snag upon the wall where Rein's left shoulder had been. The tip of his cane, though, finds its mark, thumping into the chest of the middle attacker.

The force sends the body crashing through debris, but the rightmost ghoul presses. Rein cries out as the creature feints left, then shifts with help from the wall, plowing into him. Foul breath is then upon him. Fouler claws, too, and fangs, biting into the wood of his cane. His head hits the ground, and the third ghoul from outside howls, filling the ruined inn with its own cries of anger and pain.

He kicks and rolls, tossing the creature up and over a divide, only to be attacked by the one he sent flying before. Fangs sink into his right arm. Rein struggles, taking the cane into his left to strike. But the other quickly recovers and grasps him there. Claws rend cloth, flesh. Pain, the feeling of bones cracking, and the smell of his own urine overwhelm him.

His mouth opens, but it's the ghoul that screams instead, releasing his arm from its terrible bite as a wound opens in its chest. Metal glints there. Then again, a few steps away. A blade from without. The slickness of blood is the next thing he feels when his knees buckle and the second monster lets go. There is little strength holding him up. Rein crumbles to the ground. Another person is here with him, fighting for life.

His vision blurs. One arm is ruined, the other shedding life with every heartbeat. *"Caic—"* something heavy hits the debris nearby with a sickening crack. *"Caic fel."* His bleeding trickles. Rein grasps his right arm with his healed left one and repeats the spell.

Labored breathing. Grunts. Neither his own. The Inspector attempts to stand but fails, and in doing so presses his hand against his chest. *"Ath Cuai—"* Metal rings against stone. Rein tries again, but the spell falters.

The sound of fighting has left the tavern. Curses fade and mix in with ghoulish howls.

"Ath Cuartic," Rein says.

Strength once again flows through sore limbs. He finds his cane in the wreckage nearby; with it and renewed vigor, he stands. Quietly, betraying little movement, he brings the ferrule to his lips.

The words whispered into his cupped hand and a thread from his coat combine to create the *Forme* for a spell of unravelling. He straightens, listening. The shouts and the ghoul's own cries have carried themselves beyond the main street where the inn lies. There is no sign of his savior inside.

Rein sweeps the wreckage. "Niena," he whispers. But there is no answer. Over a heap of timber, and glass he finds the carcass of one of the ghouls, still twitching, still *dangerous*. The Inspector stabs the abdomen with his cane, separating out the creature's thread. With a few more words and a quick yank, the beast moves no more.

"Niena," he calls louder, to the same result. Other voices of help call out to him in the chaos. Rein looks towards where the inn's door should be, but only darkness rules; then back, listening to the pleas of the injured and dying people crawling out of the wreckage. "A pox on the Curators for this choice."

And the Inspector leaves them behind.

Outside the sight isn't any better. Or smell. The cold is unnatural, and quick into the bones. The Inspector shudders, focusing on the sounds of steel and claw. A spell of protection is whispered on the skin covering his vitals, throat, and more. The fighting is close. He bumps into a wall, then tumbles over rocks to splash into the stream.

The water is brisk. The screams of the ghouls, as they realize someone else approaches, thick. There are more than the two that left him. Rein closes his eyes, kneels into the water. *Higgins is not the only one who knows a holy spell, or two. "Spur atrom agior lan."*

Droplets spray his hair, weigh down his jacket, dripping with both chill and light from the spell. A splash at the far side erupts into unholy shrieks, then into quiet, as the blessed water takes a ghoul. The Inspector thrusts his cane into the rushing depths, and screams another incantation at the night-swallowed shore, launching the cane and with it a torrent of water forward in a wide arc. More ghouls succumb, their cries drowned quickly by a spout of the stream. Rein follows the light up and over to the crest, walking past the destroyed remains of the beasts.

But beyond the rocks, beyond the mud and the wet grass, a fight still rages. The Inspector rushes forward, weapon raised and poised. Then stops. Something slides to the ground, like bloody meat falling off a skewer. Rein waits for the howl of victory and the return of the creature.

Footsteps instead. *Boots?* Not boots. The heaven's light spell is rekindled on the end of his cane. The impression of someone near is followed by the sight of the elf hunter.

"Niena?" There is no one here, but them. "What have you done with the girl?"

"She is not with me, or among the dead," the elf says. "I searched both the inn and beyond. Can you fight, E'tah, or are you spent?"

Already his legs weaken, and the rest of him aches for sleep, and nourishment. But he fears showing weakness around this enemy, more than the ghouls before. *No, I can't,* and, "Yes, but we must destroy the bodies here to protect the village."

"They are of no use to me."

"Wait," Rein says as the footsteps depart. "It will take me but a few moments to find their thread, and to end these creatures."

"The ghouls lay in four parts. If these people cannot deal with that now, then I consider whatever happens as fate. Or the course of nature, take it as you choose, E'tah. I have no—"

There is a swish of air, and the Inspector can't tell whether it is a sword being readied or a breath taken. He waits, expecting to get struck down by the notoriously fickle creature. Yet it is a sudden tapping, and not from the elf, that answers. Rein turns to listen. *What is this new—?* A throat clears, and the Inspector's cane presses into the mud. *You have got to be kidding me.*

The Inspector tilts his head and alters the angle of his left foot slightly. The elf straightens. Rein's visage is bleak and feral. "What have you done, Chancy?"

"That's a stupid question," the former Artisan says. "Even for you."

His knee bends and the Inspector takes a step backwards, feeling the unease in several eyes watching his movements. Rein prepares to spring.

"I'm afraid Niena won't be joining you tonight, she—" Chancy drops more than curses when Sethlan lunges first.

Threshing air follows Chancy's cry as he falls back, back into darkness. Amorphous blobs of black replace him, cutting the air as they press forward. Rein groans loudly; this was not a good plan. The light from his spell fails at their charge, letting them conquer more and more ground between him and the elf. Until they are divided.

"Bastard, don't you dare move," the Inspector says, circling with the cane held up as a sword.

Seven voices answer in unison, their reply arcane, flowing.

"It's a bloody spell!"

Gobs of black shatter at the last word, dousing Rein's light and throwing him to the ground. The seven voices split once, then once again. Words are overtaken by moans. Moans by howls and shrieks. The smell of death is upon the air.

A dirty claw glances his arm, and his magical protection throbs blue from the impact. Rein reels, swinging his cane desperately as he lurches to his feet. Around is the sound of the air being sliced. He ducks in time to avoid a grapple, but not quickly enough to keep from stumbling into another body. The thrall that tries to grip him there earns a kick to the shins. Bones crunch and break under heel. Another thrall takes the place of the first one, pawing at him, lighting up the night with the glow of the failing spell. Rein spins, twists, falls to the floor. The creatures pile in on top.

"Put deth," Rein utters.

Electricity crackles around the Inspector, and thrall, ghoul and more fly away from him. Their shapes disappear, but not their voices. And as Rein looks to his left, to see the elf fighting for his life on top of an overturned wagon, their menace returns, sweeping in upon him.

I've got nothing more. Still, he parries a slash. Then another. The attacks come now, relentless, unseen. His spell dims under the assault until the glow is barely perceptible. Rein crumbles.

The claws start to bite clothing. Flesh. He speaks the words for heaven's light, pushing with the remainder of his strength. And the monsters flee, for a moment, retreating to outside the magic's protective ring.

Anna, my wife. The light pulses, scouring those who get too close. Then shrinks to a thirty-foot radius. *Forgive me for not holding your hand.* Twenty. *For spending time in libraries, instead of with you.* Ten. *For all the travel.* Five. *For taking your love for granted.* Two. He can smell the ghouls' breath, see their wide mouths and hungry faces. *For not being able to save you.* One.

Something comes. Creatures left and right shriek in pain, and the throng throbs, pulses—fighting against a terrible force. Rein shades his eyes. Hooves, hooves on the road, and neighing. A stout rider appears fast in the middle, the darkness swarming around him, trying to take him down.

The figure on his horse shouts in the old tongue and raises his fist to the sky. The blackness bubbles around him like a boil, then breaks. Light spills over, and creatures, left and right, near wagon, or surrounding the Inspector, fall to the deluge.

From out of this a hand reaches. Then a second, gently lifting up the torn and wounded Inspector. He staggers, wiping away the blur. Shapes are the first things that appear. The rough outline of a rock, a wagon. The slender line of the elf, and the stout form that is both familiar and impossible.

"Higgins?" Rein says, wondering where his apprentice came from.

"You are a bloody, egotistical, daft-minded fool."

"Dear Lord," Rein says.

"No, Higgins is still fine," he answers.

"Where is the elf, we must—"

The sound of renewed fighting interrupts them.

"Come," Rein says, relinquishing his assistant's hand. "I have an old friend I must pay a visit to."

Chapter 45

Outside, the shrieks and howls of the dying are loudest. Outside is also where Niena thought she might gain her freedom. *Terrible, terrible freedom.*

She looks back towards the tavern and sees nothing. "Blasted mist." It covers the ground, obscuring person and thing alike. "Not like I'm heading back there, anyway. Really, wait here? Like I'd take orders from a—"

Niena slows her breath. There were footsteps in the dark near her. *At the farmhouse?* It's a former stable. *No, closer.*

She places her hand on a tall lump, thinking it a piece of equipment. The sound of her sinking into the straw is far too loud. Shrieks call out in answer. Between her and the stable. Even towards where the tavern should be. *In there!*

And into the stable she goes, gasping in time with the patter of her feet. The shrieks have stopped, but in their place is the sound of creatures stalking outside—creatures, because their pacing changes in a way a man's wouldn't. Niena retreats further inside, and edges into a table, then another.

I've run into a furniture store or something. She pauses after using a rare moonbeam to pick her way around more. *What is that? Sounds like whispering.*

In this moment, as her arms stretch back against a chair, something grabs her. A terrible strength takes her left arm, ripping her fingers from the upholstery. She lets out a strangled cry, the cold hands stealing her every breath. They take her up, up and over. Into the fresh air that is no longer fresh; death is upon it. The smell of fresh blood and further carnage ebbs and flows in a river of panicked screams as she is dragged, joined soon after by the sounds of men fighting beasts.

Pieces of a fence from outside join gravel and dirt to ruin her clothing and mar her flesh. The hands are relentless. She tries to wedge, grab onto anything. Everything. Wood planking is yanked away, the dirt ploughed by her fingers. When they stop pulling, she has already run out of energy to fight it.

On her back, yelling at the sky, Niena takes a deep breath. There are no longer any lights there, or stars. And she is not sure there is even a sky. The hands, the fingers that snatched her, have taken her far. Shouting sets the background. She exhales as all the little pains set in.

All manner of chittering and chattering pays a visit. Some sound like wild animals, chewing on nuts or roots. Others groan like men, while their footsteps tell of creatures that walk on four legs. But it is those who neither groan nor chatter, who also move through the darkness silently, which cause the goosebumps on Niena's arm to peak. These things, creatures, whisper in low voices. Every word is followed by the painful touch of ice, the memory of dread.

"Fear the moon, the wolf's howl," they say.

"Fear the night, the death's cowl," they chant.

Yet, through the whispers, this foul chattering, a song comes to challenge.

"Brave this night for no spirits prowl," someone sings.

"Brave this moon and the screech of owl," a woman sings.

The counter song has struck its challenge, and the air tips into immediate tension. The darkness closes in—and despite the pitch she can feel it, like a blind woman who reaches out and finds her coffin. Niena weeps silently for the cold.

The first voice sings again,
"Come see what no hunters dare,
Come see our dreaded maw."
Niena curls into a small package. There's blood on her lips, but also warmth on her arm. A hand, and a soothing voice, fight back.
"Leave the bow, do not draw.
Leave this place, for weather fair."
The chill retreats, the whispers die. Two green eyes look down on her, scattering a sudden light like emeralds in a torch's glow.

"It's all right," the woman says. "You are safe, for now, but we cannot stay."

"Who—?" Niena's eyes descend, rung by rung, from the lady's face. Dangling from pursed lips, an elegant neck. Last the bodice. Past a march of blue porcelain buttons, with white faces made in perspective. To the lyre. More specifically, her lyre.

"You recognize this, don't you?" The woman's smile is warm, and it is followed by a contrasting laugh. "It is yours, of course."

Looking at the silver lyre for the first time since Shenan stirs up emotions, wisps of memory. Some good: finding her way through the wild. The feel and rush of power, and song. Many bad: the death of her Grandfather Marny. The Evercharm glows brilliantly, and Niena understands that it is the source of the light framing this woman, and what is pushing back the night around them.

"As for my name? You may call me Titania."

"Titania?" In one hand the woman offers the lyre, the other, her aid. Niena considers the two, before taking the latter. And as she is lifted to her feet, a niggling feeling surfaces. "I know that name from somewhere."

Titania smiles, pressing the Evercharm into Niena's hesitant arms. "As I have yours. It is a pleasure to finally meet you, Granddaughter."

Chapter 46

Lights wink out, left and right. Above. No, these aren't stars, but the flashes of the fleeing Cultists' spells. Chancy, flanked by four loyal who remain, glares hard at the tilled ground where his agent, Sofie, was supposed to meet him.

"She was here, milord," a Cultist says. "Look."

Tussled earth. The remains of wood fencing. These tell him nothing. But the trace of magic and the pungent smell of ammonia speak of a pall of concealment. *Treachery.* "I hate your choice of tense. Where are the Udur?"

"I have not seen them, maybe they are waiting."

"They've abandoned us," Chancy laughs coldly. Flute music rises in the air, causing one of the Cultists to dig into a pouch. The Speaker leans into his umbrella. "They have what they want. Now the hunting dogs—" One hand of his feels into the bag for the sphere. It is cold and lifeless, the magic that brought them here no longer surging within. "All of the dogs can tear each other apart."

The music bounds from every side. Cultists raise their hands, prepare spells. Chancy nods solemnly and tugs at his gloves. A bark from a ghoul trails off into the night and dies. Then, as the flute music sinks, a song rises above it. The Speaker of the Teamor lowers his head and listens:

"She gave me the last bread, as the snow fell down. The grain was coarse, the meal heavy as my crown."

A blade comes between the verses of the song. Silent, precise. The Cultist from before falls to Chancy's right. The Speaker turns and scrunches his nose. He's heard this lament within the Abbey of the Forum Magicae. Another man is struck down after, the spell faltering with a gasp.

"And I stole a look into her eyes, hungry, pale and blue," Chancy sings.

Sethlan, radiant in the night, kicks a third body forward, freeing his weapon. Darkness falls off him like water. He slides right then left, avoiding a tendril-like chain spinning from the hands of a Cultist.

"The sadness held in their depths was for me and for you," the elf adds as his sword cuts chains, tendrils and lines that whip at him from every direction. Chancy straightens. With a tap of his umbrella, three pillars of light bloom from the ground and fold over. The last of his fellow Teamor fall back, but he remains in the center as Sethlan dashes forward.

"You are not Rein," the Speaker says, watching the violence of the elf's charge stop at his feet. "Where is he—where is that pompous…

A flash of light heralds the retreat of Chancy's last ally. Where the Cultist was, two figures emerge from the darkness. The Speaker doesn't need to see the Dutchman's upturned lip, or the low brow of the Englishman, to know who they are. He sneers, sensing it is the only appropriate thing to do at this moment.

"A more respectable man would know when to die," he says.

Rein squares his shoulders. "How would you understand respect? You were born low—"

"Bodchead." Salt trails in an arc from Chancy's hand and towards master and apprentice. Rein dodges left. Higgins' hesitation earns him a glancing blow. He tips and stumbles as his arm is weighed down by a sleeve turned to stone.

"The low must walk through things the high can ignore," Chancy says he tosses the gloves to the floor.

Rein's lunge morphs into a stumble, as Chancy sidesteps and plants the tip of his umbrella right in front of where the Inspector's foot lands. But his attacker recovers quickly, flowing up into another lunge.

"Lovely evening for a dance, wouldn't you say?" The Speaker catches Rein's arm with the crook of the umbrella handle. After two turns that look more like a couple's waltz than a fight, he sends the Inspector careening towards Higgins. Chancy then wedges the ferule back into the ground, smiling.

Rein, sent low, shoves his hand into the dirt.

"This must be a struggle for you Christaan. Oh, I am not talking about being shown what for by a peasant."

A poor swipe from the Inspector at the Speaker's legs is easily parried. Chancy steps back and leans like a fencer. From the corner of his eye he notices Higgins is on his feet again and searching through his pockets. Elsewhere, Rein plunges his other hand deep into the mud.

"I'm afraid I'm much harder for you to kill than a seven-and-a-half stone woman. Or was she only seven stones?" The Speaker angles his body left, but the Inspector doesn't move. Chancy squints. "My apologies. I was betting on you knowing your wife, Anna."

He pivots to his right, keeping Higgins at point. *They're trying to wedge me in.* His head briefly turns to watch Rein, who hasn't risen from the ground. Both the inspector's hands are hidden. The Speaker steps back, then slides his right foot over his left. In the cuff of his sleeve, he finds a dried rose petal and crushes it between his fingers. "Alan Ai—"

Two gobs of mud and gravel smack into his face. Blinded, Chancy steps forward and to his right, anticipating a charge. Instead, Higgins snatches salt from the ground and slaps his hands together. His guttural bark is followed by a torrent of flame that cuts the two fighters from one another and singes the umbrella's fabric just from the heat. The fire leaps from the assistant's hands and into the night as if from a spout.

I'm focusing on the wrong one, Chancy thinks, wiping the mud from his eyes and putting distance between himself and the spell. Rein appears confused ahead. His face is lit by both the spell imprisoning Sethlan and the fires from before, as they find a home among the timbers of a tall building.

"Is it your lackey's competence or my accusation that enthralls you?" Chancy turns from Rein to his assistant and back again. But it is the latter whom he watches most closely, even while addressing the Inspector: "Your ex-wife, I said you—"

He spins into a backhanded lunge, batting Rein aside and sending Higgins flying with a vicious jab to the chest. "*Solas ifrinn.*"

The Inspector rolls, and the umbrella strikes the ground where he had lain, igniting the air overhead with a deadly crackle. Chancy advances. Rein's breathing is desperate; his crawl, his scamper, barely enough to keep distance.

"Anna." The Speaker clears his throat. "You courting that radiant creature was a crime." He stabs to the right with the umbrella, missing. "Your marriage, an abomination." And then left, also missing. Sparks fill the air, singing the clothes of both men.

The air between the tip of the umbrella and Rein's face must be very hot indeed, judging by all the sweat. Chancy presses on, "I have no words for what you did to her," as the Inspector's confused gawp turns into an angry snarl.

The Speaker's weapon is batted away. Up the Inspector leaps, throwing his opponent off-guard. "I didn't kill her," he shouts. "Her death was an accident."

Higgins joins his master, and Chancy is pressed from two sides. He circles, snapping the umbrella back and forth in elegant rolls. *The lackey must get in close,* he thinks, checking Rein's cane. *He's trying to sneak a hand into his pocket, the slippery—*"Deadly accidents are a common occurrence around you," Chancy adds, his gaze tagging Higgins.

The look unnerves the assistant, distracting him long enough for their timing to be thrown. Rein lunges forward without a countermovement from Higgins. Chancy flashes a quick smile and steps to the left, swatting at the back of the Inspector's arm. The move does little harm, but now both attackers are close together, and directly ahead of him.

A twitch at the periphery causes Chancy to retreat further, angling left to a backdrop of the building Higgins set alight. *The spell is wearing off.* Higgins swings around behind Sethlan, and approaches from the right. *The bastard Christaan tries for the left.* The smell of charred timbers is second only to the heat at his back.

Time and time again, the trio orbit Sethlan in their dance. Higgins remains out there on the edge of their little system, while Rein repeats his forays into the Speaker's space. None land. Chancy, pressed, withdraws his hand from his pocket. The stench of sulphur is immediate, and flakes of the stuff fall through his fingers.

"Your friend has been accused of murder foul; do you not have any comment on that?"

"Higgins," the Inspector yells, distracting Chancy enough to strike his hand.

A cloud of yellow separates them. The Speaker, stung by the cane, retreats as far as the two will allow. He jerks his head left and right, pointing his umbrella like a rapier. The two Artisans never get in his line of sight together again, leaving him the choice of Higgins and Sethlan, or Sethlan and Rein. And the elf stirs.

"You are such a bloody coward," Chancy says.

Rein lowers his weapon. "The man who hid behind demons and thralls on his way to slaughter his brothers and sisters of the Curatorium calls me a coward?"

"Yes."

"You aren't going to walk away from this one," the Inspector says. "I'm going to see justice served, for all those innocent men and women you murdered."

Sulphur falls around Chancy, and he closes his eyes as his shoes are dusted yellow. *Masters. Betrayers.* Calling to the true Teamor. *Do I need to remind you of the pact?* The sound of cautious footsteps encroaches. *You will not save my life, I know, that is not in the contract. Only death. Death—and so I ask. There is a mountain, and fires that lay dormant within. You know the power. I need your power.*

A warm sensation pulses through, from the ground, to Chancy's head. He steps back, sweat building upon his forehead, then trickles down his cheek as the image creeps upon him. But the feeling is more familiar, less vague than the normal impression the Teamor give. He shudders first, as a woman's face scrolls past his eyelids. Then he breathes in, feeling the *Forme* of the spell enter.

The first phrases of the *Étincelle* are soft and taken by the wind, masked partially by his rare, neutral visage. A strange growl shudders on the mountainside. The Speaker then opens his eyes, the timbre of the magic and his voice rising with the rumble of the earth.

The look shared between Rein and Higgins is gone in an instance, replaced by the sound of canes dropping, and the rush of both men against him. Chancy pivots, still chanting, still armed. The ground rolls and he flows with it, using the force to strike Higgins in the knee even as Rein wraps his arms around the Speaker's torso. The two men hit the ground together, flipping end over end.

"Heathen barbarian," Rein cries, his fingers clawing into the Speaker's chin and mouth. But the spell continues till the end. Somewhere to the left Higgins stands and then yells as he is thrown to the ground by the shifting earth. Chancy, fighting for his life, claws at the Inspector's eyes as Rein's hands in turn find their way to his throat.

"Dare call me a murderer," Rein growls. "I'll kill you."

A crevice breaks near the Speaker's head just as he is forced on his back. "What do you know about justice, what do they?" The shaking intensifies as Chancy speaks. Something Anna once told him rattles around in his head, escaping with several other dizzying thoughts. "We are made of dreams, and we dream our making."

The Inspector's nostrils flare in rage, and he presses hard, and harder into the former Artisan's throat. Behind, and drifting with each second, is the elf's voice. Chancy smiles, as he can see the fire in the town grow, casting a hellish background around Rein. *May the devil take you.*

"Mannelig," Sethlan says.

Rein jerks his head, dropping the pressure just enough for the Speaker to think. He considers briefly, though a thousand choices flash in his head. With the right thumb he digs into his own cheek, just as the Inspector renews his effort to murder him.

"Christaan," Higgins' voice. "The whole mountain is coming apart!"

Hallucinations of Chancy's hated enemy blur. A young man. An old man. This middle-aged man, all seem to take their turn strangling him. The Speaker coughs and reaches with his right hand, pressing the bloodied thumb into Rein's eye. *"Ans achion gadmi a furec."*

The Inspector gasps, his eyes sparkling, before being overshadowed by the manic sneer. Chancy coughs, sputters. The last image he sees is Rein's drooling gape, before blackness takes him, and the march of footsteps carry him to his final sleep.

Chapter 47

The ground shakes, the skies rain ash, and Higgins for not the first time this day wonders what the hell he is doing with this crazy Dutchman.

They have left the town proper now, following the same road from which they came. Behind, the former village is obscured by smoke. Many of the townsfolk, thankfully, fled earlier. Those that survived the fight.

On the approach to the main river, it has become clear to Higgins that the elf means to stay by them.

"Bloody nonsense," he says, supporting Rein as they cross the bridge.

Steam obscures the river, the spray wreaking havoc upon the timbers of the covered bridge. Somewhere up ahead, the elf calls back to them. Higgins stumbles more than once as the bridge heaves to and fro. All the while, the Inspector mutters.

"I always thought I would be holding you when you babbled to the grave, but—" Higgins lurches forward, pushing, nearly throwing the Inspector towards the other shore. The elf appears from the shroud created by the steam and pulls him over too. Not for the first time since leaving that bleeding wreck of a town, Higgins looks upon Sethlan, bewildered.

"We need each other," the elf growls, answering the Assistant's look with one of equal confusion, as if his own ears aren't quite ready for what his mouth has to say. A long quake quickly takes this picture away, as Sethlan turns, to disappear once more ahead.

"'Once more into the breach,'" Higgins quotes. A tremor rocks him as he gathers Rein. "Not that breach."

Through mist-shrouded corn fields, they make their way north, not stopping until the flow of the river replaces the sound of fire and breaking earth. Here, and upon a tall mound, the three return their gaze towards where the village once stood. Though miles have been traveled hence, and a ring of smoke envelops the nearest crag, the fires burning are not coming from the village itself. They rise, and rise, touching the sky with smoke and flame.

Higgins balks, dropping the Inspector upon a small patch of yellow flowers. "That's some spell."

"Not spell," Rein mumbles. "The Chords. Plucked."

"Strummed," Sethlan adds. "As if they reached out and meddled with the music of creation itself and mixed it with a Mannelig form of magic."

"I prefer choirs," Higgins remarks.

"We need—" The Inspector falls silent, his voice conquered by distant thunder.

Sethlan steps forward, separating master and assistant. "What would you do with the Evercharm, should you get it?"

"The Construct must be preserved," Rein says, raising his head. There is a spark there, in the corner of his eyes, that catches Higgins. He leans in closer. "The Curators will know what to do."

"Will they?" the Elf says. "Everything that has happened today is because of their ignorance."

Rein looks away, as if contemplating the grass on the hillside. "They are our only hope."

"There is another choice…"

Higgins slinks back, unnoticed, over the other side of the hill. The conversation between the two fast turns from a debate into some sort of deal making.

He strokes his prodigious chin, running his hands over a three-day stubble. Birds chirp in the background, ignorant of what's being discussed, or the carnage happening merely miles away. The ground is soft. "Too soft. I hope that's not a cow patty."

And in this silence, a voice reaches out to him: *You are in deeper than you know.*

The assistant looks over his left shoulder, but there is only a bee buzzing around a white flower. The timbre was loud, and clear.

Do not bother looking for me, you won't find me. No one will. My name is Oberon, by the way. We have much to discuss.

"Like hell I won't." Higgins stands and brushes the grass from his trousers.

I'm in your head, you dolt.

"Then get out of my head, you ass," Higgins says.

A solitary word reaches him over the crest of the hill. Higgins pulls his coat closer and stares hard at a line of trees below. "They're talking about the girl," he mutters.

Precisely what I want to talk to you about.

"Bugger it," Higgins says. "I don't care about some whelp."

You do. You care about people, more so than they. That's why you can't listen as they talk about hunting down my granddaughter, and what she can do for them.

"Granddaughter," Higgins growls. "I see where this is going."

I've made mistakes. I—

"Then it is agreed," Sethlan and Rein say in unison. Higgins bristles, realizing that their duo has now become a trio.

I let my grief take over. I see this now. I wanted it all, and in doing so, I may have ruined her life. I hid the Evercharm from Niena, hoping to use it with her towards other ends. I lied, letting her think it was stolen. She's now taken up with my wife, Titania. I know what you are thinking. Titania is bad news, as selfish as the Teamor, though not as dark. Their vision is the death of thought, of nothingness. Hers would be the dearth of thought, of lives spent in blind worship.

Higgins snorts. "Wouldn't be the first. And let me guess, you want me to save her." His words fall, rolling around in the muck. He almost spits out the rest, "And you'll offer me her hand in marriage as payment?"

I offer squat. Nothing. Nada. Zero.

"Nada? Squat? The former sounds very foreign. The latter, well. Squat on you! But if it is nothing, a zero, that's not much of an offer."

I often forget the time, and place. Past or future, ahem. Keep Rein away from her. I was wrong about him, there is a darkness there. I can no longer pierce his mind. Keep him away from the elf, for elves are alien and do not care about anyone but themselves.

"This Titania too? Lord, I hate getting involved in domestics."

And yourself. Just do what I couldn't. Let Niena go.

"Higgins?" his master calls out. "Where is that blasted fat little man?"

Threads of their conversation had wound themselves into Higgins' internal one, all through. He bites his lip, swallowing back the comment that he was about to vomit forth. Instead, he sighs. "It's a bad sign when I've stopped arguing with voices in my head and just accept them."

That's a good man.

"That doesn't mean I will help," he says. "I am a man of duty but, but I will think on it." He turns away from the forest line, and trudges back up to where his master awaits impatiently. The two have apparently ended their dealings. Some accord has been struck between man and elf, and now Higgins will be employed by Rein to help track down this pot of gold. This Niena. The realization fouls his stomach.

Still, as the smoke shrouding the mountain billows, he joins them. Fresh air from the north teases their faces, telling of the coming of autumn and of harvest time. There is a determined gait to Rein's step, not unlike the wholesome spring he has had when learning of a new brewery or being invited to a ball where the host has a well-thought-of wine cellar. It is decidedly less earnest and mirrored in the stalking of the elf. Higgins straightens his coat, harks to a hawk's call. Together the three head north. North—and upon the trail of their prey.

Chapter 48

Snow falls around Niena like ballerinas on a worldly stage. She doesn't know what a ballerina is, but the thought comes, anyway. The creatures from before are gone. Only the voice of this Titania, her supposed grandmother, remains.

"Look, child, what do you see?"

Tall peaks, capped in the same snow that falls near, yawn left and right. She steps forward, taking a place on a large rock. Beyond, a wide green swatch of forest stretches, marking the white with an emerald gash from here into an awakening morning.

"Adventure," Titania says, shaking her head. She smiles. "You were going to say a long walk down, weren't you?"

Niena nods, absently, following the wave of her grandmother's hand.

"We have to do something to rekindle that imagination of yours." Titania pauses to look out towards the horizon. "Where would you go, if you could?"

"East," Niena says almost instantly, for east was Maidenhill. East was home. Niena stretches her hands on the warm stone. She reconsiders. "No, south. Or, well, wherever?"

Titania taps underneath her granddaughter's chin. Stardust melts with the dawn on her fingertips, and visions sweep with each gesture. From white shores to green hills. Under stars, under a high sun. Niena yawns, and the scenes trickle into the real world. There are the green fields they came from, then the mountain they stand upon. Its sister, opposite. Over the ridge. Over a tumble of stones, and down into the valley where farmsteads cling to the sides of foothills like lichen.   Yet where there is sunlight, so too, are there shadows. And the things that dwell therein.

"That's where we are going," Titania says. "To the next hill. To the next town, towards a quick sunrise."

About the Author

S.D. Reeves was born in 1980 in Huntsville, Alabama. He currently resides in Switzerland with an undetermined number of cats greater than zero, and a propensity for nonsense. On those cold nights where the wind steams off snowbanks, he is known to write award-winning fantasy novels. And curse his wife's cold feet.

If you enjoyed this book, please consider leaving an online review. The author would appreciate reading your thoughts.

Visit the author's website at
https://sdreeves.com/

Join his newsletter at
https://sdreeves.com/newsletter/

Follow on Twitter at @SD_Reeves

About the Publisher

Sulis International Press publishes fine fiction and nonfiction in a variety of genres. For more, visit the website at https://sulisinternational.com

Subscribe to the newsletter at https://sulisinternational.com/subscribe/

Follow on social media
https://www.facebook.com/SulisInternational
https://twitter.com/Sulis_Intl
https://www.pinterest.com/Sulis_Intl/
https://www.instagram.com/sulis_international/